FROM TIME TO TIME

(*further tales from Tipperary*)

Edward Forde Hickey

Grosvenor House
Publishing Limited

This book is published by
Grosvenor House Publishing Ltd
Link House
140 The Broadway, Tolworth, Surrey, KT6 7HT.
www.grosvenorhousepublishing.co.uk

A CIP record for this book
is available from the British Library

ISBN 978-1-83975-443-2

CONTENTS

FOREWORD

While I might never have met Edward Forde Hickey in person, I feel as though I know him very well through his writings. Since his first publication 'The Early Morning Light' in 2015, I have closely followed and enjoyed his work immensely.

As Local Studies librarian in Tipperary County Council Library Service, it is always a source of great enjoyment to see a Tipperary native remember his home, be it in the world of fiction or non fiction. Edward has a lovely style where he effortlessly combines the worlds of history, folklore and fiction while keeping Tipperary as the common base throughout his many volumes.

His lifelong attachment to Tipperary and to his Tipperary ancestors is evident from the dedications in his works e.g. 'For Grannie and Jack, who carved out the pathways of my early Irish childhood' (The early morning light).

It is very easy to see Edward's background as a student of English literature in his writing. He manages to switch from humour to sadness with ease and takes the reader willingly along the journey with him. The stories may be based in Tipperary but there are themes and subjects which are familiar throughout Ireland and so appeal to a wide audience.

Edward mentions that From Time to Time is his penultimate volume which means he will have some very disappointed readers but at least there is another volume to which we can all look forward. Edward's works rest comfortably on the shelves of Tipperary Studies and are a very interesting addition to our Local Studies collection.

Mary Guinan Darmody
Tipperary Studies
The Source
Thurles, Tipperary

THE BIG Y'HOO

1

The Daffy-Duck Circus was presenting itself again this year on the hurling-field at Abbey Cross and would give everyone a hearty taste of fine entertainment. There'd be several novelties on display, like Tom Tatters balancing the telegraph-pole on his forehead and wobbling around with it on his delicate chin before finally transfixing it onto his upturned nose. The women would be praying that he'd drop it on top of his big toe. There'd be the Yankee-Boy walking dangerously across the delicate tightrope. He had been in the Land of the Silver Dollar for the last twenty years but had been sent home in disgrace for his roguery in the whiskey-trade. Then there'd be the sliding up (and sliding down again) on the slippery pole covered in pig's grease for any lad brave enough to try and grab the fletch of bacon slung at the end of the swaying pole. Time and again, young men would fall helplessly down into the river - to the screams, roars and cheers of us all - and come out dripping wet and start all over again.

By-Jiggery took Moll-the-Man down to see the cheerful spectacle and take a look at some of the local lads trying their hands at the sports. He hated to be late and was just in time to witness (a rate glimpse indeed) what was called the Great Event – the noble art of boxing as displayed by that fighting stylist, known as the Marvellous Man, who had come to show us the action of his hefty knuckles. He had arrived from Clare early that morning to shake hands with his opponent, known as Man-and-a-Half, who had come in fresh from Tipperary Town. The two of them were tall and athletic and had the puffy noses and prominent jawbones of men that were good at their clouting trade. They had stripped down to the waist. 'Ah,' sighed the adoring women, looking at the bare hairy chests of the two hardy fellows, 'the fine manly men that they are, when their skin is laid bare for us to behold.' And they gloated lustily in the pride of these great heroes. The boxers looked like two angry hounds and before the fight had begun, they stared hard at one another for what seemed a lifetime. 'Come on, ye little pussycat!' roared the Marvellous Man, brandishing his huge fists, 'I'll nail ye to the grass'. You could see, however, that himself and Man-and-a-Half were in dread of one another and would rather have been sucking at a few pints of stout than face up to a few broken teeth hanging out of the corner of their mouths.

The boxing-match was only a minute old when that rascal-of-all-rascals, Clever Jack, who was always mad looking for a bit of diversion to the sports, cocked his little finger towards Black-eyed Suzy (a damsel from the hills) and whispered a few sly words in her ear. She gave a little giggle and with a skip and a jump took herself off to the far end of the boxing ring.

A moment later Clever Jack was seen giving her a cute little wink. The wink did the trick. The Marvellous Man was just about to deliver one of his famed sledgehammer blows to Man-and-a-Half's neck. What happened next was nothing short of a disgrace to the noble art of boxing. Black-eyed Suzy (the little hussy) lifted her flouncy skirt an inch or two above her knees. The shy young lady gave the Marvellous Man a painful little glimpse of her white thighs and her dainty mauve knickers - something he had never seen before. Mind you, it was just a little glimpse, a little peep - and only for a split second. It was enough (alas) to distract the Marvellous Man's misfortunate eye from the fists of Man-and-a-Half.

'Give him the right! Go on, ye devil - give him yeer right one!' roared Clever Jack. Man-and-a-Half was not the sharpest of scholars and Clever Jack knew this for a fact. The man from Tipperary Town completely mistook this piece of prime advice. Instead of hammering The Marvellous Man with his right fist he gave the Clare-man the most unnatural kick with his right boot – straight up into the poor fellow's private regalia, sending the Marvellous Man's pair of shrivelled danglers almost into his mouth. With the alarmed screams of him it was as if an army had suddenly landed and the world was about to end. His roars (said the old gossips) could be heard by the High 'n' Dry Men above in Diggledy-doo, 8 miles away. The ambulance men were there in an awful hurry to carry the great man back to his home in Clare, fearing that he had lost the prospect of ever fathering sons or daughters with any future wife he might get.

As they walked on passed the stretcher and the deadly pallid face of the Marvellous Man, Moll-the-Man and By-Jiggery were surprised (if not alarmed) at the fine way in which this year's sports were taking shape. They were just in time to see Ned Coffin (that impudent rascal) appearing in the gateway. The joy of the clouting match now turned into yet another bout of pure laughter when he upended a tinker-woman's stall of eggs by deliberately shoving into the gable-end of Tim-the-Stonemason. As a result, a lively (if unscheduled) boxing performance quickly took place when the enraged tinker-woman (now that her stall was in smithereens and she wouldn't make a shilling from selling her eggs) did what was natural for any good woman to do. But instead of chastising the villainous Ned Coffin she mistakenly let loose such a haymaker-of-a-wallop straight into the startled jaw of Tim-the-Stonemason (the poor innocent fellow) that the stretcher-carriers were called back in a fierce hurry to bandage the poor man's bloody nose and take away yet another casualty from the field. 'Bee-herrins,' said By-Jiggery to Moll-the-Man, who was wiping the tears of laughter from her merry eyes, 'this Daffy-Duck Circus is a good deal better than last year - it's as good as a bleddy wake'.

Dressed in their two distinctive hurling-jerseys and their white hurling-togs, the men came out for the great battle, the tug-of-war. On this occasion the glamour of them as they reached the field outmatched the shouts and clamour of the crowd. The women gazed at the height and stature of these noble warriors and sighed in wonder at the shape of such towering heroes. The older ones (may heaven forgive them!) wondered what kind of precious machinery was shyly hiding behind those thin little trouser-togs and the pleasures these unmentionables might give a woman.

The contestants dipped their hands in the bag of flour and spat on their fists. They went to their marks and dug their heels into the ground. A shout went up and all eyes were glued intently at the shivering ribbon on the middle of the rope. Tom Tatters blew the whistle and the tug-of-war began. With every heave of their sweaty sinews and every intense gasp of their jaded lungs the team from the town were on the verge of victory when a certain comedy-maker from the mountains (the Slasher's father I think it was) enticed a pretty young miss to enter the fray. She was soon to bring pure havoc into this manly contest. For the brazen little hussy (and that's what she was) strolled over behind the lynchpin tugger on the town's team (*Wiggy-Wagger*) and with a yank of her fists pulled his hurling-togs down round his ankles. Instant panic ensued – so much so that the whole undignified team collapsed like a folding concertina ('*Ah lads! Ah lads!*') as the poor fellow vainly tried to hide his private credentials from our view. Oh, the commotion! Oh, the disgrace of it! And then the blazing row rose up between both sides and the fists went flying in a far livelier battle than the tug-of-war itself - a good deal of coppers having already changed hands and neither team winning the laurels on this illustrious day.

We named the rattle-trap-of-a-bus the Ould Buzz. It came down by Echo Bridge to take those without bikes into the Show Fair. We were packed into this contraption like a pack of horseflies. The windows were kept wide open to let in a drop of air and let out the smell of the men's beer-stained mouths and pissy trousers before we were all knocked kicking without ever having the chance to get inside the showground. There were arms and legs poking out everywhere and from time to time the swaying branches of overdeveloped trees came whipping in through the breezy windows and ('Be-chrysht!' screamed Red Scissors) cut the jaw off of some of the men, almost blinding them. Whereupon they lost their temper and shouted the most unprintable curses against the trees that Lord Manners had planted on his estate many ages previously. And then the women screamed like lunatics when their Sunday-best hats were knocked askew by the intrusive branches. The men (bold devils) took this opportunity to squeeze ever closer to them and prevent them from toppling over as they gallantly helped them to fix back their hats and pins. The overcrowded bus (ah, the dirty heathens!) gave them this one great chance in the year to grab hold of a woman's waist and rub their eager old bodies up against the bellies of one or two young damsels as well.

Tom-the-Bee put on his best boots and hopped up on the ass-and-car and went into town to buy a suit of clothing fitting for his lovely son, the Big Y'hoo. The money in his fist was from the sale of six hurley-sticks that he'd recently planed and hooped and the sale of his sow's four little piggies. Once inside the town, he spent a hatful of money on gifts and treats to supply his son with what we regarded as the symbol of new manhood - namely a stiff white collar, a fine pair of brown boots with the shine in them like a stallion as well as a new shirt and a pair of corduroy britches. Did ever a father love a son like Tom-the-Bee did?

When he got home he went to the haggart and cut the Big Y'hoo a switch, which he carefully paired into a handsome ashplant. He showed his son how to put the dab of butter on the caps of his boots and around the handle of his new ashplant so he could walk with the step and swagger of a military general. He let his son put on the new clothes for a moment and then he marched him out from the half-door and stood back to take a look at the grand style and dazzle of him. Yes, he was a handsome young gallant - and in a year or two he'd be off to town, *damseling*, just as he himself had done in the past. There was, however, a second dimension to these comely preparations; on the following Monday he was planning to take his horse-and-cart (not the ass-and-car this time) to the lord's back kitchen and present his son as a prospective ploughboy for the estates. A sound-thinking man was Tom-the-Bee.

A few of our older children thought they might have the prospect of a great day's outing to the Show Fair – that is, if their parents had the price of it. The Big Y'hoo was no exception and his feet were itching to go. Nothing would stop him – especially as his father and mother (Bridie, of whom little is known, she being so very shy) were unable to get to town themselves, what with the turf to be saved and the ass needing a new set of shoes. Tom-the-Bee had charged him with the task of oiling the scythe and cutting back the briars that were suffocating the edge of the haggart. But as soon as his parents had left the yard he pelted the scythe into the ditch. Let it lie there to hell.

His older sister (*Lucy*) had been charged with giving the younger children jobs to do whilst she herself aired the sheets on the stone-wall. The girls helped her clean and polish the crockery and cutlery and the boys chopped up logs and used the hand-axe to make kindling for the fire. The smaller girls (anxious to be good) held out their elbowed arms and carried in armfuls of logs and threw them ('look, see how big and strong we are!') in under the stool near the fireplace.

The Big Y'hoo washed his face in the stream and gave his hair a good rinse with the carbolic soap before giving his body and arms a similar dose. In the stream's reflection he screwed up his face to examine any little blemish he might find there. He took his father's cut-throat razor and shaved himself for the first time in his life. He didn't make such a bad a job of it, with only a few nicks to his jaw, which Lucy covered with a bit of baking-powder. He put on the new britches and matching shirt and Lucy put the finishing touches to him by patiently showing him how to don the white collar. He put on the brown boots and made sure to dab them with the butter till they glistened – then added a bit of butter to the knob of his ashplant. In his eyes he was as handsome a devil as any of the rich farmer's sons, who regularly passed out the mountainy men's ass-and-cars in their silver-railed pony-and-traps on their way to Mass.

Lucy ran the soapy water through his hair so as to stiffen it and she streaked it back down his poll. Finally, she sprinkled their mother's brilliantine on him. With his new finery, he strutted amongst the bemused hens, ducks and geese, none of whom were able to grasp the beauty of this moment. His brothers and sisters gaped at the dash of him as he whisked a couple of flies from the ass's dung. 'Oh, the bleddy eejit,' whispered the wayside fairies for he lacked the townies' walk and the salty wit that made them more than a match for a mere mountainy boy. Before this day ended he'd be given the sharpest of elbows by some of these scholarly boyos, who were forever trying to put lads like him back on the mountain-top where they belonged.

He now made his first mistake and stole his father's Sunday bike from the turf-shed. A man and a bike had the perfect chance of enticing a young damsel onto the crossbars and investing her with his mountainy charms. Then the Devil found a little hiding-place inside his head. What on earth made him steal his mother's green banknotes from the tea canister half-ways up the hob – and her six silver coins from the polishing-rag behind the shoe-last in the press? Poor Bridie! As shy as she was, she'd put the pickaxe-handle across his back when she came home from the bog and found her treasure-trove missing.

That's not the whole of it: with an inspired eye he saw his father's gilt pocket-watch-and-chain (the gift from the Abbey

Cross hurling-team), which for years had been hanging undisturbed on a nail inside in Tom-the-Bee's bedroom. What on earth made him steal that too? He'd surely go to hell for this great sin. The watch-and-chain had always been his father's pride and joy - the reward from the hurling-team on the day he lost his top teeth when a hurler from Thurles sent the slither ball up into the roof of his mouth. Yes (I hear you say), a silver watch-and-chain was a small reward for a man with no teeth to call his own.

With the money jingling in his pocket and armed with the gold watch-and-chain, he powered his bike towards the Show Fair and its Big Tent where the red-faced jolly-boys were already consuming gallons of stout and whiskey and all sorts of dreamy merriment were waiting to warm his spirits. He couldn't wait to buy a few good pints of stout for himself and find himself the grandest young damsel. The drink would give him the jauntiness to roll her in his arms in some shady nook for the whole afternoon. In short, he was the happiest yahoo in all Tipperary - at peace with the rest of the world.

2

The town was not like Fair Days when the streets would be lined with carts of pigs and droves of cattle and the shop-windows lathered in dung. The shopkeepers didn't mind their filthy shop-windows a bit. Fair Days brought in heaps of money from the sale of animals and their shop-tills rang with silver coins from the drunken old farmers, whose poor wives stood helplessly at the edge of town. Bravely (for their jaw might get a slap or two in the evening from their embarrassed men) they pleaded with their husbands (*think of the children, think of the children!*) to stop drinking and come home for god-sake before all their sales-money landed in over the counter.

No, today the streets glittered with women in their best dresses and one or two brooches in their lapels. The men walking stiffly in starched white shirts and wore their best suits or sports jackets. Big people, small people, thin and fat people – more people than the Big Y'hoo had ever thought existed and they all surging ahead of him, the rhythm of their clattering feet all reaching towards the showground gates.

Above the din he heard the impulsive shouts of the red-faced men (Red Scissors and Rambling Jack among them) and their ashplants waving their greetings. 'Blasht ye, Noolah, it's younger ye're getting – I thought it was yeer daughter!' The yarns and the laughter - it was like a farmyard of hens when the fox arrives. At Goosey-Goosey-Gander's eating-house he saw a yellow-haired tinker-woman and she singing *Tipperary so far away* – with the words all back-to-front so that, whenever she couldn't remember a line or two, she'd make it up on the spot out of some other song. She put out her hand towards him (*Gimmee a copper, go on, do!*) and he gave her the first of his mother's silver coins. These tinker-women were the most tuneful of singers but by nightfall - and after they'd gulped down a fair share of the black stuff - they might be seen having the fiercest of hair-pulling battles with one another (their babies and men meanwhile sleeping soundly at the corner of the alleys). And God help any of us trying to stop their amusements for it was then that the two of them would join forces to beat the pulp out of the rest of us.

Further up the road he came on a second tinker-woman, her basket laden with apples and oranges, bananas and chocolate. She was well into her fifties and wearing her blue-green tartan shawl and barefooted like all the tinkers this fine summer's day. A group of townie boys had come up behind her and were imitating her sales-cries (*banannahs, appells, oringes, chucklets*) and trying to steal an apple from her basket with a view to hitting her on the ear later on with what was left of it. He saw the poor woman and her basket slip in a heap of horse-shite, her apples and oranges flying into the air. It was as good as the Daffy-Duck Circus (thought the Big Y'hoo) as he saw her exploding with rage and laying into the amused crowd of boys with her empty basket.

Just outside the entrance there was a tinker-boy. Two of the gatekeepers had stopped the lad going in - not until (and they smiled and winked at one another) he had sung his homespun version of 'The Valley of Sweet Slievenamon'. Once more, the words of his song came out all wrong. But he had the voice of a blackbird and left the onlookers wiping sentimental tears from their eyes as they listened to his delightful strains. When he'd finished and made his bow, they grabbed him by the seat of his britches and hoisted him into the air before passing him over the heads of the cheering crowd and into the Show Fair.

The Big Y'hoo followed in through the gate where he saw a young dancer attempting a makeshift hornpipe full of complicated hops and leaps on a half-door and knocking several splinters out of it. His father was rasping away on his fiddle and staring into the heavens with only the whites of his eyes showing and the horsehair of his bow hanging in shreds from the attempts he made to destroy the heart of the fiddle with the rage of his music. The onlookers (already well-oiled with the early day's fine bouts of drinking) started to shout and pelt their caps and ashplants good-naturedly into the air. The father was snaring in the heaps of coppers that were thrown down on the carpet in front of him and we wondered would he ever get to carry it all home or would the drinking-shops get their hands on it. We knew the answer for the father and son would be as drunk as two mules by nightfall.

The Big Y'hoo now turned to watch the high-stepping horses wending their way through the crowd in order to get to the start of the show-jumping. There wasn't a trace of dung on their plaited tails. Fine young damsels were astride their backs (a step or two in class beyond the reaches of himself) and they wore black jackets and hats and tightly-fitting cream trousers. Our dreamy hero took note of the shape of their arses as they cocked their whips in the air and bounced up and down on the horses, skilfully manhandling them. They were almost as noble in form as the horses themselves.

By now he was well and truly embracing the life of the Show Fair as he headed towards the Big Tent where he passed a number of women setting off at a smart pace to the displays of caged hens and geese. Some of them branched off for the agricultural hall where there were all sorts of fine exhibits - the rug-making and the bread 'n' cake making as well as the huge vegetables that had surely been blown up with a bicycle-pump. Many of the men had lost themselves amongst the machinery – the pulpers and ploughs, the forks, spades and rakes, all as shiny as pins. A few arthritic old farmers were leaning on their sticks admiring the cattle while their sons dug their fingers into the rich wool of the sheep. The sight of it all – you'd never think there'd been wars or famines or a scarcity of anything in Tipperary.

The Big Y'hoo sat on a high stool inside the Big Tent. From time to time one or two flirtatious young women gave him the glad eye and cocked their glass of ale in his direction and added the odd little bow and even a flaunting little wink or two – or at least he thought they did. The stream of their silvery laughter seemed to catch him by his heartstrings and after one or two glasses of stout he found himself sheepishly smiling back at them, a new longing throbbing in his throat. Amongst all those pretty creatures the eyes of one young damsel drew him from his drink. She was from the lower end of town and at the age of 20 was known for her ability to charm the legs off of an ass. Her father was a harness-maker, more often than not out of work and her mother was a little too fond of the gin-bottle. To escape from household drudgery this girl-of-the-town had developed a spirit for fun and frolicking and went by the name of the Bowery Maiden.

It's amazing what a few pints of stout can do. For with her heaven-sent eyes and those smouldering looks of hers she was soon murdering the heart out of him. Her hair (had the befuddled lad the words to say it) was the jackdaw's wing and her skin was the unblemished white of fresh milk and she had the black soot-drop delicately embroidered on her porcelain jaw and her vivid mouth was as red as cherries and she was wearing a flowering flouncy frock that swelled out here and there suggestively. She again winked her roguish eye at him and he (poor scholar) attempted to give her the wink back and called for another glass, this time of the whiskey (*'Gimmee the rale shtoof!'*).

And then, as though carried across the tent on the wings of an angel, he found himself miraculously seated next to her and gawking at the charming rise and fall of her laughter. After another whiskey he began to admire the detailed style and grace of her and the rotundity and curves of her, the disturbing way she crossed her legs and then clasped her knees together (the little devil). It was as though the world had changed from a dull white to a dazzling silver for nothing makes the world so merry and bright as looking at it through a glass of Irish whiskey. And as the stream flows to the river and the river flows to the sea, the sting inside in his eighteen-year-old body drove him further and further into the sway of her - so that the money (much to her delight) began burning a hole in his pocket as though all the coins were anxious to get loose. An irresistible wave of emotion had crept through his veins and there was nothing (he said to himself) that he'd like better than make a raid on her.

But she - though not much older than himself - was far superior to him in her knowledge of life's mysteries. She accepted a small glass of whiskey from him, which brought a pink flush to her cheeks, adding to her beauty. By now his tongue was as dry as alum and the lustful leer in his eye told the Bowery Maiden that he was like a lost flower looking for a drop of water and that she was the very thing a poor lad like himself would be needing.

The day was beginning to pass quickly. The Bowery Maiden had brought her bike (she said) to the rear gates of the Show Fair and the wheels had been somewhat buckled by the horses treading on them. Would the Big Y'hoo take a look at it? - her lame excuse for beckoning him out the gates and into the spidery web of those forbidden pleasures, which she knew only too well.

The drink had made him full of confidence. Wasn't he the worthy companion for this pretty damsel (said he to himself) - a man who could hold so much of the black stuff and whiskey inside him, a man who carried in his waistcoat-pocket his father's watch-and-chain and he swinging it casually round and round in his fist as they paraded out the tent and across the showground field.

With his arm around her, the two of them strolled behind the heap of bikes, the girl leading the incautious lad out under the wire fence. They walked across hidden fields, their faces turned towards the sunlight burning down on their heads. The

Big Y'hoo reached out for one or two wildflowers, which he gave to his damsel. She in turn reached out for armfuls of white clouds that were strewing the blue of the sky as she danced ahead of him. The breezes bowed the tips of the poplars and seemed to welcome them till they could hear the purling merriment of Fishing River, a laughing place for sunbathing, for swimming and secret joys.

They slipped down the slope and hopped over the wall, following the laughter of the liberal fairies till they were beyond the mill and the dashing pool that had drowned poor Feckless Mary the previous year. They had reached Fairyland and were lost amid the ferns. The branches of the trees crept down to make a grab at them and hold them back. The wagtails flew back into the briars to tell others of the boy-and-girl's intrusion into their secret recesses.

By now it had begun to dawn on the Big Y'hoo that, though he was wearing his new white collar, he was still little more than a big soft child. The wind in the trees seemed to be laughing at him and telling him the very same thing and to go back to the tent. There were drops of sweat on his flushed cheeks - not so much from the sunshine (little of which he had seen in the tent) nor yet from the effects of his carousal with the drinking-glass. No, these were the sweat-drops of real fear for the back-breaking beating which his saintly mother would give him if she ever found out what he was up to. He shuddered to think that all the previous goodness taught him by his parents was about to be dismantled and there was nothing he could do to prevent it. But by far the greatest fear was the knowledge that he would fry in hell for the sin he was about to commit if he gave way to this bouncing young temptress.

They lay down and listened to the nearby song of the river. The Bowery Maiden took the ribbon from her hair and unwound her dark tresses so that he might see their sleek luxuriance spreading round her face. She lay back in the ferns and the Big Y'hoo gazed at her like a cow looking at a field of after-grass. She sensed his inexperience, his uneasiness and the priest-ridden anxiety, which was going on behind his eyes. What good is life (she whispered to him) if we don't pause now and then and make sure we're alive? She'd lead him into new realms of mystery and invent her own type of music for him. There'd be no more delight (said she) in those childish games he once played on the riverbanks alongside other children from the hills. All that sort of nonsense would seem like a child putting his hand into a biscuit barrel, so tame and so trifling. That's what she said.

As the moments went by he started to learn a new song. Awkward lips were pressed to awkward lips and trembling fingers played quivering music where no fingers had ever played before so that this new man seemed to have slipped out of the world. No gold or silver (not even the fine mansions of lord and lady) would he have exchanged for this heavenly moment. Such furtive delights were beyond the bounds of Father Honesty in his confession-box. The Bowery Maiden was truly the answer to all his pagan prayers.

'Aren't you the bull-of-a-man!' she sighed and he in turn toasted her apple-cheeked beauty and the soot-drop painted on her jaw. 'You are lovelier than all the young mares in the Show Fair,' he'd have said, had he the words. The Devil and those liberal fairies now sat down to tea and carried the boy and girl off to a new and dangerous world. The Bowery Maiden threw off her dress and knickers, putting caution to the winds, splashed her legs out into the sally-hole, frightening the startled trout with her beauty and setting The Big Y'hoo's eyes clean out of their sockets. Before he could catch his breath, she dragged his togs off of him with a delicacy, which would have pierced the soul of every youth in the hills. There and then, in the shivering river, they horse-played to their heart's content.

They came out from the river and in their natural finery sprawled amid the ferns to dry themselves. There wasn't a breath of wind and no leaf stirred - just the sun dappling coolly through the trees. In this profane playfulness he was about to commit his first big sin (apart from stealing his mother's money and his father's watch!) - the sin that Father Honesty had warned him against. Let it all go to blazes (thought he) as he placed his arms round this strange woman whilst Fishing River tried to hold itself back as though frozen and yet all the time on the verge of crashing uncontrollably on towards the Limerick River. And then, just as when a gunshot is fired and the little sparrows and their distorted cries fly away from the gate ('Ah!' she thought - and 'Ah!' he thought) there came an aching music, pitching and rolling like the river's own song and in his flaming eyes their shone pins of liquid glory - Ecstasy.

But a short while afterwards there followed a change in him and, having indeed experienced a very wonder, there was now a dishonourable sadness in his heart. He could hear the haunting reprimand of the angry wind among the riverside trees. What have you done? What on earth have you done? He was sure the great God-in-heaven would seek him out, would find him lurking in the ferns and send him an unmerciful punishment like any common thief in the orchard, he was sure that poor Father Honesty in his confession-box would die of an untimely stroke when he unfolded to him the tale of his sinful enormities.

For any young man that had slaked his thirst as the Big Y'hoo had done, the time of fun and frolicking had to give way to a quiet grey time, to a leaden drowsiness and a desire for sleep. Our dizzy hero passed his hands over his eyes as though he had a hurt in them from the sunlight and soon he was in dreamland. The Bowery Maiden smiled down on his whitewashed features, the big baby that he was. She would have loved to smother him with her kisses but her thoughts all along (ah, the wiles of a girl from the town) had been far more inspired by a cruel craftiness that would now cause her to forsake him and direct herself back into the mists of the show-fairing merriment and gaiety. Ah, the innocence of a mountainy boy - never to see again this bewitching banshee, who had filled his spirit with so much sweet-as-honey pleasure.

She looked at the youthful snores of him. Then, quicker than you'd squeeze a lemon, she stole from the pockets of his britches his mother's precious coins, the few that were left him. She raised her eyes skyways to some pagan deity (thank you a thousand times, she said) and she then stole from his hip-pocket his father's priceless watch-and-chain. Even the *liberal fairies* hung their heads in shame at what she had just done and one or two of them wept.

Her heart pounding, she backed away silently through the ferns, leaving nothing but the ghost-of-him behind her. Then, cautiously looking round her, she scrambled into her dress and knickers and for a final whim (her cruelty and playfulness combined) she hid the forlorn lad's britches behind the trees near the stupefied cattle on the riverbank. She could have burst with the explosions of stifled laughter that came rising up in her chest. Racing across the field, she dipped under the wire fence. Rounding the heap of bikes, she was soon joining in the merrymaking of the crowds.

The Big Y'hoo opened his dull eyes. Foggy clouds seemed to be bundling themselves in his brain and the wind from the river blew cold and made him shiver. Far better had it been if he had never awoken from the obscure shapes of his sleep for there was nothing around him but spider-web stillness – just himself and the soul of the river. He now realized that this cruel woman had bewitched him and was clean gone. His mother's money was gone. The watch-and-chain of Tom-the-Bee was gone. His clothes had hurried after them. If only he could pluck out the thorn that was now in his heart. He, who this day had lost both his virtue and every stem of sense that he was born with, had paid a very dear price for his youthful sins-of-the-flesh. He bawled as any sick child would bawl. He bawled for his father. He bawled for his mother. He bawled to God-in-heaven that his ribs and backbone would not be entirely shattered by Bridie and Tom-the-Bee when he got home that evening.

He at last found his clothes and crept shamefacedly towards the Show Fair and in across the wire fence. He saw his father's bike - the only thing he had to throw at the Bowery Maiden, his eyes all the while searching among the knot of people for the scheming woman. The hatred that now took a hold of him (a hatred against all women) no words could describe.

3

In his clamping boots he staggered with his bike towards the gate and made his way out onto the lane. He teetered down Jinnet Street and out of the town. He cycled towards Abbey Cross, in the direction that some faraway instinct told him was the origin of his birth – home. His mind was full of remorse, full of sorrow for all his misdeeds: the thievery, the drinking, the lovemaking. He'd confess to the priest his theft of the silver coins and the theft of the pocket-watch. But the riverside debauchery, for which hell's gates were now summoning him, this he could never mention to Father Honesty in the confession-box – such was his shame. Ahead of him the hills and the smokiness of Chieftain Hill rose steeply and he was too weak to ride uphill. He could scarcely put one foot in front of the other. What would his older sister, Lucy, think of him? What would his little brothers and sisters think of him? One final effort had to be made and, like any man-of-fashion, he made a fair attempt to mimic the hero he had been this bright morning. Himself and his ringing brogues came walking round the bend at Abbey Cross. He turned up the road towards home, holding his bike as nonchalantly as he could, his hand pressed down on the saddle, his nodding head in rhythm with his plodding boots.

In front of him he saw four of Moll-the-Man's children (Lippy, Philly, Young Jim and Leppity). They'd come out gathering those shy little strawberries that hide beneath the foxglove leaves and, with their parents in town, were looking for news of the Show Fair. They scrambled up onto the ditch to get a closer look to see who was heading their way. It was the Big Y'hoo - the very fellow to amuse them.

'Tell us the news, blasht ye. Tell us the news of all the fine show-fairing and who was in it,' said Lippy. They had several questions for him, so anxious were they to get the news out of him - these poor scholars (he thought), who had never owned a suit between them, who had never worn a hard collar, who were still in their short britches (even Lippy had never worn a pair of long britches).

At the sight of the Big Y'hoo and all his finery, a feeling of hatred (never experienced before) had wormed its way into their hearts - not so much against the Big Y'hoo, but against the starched white collar they could see him wearing. They loathed it for the rank in which it placed him above them.

'Go 'way, ye pack of basthards!' roared the drunken youth. He knew it was time to strike out at them this day of all days and he being a new man – 18 and with the first hair on his face and allowed to wear his new white collar – he who unknown to these children had been celebrating his manly life with the sowing of the wild seeds of love.

The children had enough of his posturing. A bit of bear-baiting would be better sport than picking wild strawberries for their mother's jam-making and they began dancing round him, lifting their legs in the air and shouting abuse against all who ever came down from the mountains and against the mothers that had given birth to them.

Out stepped Lippy to challenge him. A dim light of warning glowed behind the Big Y'hoo's eyes as he tried to collect his sad thoughts. He didn't know whether it was in jest or not that these boys were raising their fists. 'Step out of mee way, ye blashted whoors!' he roared but they laughed all the more at him. They pulled at their ears and poked out their tongues and made grinning faces at him.

'Tis yeer hard white collar that we want,' they shouted. 'Coom on, blasht ye, give us yeer collar,' they chanted. And then the whole road echoed with 'Fight! Fight! Fight! - ye ashy-arsed basthard! Be a big man and fight us, ye Big Y'hoo!' The Big Y'hoo tottered this way and that like some enraged bull while the children swore they'd snatch off his manly collar and run off home with it as a keepsake.

'Coom on,' they shouted again – their impudence growing stronger as they jibed at him with their fists. Lippy stood at one end of him and his brothers at the other end, flexing their knees and peering at him from behind their closed fists. 'Boo Boo! Shoo Shoo! Yah Big Y'hoo!' they shouted devilishly.

'Is it fight ye want? he roared, a note of triumph in his voice. He'd not let them rape him of his collar. 'Mee family is dacent and I won't let them down,' said he, one hand protectively touching his collar. The spit glistened on his lips and with that he struck out blindly at the head of Lippy. But, just as the rabbit is no match for the ferret, the poor drunken youth was no match for these high-spirited boys and their hatred. Fair play to him - he clouted his fists into the heart of them, raining down blows on their backs and skulls. Blow for blow they struck back at him, Young Jim and Leppity driving in behind and underneath his legs, tried to unbalance him and topple him to the ground. Once there, they'd have him at their mercy.

It wasn't long before they had buffeted the poor devil's head till he was black and blue - chastising him as never his father could have done. He wouldn't go down. He was as strong as an ox. He stumbled across the road towards the ditch and staggered up onto it as though he were about to make a big speech. Lippy, like a dog and a deer at bay, leapt onto his shoulders and fastened his nails on the prized white collar. No badger, no terrier ever held on so tightly. In an almost death-struggle himself and the Big Y'hoo fell like two huge trees and toppled headlong down the dyke, landing in a sea of nettles.

The Big Y'hoo felt strangely dizzy and numb, thanks to the cursed drink. You'd think he was dead. He saw the hardness of Lippy's face above him and the hardness of the earth moving speedily towards him. Oh, merciful God - he hit his head on a discarded pick-axe frame and onto the stony base of the ditch. He felt as if an ass had kicked him and a small bloody lump appeared on his forehead. It was a wonder his head wasn't smashed like an egg. He lay grotesquely in the heart of the nettle-bed and darkness overwhelmed him.

Unaware (it is hoped) of the poor lad's injuries, Lippy wrenched off the hard collar and climbed back out of the dyke. His brothers ran over and peered in at the Big Y'hoo. There wasn't even a whimper out of him. Their little sister (Battlin' Sal) ran down the road to see what all the commotion was about and she followed them as they ran across the rishy field.

'We have the collar! We have the collar!' They were full of their simple triumph and were throwing the once-white and now dog-eared collar from one to the other. Not one of them bothered to consider whether the Big Y'hoo was alive or dead!

The sun had turned to nothing and the *mysterious fairies* came and gazed down at the Big Y'hoo and the blood drooling from his brow and his face as yellow as a bad moon. He looked like a dead crow and they wept for him.

Many hours later the harsh morning sunlight dropped on the white-faced ghost of the Big Y'hoo. His head hurt crushingly and his body was sore all over from the stinging nettles and the hurricane of the children's fists. Then he heard the vague crowing of the cockerels and the songbirds' cheerful songs. Where was he? It seemed but a moment ago that he was holding the young woman in his sweaty arms. And then he felt the bloody smears on his face and in his matted hair. He was rigid with cold and traced his unsteady steps to the stream. He had lost his collar, the symbol of his manhood. He had lost the silvery coins and the watch-and-chain. He bathed his face in the water and an irresistible wave of sadness welled up in him. He lumbered home across the fields, knowing well what was in store for him when his father and mother would see the sorry state of him and learn the truth about the fine day's outing he'd been having at the Show Fair.

In the early evening Tom-the-Bee, sensing that something was wrong and having been informed of his son's gaudy show in the Big Tent and his liberal beer-swigging and his high and mighty swaggering, found he was no longer the owner of his prized watch-and-chain. The sudden change in this kind-hearted man was something to behold as a raging venom boiled up inside in him. The rage of his wife was also as hot as a boiled spud and she vowed if she got hold of her son she'd nourish his hide and take the hatchet to him.

At the sight of his besmirched son staggering in along the haggart, his father reached for the rifle on top of the hob. He took the box of cartridges from the press and marched back into the yard. 'By the limping tinker - here comes mee little sugar-shite,' he roared. 'I'll put an end to his gallivanting!'

The Big Y'hoo was no fool and fled as though his little arse was on fire. Across the thistle-fields - across the bouhilauns - he fled, leaping the wire fence at Moll-the-Man's orchard and the stone-wall at Shy Dennis's cowshed. The Daffy-Duck Circus would have been proud to see the leaps he made. The volley of the rifle-shot came just above his head, resounding like thunder off of Red Scissor's hayshed. The terrified youth (like the pig at death's door) was sure he was going to die and he filled his britches with shite and landed in yet another heap of nettles, stung in a hundred places. And there, whimpering himself to sleep, he slept for the rest of the day and night rather than face the wrath of his father and his murderous gun. If a volcano hissed beneath his feet he would not have stirred a muscle from there.

Meanwhile the Bowery Maiden came running like the wind into her mother's yard. Her grandmother was sitting on the stool outside the half-door, the customary little black dog at the heel of her wellingtons. 'Mother! Mother! she announced, brandishing the stolen pocket watch-and-chain. To her surprise neither her mother nor her grandmother shared a bit of her joy but both proceeded to beat her out across the lane with the yard-brush till the blood ran down her legs. Thinking that she was about to die, she fell in a heap at their feet and begged for mercy.

That same evening, when the Big Y'hoo was still lying in his cosy bed of nettles, his conqueror was led into Tom-the-Bee's yard with her crestfallen shame. She begged him to forgive her. She returned the stolen coins, adding a few of her own to make up the tally. She placed the stolen watch-and-chain back on the nail as though nothing had happened and, like the simple fool that he always was, the kind-hearted man shook her by the hand and sent her away with his blessing.

When next evening came on and the cows were heard bawling to be milked and the asses and sheep - the hens and the geese - were all composing their own tunes, the Big Y'hoo (not knowing which way to turn) headed towards his home. 'Women! What are they?' said he to himself. 'Nothing but a shower of basthards that can land a lad like meeself into such a heap of trouble – into such a heap of nettles.' He came in the half-door and into the sobbing arms of his mother and father, both of whom withheld the murdering of him with the hatchet and the fierce gun. It was the passing of a youthful storm (they said) and they forgave him as only a mother and father could. He knew now that he was not yet a man, but still a child. He had indeed celebrated his 18th year on earth - had seen Joy – had seen Pain - and these two feelings would stand him in good stead in the coming years.

Inside in the town the lemony lights of the street lamps were again lighting up as if nothing unusual had happened. These lamps brought a cheer to the drinking-shops of Jinnet Street and to the railings round the market square. In several places the resounding songs continued to be sung out. The laughter of the drinkers beckoned the merrymakers to come in and spend their last few coppers before finding their way home from the bustling Show Fair. Beneath the new moon's lustre the tinker-women marched off through the back lanes with their bemused babies wrapped snugly inside their tartan shawls. The night turned black and the curtain came down on the town. It was just another day in the lives of us all.

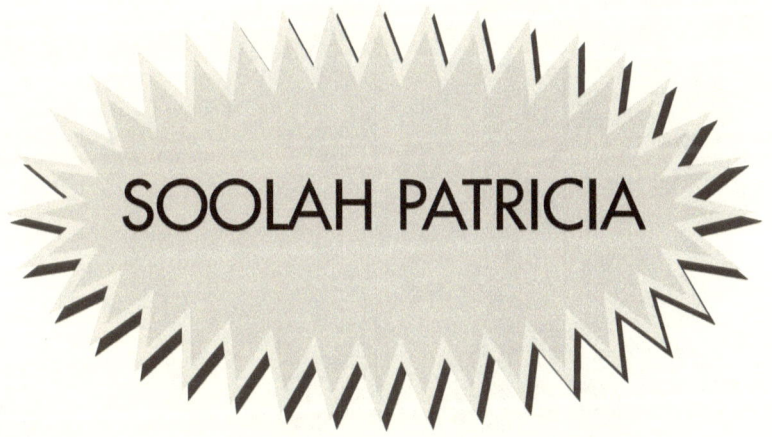

SOOLAH PATRICIA

1

It was the time of the Troubles. In the battle up around Mureeny the big guns of the Tan soldiers kept pounding down on our own young lads, some of whom were but a day out of school and still looking for work. The fighting went on from nine in the morning till four, eventually leaving six spattered corpses in the yard outside the church door. The children stood in the nearby field and looked at the dead youths through the bars of the haggart-gate. The mothers came running down the lane and with hushed breath crossed the churchyard. They looked at the carnage – at the bodies of their sons and their youthful idealism, fighting for Ireland's freedom they'd been told. It was a sad sight and there was nothing glorious in it. They took off their aprons and threw them on top of the bloody bodies to cover them. Then with feelings of pure distain and cold fury they took their miserable way back home and only then did they tear out their hair and cry like a pack of sick donkeys. They never got out of bed for the next week and a half. And then they put on their long black robes for another year. They were grey-haired for the rest of their lives.

The following day the children ran around collecting the spent cartridges. They got hammers and proceeded to hammer them into the church flowerbed, making a reverent circle of them in honour of where our fighters had died. There wasn't one of the men who now hadn't thoughts of sheer murder on their minds. They'd have liked nothing better than find a few stray Tans and take them out behind a rock and cut their throats with the reaping-hook. But enough of this sad old talk.

2

Ever since the events of that wretched day Tippity had been working with his small band of rebels in the pine forests on the far side of the Little Bald Plain. Each day he'd been watching the Tan soldiers driving proudly by in their tender-vans, sitting back-to-back with their rifles pointed towards the ditch in case a little leprechaun might leap out at them. To see them parading the countryside as though they owned the damned place filled him with anger and he couldn't wait to send them off to a quick death.

As soon as their vans reached Echo Bridge, he and his band crept out from their hiding-place and loosened the pins on their grenades They lobbed them from inside the ditch, killing half a dozen Tans and leaving their limbs round the road. That's when their colonel (*Perilous Joe*) showed he wasn't a pure fool altogether and ordered his soldiers to put wire cages round their vans so that Tippity's grenades would roll off and explode harmlessly on the road.

'I'll take the smile from off their faces and teach them a few Irish manners,' said Tippity to himself. He spent the next few nights fixing long steel hooks onto his grenades so that the next time his comrades pelted them at the vans, the hooks remained fixed on the nets, preventing the grenades from rolling off. Once more the explosion split the air, blowing the Tans (thought Tippity) back to the hell they'd come from.

Rage! Rage! We didn't know the meaning of that word till a few days after Tippity's attack with the hooks. The soldiers' anger turned into something like a tornado and at any hour of the day or night they'd rattle their boots round the depths of every yard and haggart – into our hen house, our pig house and cowshed. They charged into every room and destroyed what bits of furniture we had. We saw (even the children) the insatiable hatred in their eyes at not being able to get hold of Tippity. In the morning we were left picking up the broken bits of our tables and chairs and spent hours trying to glue them back together. It was clear that the Tans wouldn't leave us alone till they'd given Tippity an unmerciful death and left him to rot abroad in the bog for the eagles to dine on. However, after days searching for him, they could see they'd have to resort to a more sinister tactic than wasting their days tracing Tippity's footsteps out across the bog. This was their devil-of-a-colonel's own crafty idea.

So, on this fine spring morning we heard them clattering their van up the hill and testing the strength of their lungs as though they were a crowd of angry bulls fresh in from Spain. They went out passed the forge and headed along the Little Bald Plain till they came to the farmhouse where Tippity's father (*Old Tim*) was whittling a smart finish to his snare-sticks. They jumped down from the van and pounced on the old man, ignoring his feeble protests. They dragged him out of his chair and tied him to his horse-and-cart in the hope he'd squeal for mercy like one of our cornered pigs. Then they stripped the shirt from off of his back and flogged him mercilessly on the boards of his cart. Fair play to him - Old Tim had the same lion-hearted courage as his son. There was no way he was going to betray Tippity's whereabouts - no matter what price he'd have to pay with his tortured body. What sort of father would he be if he told them the plans his son had been making for the destruction of their hated foreign barracks round the hills of north Tipperary?

The soldiers steered the van up as far as the half-door, kicking the chair and Old Tim's basket of snare-whittles out of the way. They dragged him across the yard to the back of the van where they lashed his ankles to the tailboard. Then, with the old man strapped down, they thundered across the stream and headed for the unmade road where they picked up a bit of speed. At every turn of the wheel the old man's skull was hopped off of the stony road. Had the wicked whelps no fathers of their own back in their own country?

The children ran out from the haggart and stood on the flagstones to see what all the noise was about, not knowing that their morning was about to be turned into a cruel fantasy. They heard the roar of the van and then they saw the savage carnage and the blood dripping from Old Tim's crushed head (*mee head! mee head! sweet suffering Jaysus, mee feckin' head!*), splashing behind him on the dusty road and spattering the trees and bellflowers. A pig, stretched out on the horse-and-cart for an uninvited meeting with his slaughterers, was a sight all our children knew well, having seen the sad pig's blood spattered on the straw of the cart. But - to see the murder of an old man who had never put a single bad word passed his lips – that was something else.

Would the children ever forget his dying screams? The very stones must have risen up at the sight of what was happening and all because the Tans couldn't get their filthy hands on Tippity. And after seeing such unbelievable savagery for the first time in their lives they were filled not only with sorrow and pain but with a fierce anger against these soldiers from abroad – an anger that would never leave them.

'We'd give the world to set our two eyes on Tippity,' laughed the Tans, pointing back at the young rebel's dying father. But with his last feeble breath he told them go feck themselves – put their filthy noses up their mother's arses. Then his soul fled away over the hills and on towards the Beyond – to a far better place where life's troubles would be gone from him forever.

The soldiers turned the van round and wheeled the old man back up by Free 'n' Easy's stile. They entered the yard and unharnessed his ankles. Their anger was now sated and they laid his battered corpse down in the yard - almost reverently. The hens, ducks and geese (weren't they the wise ones?) scurried away into the silent haggart but Lancy (Old Tim's sheepdog) was utterly bewildered and sat beside his dead master, frantically howling and licking the bloodstains from his face. The sow was next to hurry away and hide herself in the depths of the haggart dock-leaves. Her turn might well be next.

The soldiers went out past the pig house where they found the horse's tackling and harness inside the stable-door. They made a hurried fire from the twigs round the woodpile and brought out dead ferns from the side of the cowshed. The wind rose up around them and soon a blazing fire was heard rustling. It filled the yard with thickening smoke before turning red and blue on itself. They threw the tackling (the collar, the blinkers and haymes) into the fire. For a minute or two they thought about putting a torch to the thatch of the sturdy old house. However, even their black hearts protested at doing the likes of that. Instead, they crossed the haggart where they set fire to the two cocks of hay. Its blaze would be seen below in the valley and in the top windows of the Big House – if not as far as the distant streets away in the town. The burnt hay would be a salutary lesson for all young revolutionaries and knock any vague plans they had out of their patriotic little heads. News of Old Tim's murder was now going to spread far and wide – up through the hills and out through the bog and as far as Chieftain Hill and maybe even into the ears of God Himself above in his heaven.

The day was drawing on. The soldiers seemed to regret their recent action and to sober up a bit. After all, they were only youths from inside British jails or else out-of-work labourers, looking for excitement and anxious to earn a shilling or two in support of their wives and lady-friends back home. There was now a mood of foreboding in their midst as they sat on their haunches round Old Tim's dead body. Their hats rambled down sluggishly over their faces as though to hide their guilt. Each soldier seemed locked inside in his own lonely isolation in that strange luminosity of the day's twilight. They made Old Tim as decent as they could and covered him with a blanket from the house. After a while they took out their fags and began putting smoke to the heavens in an effort to calm their nerves. They began to talk thoughtfully to one another and to recollect the morning's events. Their voices took on a hushed and subdued tone. 'What have we done? What on earth have we done?' The sun was beginning to go down, tinting the clouds with bright hues so that the late afternoon seemed to glow round the dead man with a hazy lemon light. The ditches too seemed to take on a delicate blue from the sky and the mountains. Already the evening flies were gathering in around the body and were waiting to lay their eggs.

At last, blessing themselves to ward off the wrath of God, they hauled themselves into the van and clattered out of the farmyard, the wheels rumbling heavily on the gravel and the soldiers resting their chins reluctantly on their guns as they passed down by the forge and on across the river before vanishing towards their barracks. The children came out and stood dumbfounded on the flagstones and watched them pass by for the second time that day.

3

Soolah Patricia (she was 15 at the time) was the youngest of Old Tim's children and the only one still left at home. On the afternoon of her father's death she was coming home from the church in the village. She was a girl of apple-bloom with bright cornflower eyes – *the smiley one* we used to call her for she usually had a smile on her as big as a watermelon. Her mother (*Nora*) was still in the hospital after a neck operation to remove a goitre and had ordered her daughter to go across the fields and bring back the two gallons of holy water from the church barrels to give her father's farm the blessings of a new life - blessings for the cows and the sheep, for the ass and the horses too, who would soon be going out to plough the Seventh Field, blessings that would bring good fortune to her family (little did the poor girl know what had just happened) and good fortune to her own small patch of cabbage-shoots which one day soon would sprout up in the hot sun.

There was a stream of other girls walking home alongside her, lumbering along with two heavy gallons of holy water apiece. The younger children stopped their play as soon as they saw her heading towards the mountain path that would lead her to her father's half-door. Not one of them had the heart to confront her and tell her the miserable news about the horrendous scene they'd witnessed a few hours earlier.

As soon as she crossed the yard she felt a ghostly creepiness in the air – no bird singing, no leaf moving. Then she smelled the pungent stench of the burnt hay cocks in the haggart and she saw behind the pig house the horse's tackling – just a few small bits of sad burnt leather. She gave a roar out of her that almost caused the dead spirits to rise up from their tombs in the graveyard and she ran in the door to the Welcoming Room. The neighbours had beaten her to it and had straightened out whatever few sticks of furniture they could so as to make the place decent. There was a crowd of tearful elderly folk sitting on chairs like ancient statues all along the walls, their rosary beads in their fists. They had pulled the settle-bed out into the middle of the floor and on it they had laid the battered body of poor Old Tim. In spite of his suffering, he was now as peaceful as a sleeping child, with a crucifix in his clasped fingers. If Soolah Patricia were to die this very minute nothing could be worse. She felt her heart was about to burst asunder and come out in bits through her ears and she threw herself across the settle-bed before falling like a shattered dish in a deep faint.

When morning sunlight broke through the clouds, bishop High-Hat and half-a-dozen clergymen came on the scene. They led our sad procession in along the gravel path inside the cemetery gates of the graveyard. The funeral bells tolled mournfully. There wasn't a soul that didn't attend and draw comfort from fervently reciting their rosaries for the soul of Old Tim – that is if you forget about Tippity, who didn't dare set foot amongst us as well as his saintly mother, who was still strapped to her bed inside in the hospital. None of us had the heart to ride into town and give her the sad news about Old Tim. Even Soolah Patricia had recovered her spirits enough to get herself in as far as the side of the grave. But to our astonishment the poor girl was as silent as the grave and she never shed a single tear – not one.

The mournful coffin was held aloft. Then it was paraded three or four times round the graveyard before being rested gently on top of the boards at the graveside. The obsequies for his soul were solemnly recited and not a dry eye was seen among us (except for Soolah Patricia). The bishop was a wise man and he took this opportunity to remind us of Jesus on his cross. He said how our Saviour forgave his murderers. He said that if it was good enough for Jesus to do so fine a thing it was surely goods enough for the likes of us and that we were to try and follow in his footsteps. He then roused our spirits and said we were to forget despair and that a new day was dawning and that Hope and Freedom were fast on their way to our downtrodden land. Meanwhile, above in the clouds Old Tim was looking down at us and smiling to himself at the grand and holy show being staged in his honour among his friends round the hills. A few minutes later we took our silent boots and rosary beads home with us. In spite of the bishop and his fine words we felt that a fierce cauldron of hatred was about to bubble up and not one of us knew where it would end up.

Next day was the day that Soolah Patricia left her childhood firmly behind her. She'd had time to think clearly not only about the tragic death of her father but to compose a plan as to what she should do. She knelt down in the yard and made a solemn vow to her father's memory. 'Perilous Joe may have the brains of a pope (she thought) but it won't do him a bit of good for as sure as I'm mee father's daughter, he'll find himself rotting in hell before tomorrow's sun goes down. This I vow.'

She climbed on top of the galvanized sheeting over the pig house where Old Tim had always hidden his rifle. She knew he used to keep a box of cartridges in the press cupboard when he was alive. With the gun and the cartridges, she was like a hen about to lay an egg. That night she couldn't sleep a wink and when all was quiet she stole out the back window and headed across the fields. She hid the rifle in the depths of the grove surrounding the Big House and returned home.

Next day, in honour of her dead father, she put on his best boots to comfort her sorrowful heart, stuffing them here and there with bits of brown paper. She left the yard and with a mixture of fear and excitement she ran through the tangled undergrowth until she came to the woodland bordering the Big House. She lay down low and she waited. She knew that Perilous Joe would soon be arriving - himself and his posh motorcar, the blackguard that had ordered the torture and death of her father. She'd give him a welcome none of us would ever forget. In spite of herself she was shivering and she asked God to forgive the evil that was in her heart.

The light was beginning to fade and it would soon be dark – darker still for Perilous Joe (she thought). He'd soon be at the gateway of the Lodge. He'd get out of his car (she could picture it) and ring the bell at the gates. But he'd never get a chance to steer his car down the avenue and circle the lake in front of the Big House. Her gun would see to that. She made the sign of the cross on her forehead and continued to finger her mother's rosary beads. In her pocket were the two waxy apples that her father had given her the previous week for the journey to the church to fetch the gallons of holy water. And now - to steady her nerves - she chewed them till there was nothing left, not even the core. Her soul might be empty but her heart was aflame as she pictured the wicked Tans and the disfigured body of her murdered father and the bloodstains on his jaw. She could hear the howling tears of Lancy, their faithful old sheepdog. She could see her heartbroken mother too, who had at last been told the sad news – could see her throwing off the blankets inside in the hospital and bewailing her lovely man. And she longed more than ever to see the blood of Perilous Joe reeking the ground at her feet.

And then she heard the purr of the engine as the car came around the bend and halted at the Lodge gate. Her fear and anger were almost too much to bear but she knew what she had to do – one death for another death for the sake of her beloved father. Not a wink would she sleep till it was over and done with.

The colonel stepped out of his motorcar. He went around and opened the passenger door for his young lady-friend, Miss Raffles from faraway Bow. Soolah Patricia gazed at this stylish young girl – a girl no more than a year or two older than herself and as slim as a yard-brush with a dash of red paint on her lips and white powder on her jaws.

It was time to act and in the blink of an eye she leapt in front of the great man, a blizzard of hate scalding her eyes as she pointed the gun at him. 'Let you run,' she gestured, motioning the rifle towards the hapless Miss Raffles. 'Run for yeer life!' But, so great was the fear that gripped the English girl that her limbs had become as soft as sugar and she stood there, transfixed and clinging to the handsome colonel's jacket. He tried to protect her, his arms around her shoulders.

Soolah Patricia thrust the heel of her rifle into his chest but he merely spat his spit of contempt back into her face. 'So, ye'd give anything to set yeer eyes on Tippity, would ye?' said she, wiping the spit from her jaw. Perilous Joe had never seen such rage as this – and she so young, the fierce rifle in her fist.

'I'm Tippity's flesh-and-blood sister,' she cried and her eyes were full of tears. 'And now – for the last time in yeer miserable life ye can set yeer sights on the sun – the sun, which my poor father can never see again.'

The colonel hadn't time to utter a word or say a prayer. And even then – his terrified young lady-friend didn't make a run for the trees but remained frozen by the side of her man. There was no escape. She was on her way to meet her Maker. Soolah Patricia discharged her bullets – *CRACK! CRACK!* – into the man responsible for her father's murder – himself and his young mistress. The rifle-crack shook the forest pheasants from their reverie in Jonjo's nearby potato-field while the sun refused to shine and the winds brought down angry raindrops. The simple Irish girl had blown out both their temples. The smoky stench of blood and burning cordite filled the air and bits of the colonel's skull clung to the wheels of his car. She had dreamed about this moment the minute she'd imagined her father's skull hopping off of the road and she wiped the colonel's blood across her cheeks. Before the gatekeeper could raise the alarm, she threw the gun into the lake and darted into the shadows of the evening. It wouldn't be long (she thought) before the news got around that the colonel was dead. And what would Tippity do then? For it'd be on him that all would turn their suspicious eyes.

She continued her homeward way till she came to the river where she halted. She wiped the blood from her cheeks. She removed her dress and stepped into the shivering river. She could feel it welcoming her, could feel it wrapping itself round her and cleansing her of her sin. She ran home and entered the Welcoming Room in a pure daze. She knelt beside the settle-bed where her poor father had recently been laid. Bowing her head in serene contemplation as though he were still by her side, only then did she shed tears by the bucket-load.

By this time the yard was chattering with the last of the blackbird songsters scurrying to their roost. Dark clouds began slowly spiralling across the moon and all nature seemed to be peering down into Old Tim's yard. She got up off her knees and looked out the half-door. In spite of her tears she was in a state of blissful ecstasy as she hopped over the singletree and into the haggart. She headed for the ploughed fields and with the holy water she began to bless the sacred soil before giving a final fist of it to the ass leaning in over the gate.

THE GIRL WE
CALLED IMAGINE

1

Our men often got into rows over the flow of the water in their streams or over divides of land and ditches and many a raging battle with pitchfork and cudgel they'd had in the past. But when it came down to it we were all joined together at the hip for we knew we were the true Irish and that the high and mighty English lords were a bunch of trespassers - at least that's what you'd hear the likes of Warbling Will and other men saying. The quicker they marched off and hopped on the cattle-boat, the better it'd be for us all, including themselves, so that we could live our lives in peace with our own little bit of pride left in us.

The women, however, rarely possessed so sharp a dose of hatred as the men, though Soolah Patricia had had more than enough reason to turn vengeful following the Tans' cruel murder of her father. They had enough on their plates to get through the day-to-day grind of scratching out a living for themselves and their brood of chicks. Often, they didn't know where the next day's bit of bread would come from. As mothers they were certain what should always be first on their list - their children had to be clothed and fed and their brains to be nourished with more than a watery bowl of stirrabout if they were ever to make a name for themselves in the schoolhouse of Dang-the-skin-of-it. And they'd warn you (if their men gave them a chance to get a word in edgeways) that we should keep our mouths shut tight and should tolerate (if not love) these rich landowners in spite of their foreign ways and titles. Only a mother could have such feelings as this. Without the gentry (they'd say) where would we have been by now? Dead and buried long ago – that's where. Hadn't men like Lord Manners, Lord Damocles and Lord Dungarees always behaved scrupulously – saving our forefathers from starvation during the merciless Famine. Hadn't they opened their granaries of oats and always supporting the poor like ourselves, who would never have been able to turn our hands to a brown ten-shilling-note without their help? Ah, the romantic women – they could see those fine rich lords stepping out from their grand mansions and reaching out their hands to our people. Could see them giving the men part-time seasonal work at ploughing and harvest-time and during the pheasant and partridge shoots. Could see their rosy-cheeked daughters given work in the kitchens and bedrooms of the Big House and serving at mealtimes, ensuring they had the odd few shillings at the end of the week to bring home for the table and feed the younger children. Could see how sons and daughters alike were getting an extended education, learning new skills in field-husbandry and gardening (the sons) or in cooking and dressmaking (the daughters). That was how the world had always been oppressed and, foremost among the women, Dowager's wise old head would remind her husband (Warbling Will) of this fact and throw it back in his face. It was a pure disgrace – all this patriotic nonsense in the men's heads. Would this simpleton-of-a-husband-of-hers ever get a stem of sense?

You'd often see the women and men working together in the fields and woods, beating the flax and rising up the pheasants with the pointer dogs. They were like a little family of happy song-thrushes (the men as well as the women) and you could write a poem or paint a picture about them. The Big House was their home-from-home on these occasions. That was the bright side of the sky. But life wasn't that simple and Dowager would shake her head for she knew that this was only half the story, knew where the dark clouds lay and where other even darker clouds were looming. The Devil (she'd say) had never left the hearts of the more hostile men in our midst – especially those cold-eyed articles with no sons and daughters working for the Big House. She'd heard them say that acts of kindness from the hands of the high-and-mighty gentry had always been done to further their own interests – even during the Famine Days when they needed a constant workforce to keep their estates alive and well. Oh, the miserable lowborn heathens (she'd tell you) to be saying such awful things! And she'd insist that all of us (men, women and children) ought to get down on our bended knees and thank God that our sons and daughters were so well fed – with a shine in their eyes and hair. And though Warbling Will couldn't keep her quiet all the time, there were occasions when she felt she was as helpless as the rest of the women, who were never allowed to make a political statement of any sort, knowing they'd always be in second place to their men. It was a constant tug-of-war - the hearts of the men and the hearts of the women pulling in opposite directions.

If you were a magician – if you could look inside our men's head or see deep into their hearts - they'd tell you that they had inherited neither education or wealth. They'd tell you that they'd always felt inferior to the foreign settlers with their mighty estates and their lofty ways, their long tweed overcoats, their smart farting-jackets and their plus-four trousers. Dowager half- guessed the truth. She could see why Warbling Will and his fellow-men sometimes behaved like those heavy storm clouds gathering in across the bog while she and the women went on twisting their way like a scampering stream through each day as best they could. Nothing would ever change (she felt) because intimate conversation was rarely if ever a part of everyday life between a husband and wife. They were always too tired at the end of the day. The women, therefore, kept their innermost thoughts and feelings locked inside their hearts until they stepped into the confession-box where they could let Father Sensibly know what was troubling them. God forbid (they told him) that they'd ever get their men's rancour into their souls. All they wanted from the day their children entered the services of the Big House and curtsied before the lord and his lady was a genuine respect for themselves and their families, a recognition that they were part of a noble race – the Irish. That was one thing (they told their priest) that they had in common with their men: they were proud of their race.

2

And now we come to the girl we grew to know as Imagine from the day she arrived. Her true name was Imogen and she was the daughter of Lord Politely. She had a shoulder-length mane of saddle-coloured hair, soft were her cheeks and (unlike the rest of us) her teeth were as white as milk. She'd remind you of a swan with her classical long neck and her arms and fingers as slender as grass. She seemed to be forever cheerful, always smiling on rich and poor alike – with a genuine sense of God's goodness and a belief that all mankind (be they from the native sod or elsewhere) were equal to one another in the eyes of the Lord for they were born in his own image and likeness, weren't they?

It was the children who first noticed her – not long after her arrival and her wedding to lord Plus-Fours. Whenever they saw her riding by on her spanking pony (*Rosetta*), they'd run out to get the smell of the new leather on her boots and the pony's saddle and the warm cloud of fragrant perfume wafting in the air behind her. They clapped their little hands ('If only we could grow up to be like Imagine!') when they saw her stopping at the flagstones to greet them.

Whereas we had our own well-trained horses for going to the creamery or fetching back the turf from the bog or yoking them up to the plough, it was simply for pleasure that she rode her pony – going off for a day's adventure into the hills for she loved nothing better than taking in the mountainy breezes, contemplating the rivers and woods and the harmonious haunts of our Irish fairy-folk, those spirits of the wild places that we all knew so well.

Like the children, the women too found her a sight to behold with her long red cloak and green skirts, with her blouse the colour of a pigeon's throat and her gloved hands expertly mastering the reins. It soon became a daily routine to see the two of them passing by (herself and the pony).

She became so engrossed in our daily lives that our women treated her as though she was one of their own and soon forgot to call her Lady Plus-Fours. Nor did they dare call her by her first name (*Imogen*), which was far too familiar a way of talking to any member of the gentry. Instead, they found themselves going further downhill and labelled her with a well-meaning but slightly outrageous derivative of her Christian name, addressing her simply as *Imagine*. And whenever women stopped her in her riding and gave her the traditional little curtsy they'd always follow this up with a bit of news like 'Timmy's Kerry-blue cow fell into the drain' or 'Fatty-Matty lost his pocket-watch in the potato-field.' This seemed to entrance her and she'd cock her head to the side and listen to each new bit of daily gossip, seemingly captivated by the long-winded embroidery of our women's speech and the musical accents of their words and phrasing. She'd place her gloved fingers thoughtfully to her lips and murmur, 'Imagine that! Imagine that!' It was as if she was signalling her utter disbelief that such-and-such a mundane pronouncement could ever be true. And anxious to stay as long as she could, she'd draw on the reins in case the charming Rosetta might be getting a bit tired from listening to all this human chattering. Indeed, the poor animal sometimes lost all patience with her and could be seen tossing her creamy mane and pawing at the ground and getting ready to make a bolt for the hills at any minute.

As a result of this quaint little habit of hers *(Imagine this! Imagine that*!) our women began answering her good-naturedly as the weeks went by. 'Yes, it is indeed a grand morning, Imagine,' or 'No, I didn't see your father with his shotgun out this morning, Imagine.' She may well have mistaken such talk as another example of our broad-vowelled way of saying her name. However, we began to believe that she liked this friendly misnomer and so, *Imagine* became her name and *Imagine* it was going to stay.

Perhaps she realised how privileged she was to be the only rich lady in our midst ever to have been given this personal honour of the friendly name (like Jack-the-Herd, Moll-the-Man or anyone else we knew). And she took to her new name with an undisguised pleasure and even wore it (we felt) with a good deal of pride.

As far as anyone could recall this was the first time that any of us had spent more than a few seconds familiarising ourselves with any member of the established gentry. For there wasn't one of us who hadn't had it drummed into our skulls since childhood that there was a mighty big difference between Tipperary's rich folk and ourselves. It had always been the custom to speak only when spoken to by the high and the mighty. However, we soon heard from Father Sensibly and Doctor Glasses that Imagine had her fine manners and delicate touches brushed into her from an aristocratic school in far-off France as well as the Ladies' Academy in Cheltenham Spa across the sea – all topped off with a season of regattas and balls amongst the rich folk in Dublin's rich suburb of Rathlofty.

'Who would have thought it (whispered the old gossips) – for us to have taken a shine to a young lady from Cheltenham Spa and Rathlofty?' But (we could have interjected) the reason was because she was a young girl not above inspecting our pig house or helping an old lady with an armful of sticks for the fire. Of course, we soon learnt that (though very young) she had been married off by her father (*Lord Politely*) to Lord Plus-Fours - and he 30 years her senior - simply for his vast acres of land rather than his handsome bearing or courtly manner for he had neither of these and was indeed a rough sort of diamond.

In contrast, you'd have to laugh when you saw how our tongue-tied men with their inbred shyness didn't know what to do with the ladylike Imagine except to shuffle their hobnail boots, bury their nervous chins in their topcoats and take off their coy caps before giving her a stuttery cough and making her a confused little bow when they'd rather be making a quick dash for the hills. It would make you sick to look at the carry-on of these old hypocrites. On the surface they appeared well-mannered and polite when they met her but with their ingrained hurt and their long-term anger, with their animosity against those whom they thought too grand or far higher up the ladder than themselves – what they'd like to be doing was giving her the spit from their mouths, the snot from their nose and a kick up the arse. Of course, Imagine and her innocence hadn't a notion of all this bitterness in our men, having never spent time talking to any of them.

There was one exception to all this. Imagine found she had a special affinity with My-Son-Jack. The bond between herself and Dowager's eldest son went back a few months earlier, back to a day in springtime when his star was set to rise sky-high in her eyes. A storm came on suddenly like a glowering rash from beyond Corcoran's well and there were several bolts of lightning followed by drum-rolling thunder above the creamery road. Straightaway the whinnying Rosetta turned into a lather of sweat, forcing her to make a sudden bolt so as to get away from the lashing rain and reach safety. At that same moment My-Son-Jack was bringing in an armful of logs from behind the pig house. His eyes nearly fell out of his head when he saw the distress Rosetta was in and how Imagine was getting thrown indelicately around the bushes. He pelted the logs inside the half-door and, heedless of the downpour, raced out across the yard stream to tackle the deadly danger that faced the helpless girl and her pony. In a flash he was at her side and snatching at the reins. Bravely he fought with the pony and, knowing (as he did) the nature of any stressed creature, he managed to restore her to a state of calmness. It was something of a miracle when into his arms the senseless Imagine fell from off the pony's back, when into his cornflower-blue eyes she found herself looking once she came back to the world of the living with her peace restored. From that day forth she felt that this young man, unlike those other aristocratic toadies above in the Big City, was the sort of man who could take on the world for her if she ever asked him. She knew it. Maybe he did too.

After that she couldn't keep away from Dowager's door. When she'd stop her pony at the flagstones before making her way on up the hills, the younger children would stop playing in the Bluebutton Field. They'd run excitedly across the haggart and over the singletree – just to get a look at the latest fine clothes she was wearing (their lovely warm colours) and the beautiful pony she was riding. For a lady of youthful years Imagine was discretion itself on these occasions and had the good sense never to put her foot inside the half-door and embarrass Dowager. It was as if she knew (though how she had learnt it, we couldn't fathom) that a little cabin with a pile of children in it would often be dirty with an untidy jumble of boots and coats all around the floor. 'Are you decent?' she'd say, waiting politely on the flagstones until Dowager smoothed down her hair and undid the straps of her apron so that she'd come out to greet her politely and mannerly. Imagine then tied Rosetta to the grove's singletree over the road and began cleaning the mud from her boots in the yard-stream.

Those days (God be good to us) were very fine indeed for a short while – that is, on the surface they seemed good enough. If one left the men to one side the spirit of Imagine was at one with the rest of us. We were at one with her – like the two sides of a windowpane. Each day she was able to go off on her peaceful rambles up through the mountains, hunting the woods in search of wild birds – especially the small greenfinch, the linnet and the corncrake. She was able to sit for hours amid the wildflowers and the rare species of butterflies – examining all sorts of mushrooms and faunae. And just before the sun lowered itself and the chorus of grasshoppers took its place the children would see her returning with her arms full of nature's treasures – unusual flowers for her presses and various leaves for her scrapbook. It was clear to their mothers that this gentle soul had the same love and appreciation of the beautiful countryside that we all had in our hearts – even the coarsest of our men. If time allowed, we might see a lump of fresh cow dung hardening in the noonday sunlight. We'd stop a while and gaze at a wily old crow standing alongside the new dung. He was patience itself. He was waiting – waiting for the dung to harden. Then he'd lift it up with his beak. He'd turn it over and then (what he had been waiting for all along) there appeared before his eager eyes his next dinnertime banquet – all the little pink and blue maggots underneath the cooked lump of dung.

That old crow had patience. Imagine had patience too in her search for rare plants. The rest of us had patience as well – either in catching the little birds in our cage-traps or in setting out our snares for the rabbits. We were full to the gills with patience – all of us.

But even that old fairy-woman, Patience, was soon seen not to be satisfied. Talk was one thing. Action was another thing. And some of our men said that it was high time for a change in our country – time to bite back and wave the green flag of Ireland above our heads. Above in the Big City there were men who had already run out of patience and were preparing to strike a blow for the freedom of our land. The streets of the city were soon to be turned upside-down. It was the holy season of Easter – a time when the world was saddened as it recalled the events that led to poor Jesus being strung up on his cruel cross. And just as Jesus had risen up from the dead it was now their own time (said the rebels in the Big City) to have a bit of guts and rise up and show their manly faces. When a cow strays into a neighbouring field we hunt it back to where it came from (that's what they said). And the foreign settlers were in the wrong field (they said). And many of our own men had to agree with them. And some of our young men had already begun to make little escapades out into the hills where they started marching and drilling and preparing for the skirmishes that they knew would come. The old gossips reported what was already happening above in Currywhibble where Patsy Boon was daily leading his bands of young men as they came out from the church gates after Sunday Mass, leading them out passed the-Valley-of-the-Pig for the gun practising. Why on earth hadn't his mother been able to put a stop to him? For without proper army training he'd be of little use or no use at all when the call to take up arms was sounded. And indeed, that same poor wretch was soon to be chased up into the hills at the foot of Chieftain Hill where he starved to death beyond in Mureeny. May God be good to his soul – a youth with a heart and a love of his land and he dying at the tender age of 33 from neglect and consumption.

Once more the women shook their heads and sighed. Now that the fighting began to spread around the Big City and was soon to travel like an escaped fire down towards our countryside, they could see that we were going to get a few licks of it before long and they were filled with worry – thinking which son of theirs might be killed in a battle before the year was out. Oh, the stupidity of our men (said they to one another). It was always the men (they said). It wasn't the women that forced themselves to lift the pitchfork or the pike in days gone by. It wasn't the women (they said) that went off to do the fighting to regain our land and suffer the dire consequences of even greater repressions against them and their race.

3

And now the dam of patience was broken and the haunting hour had come. There wasn't a man (even amongst those that were earning their keep below at the Big House) who wouldn't relish taking up the gun to destroy the presence of the foreign settlers for once and for all. For, when all the unravelling was done (and in spite of the kindly ways in which the Big House had always treated us) our men felt themselves tainted by the way the fat of our land had always come to belong to the rich oppressors alone.

Oppressors? Few grown men knew the meaning of this word. But, sitting on the upturned ass-and-car and playing with the cat and her kittens, even the children came to understand what their fathers' hearts were telling them. There'd be no satisfaction – not until the last of the foreign settlers had gone back over to John Bull could Tipperary and the rest of Ireland wash its hands in the river and perform the cleansing ritual.

Dowager cursed out loud when she heard the men using such outrageous talk. She couldn't forgive them for their thoughts. In her as in many of the women who had worked in the service of the Big House there was stamped that little bit of light-hearted girlishness – that womanly feelings of romance when she thought of the fine carriages and the fine men and women and they dancing their lives away. Warbling Will, when he heard her whispering these thoughts into his ears in the marriage-bed would turn his back on her in disgust. 'Women and their dreamery (he'd say).' A stop would have to be put to it all.

But thanks to Imagine it was not going to be easy for the men to have it all their own way – despite the way they were nurturing their children in the school of hatred. The women's young friend had the manners and the means to counteract some of the rebelliousness growing in our midst. She was almost a big sister to our children. She allowed them to pat her pony. Then they ran back into the Welcoming Room and came back to feed Rosetta with generous handfuls of their mother's stolen icing sugar. Imagine handed them out sweets and gave them the odd little present such as the spinning top or the penny go-cart or even the wind-up clockwork car. The Christmas after her arrival she lit the little fairy-lights on her fir tree in her yard. She put out a rich display of cakes and jellies and rice puddings for all the children. She gave them brightly-coloured parcels, one for each child. Imagine that! Imagine that!

The men stamped their feet like delirious little leprechauns. Imagine was this! Imagine was that! Imagine was a right royal pain in the arse (they said). She had become a goddess (they said) in the midst of the women and their children. She had flown down (they scoffed), from the heavens as though she was a pure angel. They could see (couldn't any fool?) that it was into Imagine's face that the children spent their mornings gazing. They loved her. They took a pride in her that no man could fathom. It sickened them to death. For godsake, had their own children forgotten to love the land they were born and bred in?

Then the time came (it had to come) – the time for Tipperary to take swift action and get back the land. The men knew that the neighbouring British barracks had a dozen armed soldiers inside them to keep us poor scholars in our place. One fine morning the creamery carts were making a final push along the Saddleback Ridge from this side of the Limerick Glen. The men had chosen the older children to drive the procession of ass-and-cars on this last bit of the homeward jog. They would be unmolested by the soldiers. Amongst the milk tanks they were smuggling up to the rebels several rounds of gelignite.

When they reached the chosen spot in the pine forest the children handed the sticks of gelignite out among the men. By now it was noon. The men piled themselves and their sharp-shooting guns inside the ditch at the four sides of the barracks. A few of them ran out from the ditches and threw the gelignite in through the windows of the barracks. A few seconds later the barracks went up in shimmering flames. The eyes of the sharpshooters were fixed on the door and on the roof of the barracks. The young Tan soldiers staggered out helplessly onto the roof. They were like little bunny-rabbits that wait to be gunned down above in the-Valley-of-the-Black-Cattle. The shrieks of them – they were shot to pieces and their bodies were left there to fall down into the flames. The men of resistance were seen to wipe the spit on their trouser-legs. They were shaking hands with a hatred that their women wouldn't have been able to comprehend or believe. And God in His heaven bowed down and wept.

The church began to vilify these men and to excommunicate some of the more vicious ones and bar them from receiving the host in Holy Communion. The rebels sent the children with messages to the clergy house, which they posted through the door. The priests were being threatened and marked out for a bullet or two (said some of our fighting men) if they didn't guard their tongues on the altar and stick to their rosary beads. No pope, no church would prevent the course of progress and quieten the urge to fight and restore the ownership of our land. Thus, spoke the voice of the freedom fighters.

As though nothing strange had occurred, Imagine continued to wander through the hills, the little poetess that she was. To give them their due, the rebels avoided confronting her. For even *they* were afraid of their own mothers and knew that the famed yard-brush would redden their arses if they so much as looked crooked at Imagine.

An evening came on, rosy and pink and with the setting sun covering all the valleys. A haycart rolled along the mountain road from Slack-and-Tack. It drove in through the gates of the Big House. Tied together on the haycart were twelve mattresses to be delivered by way of the servant's back door. 'These are for the bedrooms,' said the haycart's driver. Inside the mattresses were a number of guns and ammunition for the hands of the rebels, who had staked themselves inside the back corridors of the servants' quarters or had hidden in the stables during the course of the night. The rebels had filled a bucket with gelignite and this was accompanied by a fuse and detonator – to be ignited during the night from a hundred yards away behind the stable-block.

And now events turned bleak. It was a windy night and during the early hours of the morning (heavens help us) the Big House was shaken - *BOOM! BOOM! BOOM!* - with a mighty explosion and went up in iridescent bubbles of flame and heat, leaving nothing but a smouldering 30ft crater behind it. In their nightdresses the delirious servant-girls (and the sweat coming out of their foreheads) ran out onto the lawn with the fear that a rabbit feels before the eyes of the weasel. The sky was just a bruised orange fire with swirls of roaring grey and black clouds of ash and dust all around it. The curious cattle had come up onto the lawn to study the burning house. Miraculously (we later heard) there wasn't a headless beast amongst them. Curl 'n' Stripes' mischievous sheepdog (*Swanky*) was out chasing lambs and had run onto the lawn and scattered the entire herd. Not another soul (including Imagine) was hurt either, not one of the servants was hurt, not a stray cat or dog was hurt. However, Lord Plus-Fours had had his tail well and truly singed (said the rebels) by the exploding bucket of gelignite. The Big House, symbol of the foreign settlers and of overseas rule, had vanished from view and lay in bits in the yard. Not a wrinkle of its former glory had the rebels left behind.

After setting Rosetta and the rest of the mares free from the stables, the bewildered Imagine came out in her jewelled slippers and her father's greatcoat. She brought out a bag of straw that had not yet been burnt. She placed it in the unscorched grass next to the lake where she had so often sat and fed her carp fishes. By now the wind had bundled the clouds of ash up high in the dappled moonlight. Limply and for a long while she sat on the bale of straw, silent and absorbed in the deepest shock. A slight rain (just a mist) was falling round her in the blackness. She leaned forward with her finger on her lips, shaking her head from left to right, demented.

'Imagine, oh imagine, that it should have come to this!' she cried as she tried to hold back her desperate sorrow and her salty tears flowed down the furrows of her nose and into the lake. Like Zachary in the Temple, she began to stammer and stutter. She began to lose her powers of speech as she gazed at the destruction of her home, the unrecognisable bits of her furniture in the devastated rooms, the gilded pictures, the broken porcelain and her mother's grandfather clock – a gift to herself on her wedding day, now in sad pieces in the former hallway.

Before utterly losing her voice, she bawled out a last wailing cry, the final words the rest of the household would ever hear from her as she lifted up her eyes to her ancestors beyond the clouds. 'I will stay here. I will die here in the flames of this fine house. Go on, you wicked cowards, shoot me down like a wild dog. Make an end to it all.'

What kind of a rape was this? It was as though she herself had been gotten hold of and utterly destroyed. How could the men have stooped so close to the gates of hell and dragged the heart out of her body? She might as well have been consumed in the flames?

When Dowager and Moll-the-Man came down they saw the place like a burial pall. They saw poor Imagine sitting beside the lake, shivering like a lost lamb – her once-stately face full of distressed tears and blackened with soot. They couldn't believe what had happened; their hearts couldn't swallow it and it made them shudder to see the state of Imagine. And as they cradled her in their arms and tried to whisper soft words of comfort to her, they heard the last croaky whispers she was ever to make - that as far as this world was concerned she was as good as gone from it, as good as dead. With the drizzle now thickening round them, they drove back home, the rest of the grey countryside again asleep and hushed. They knew that their young friend from over the water no longer wished to live. And it was then that the two women sat down and began to cry heart-achingly like two sick donkeys. Imagine that! Can you imagine that!

A drooping Lord Plus-Fours came out from the coach-house with the horse and carriage and took Imagine away. The next day the creamery road was full of dark shadow when the news got out that Imagine was gone. The children sat mournfully on the wobbly singletree and for once in their lives they didn't have a single word to say to one another.

From Tipperary to the Big City was the most heart-rending journey that Imagine could have ever made. The reunion with her parents, when her husband drove her into the yard of the Big City mansion in Rathlofty, was a vale of heavy tears, almost as bad as when the women of Jerusalem cried their hearts out on meeting their beloved Jesus and he so utterly damaged and destroyed. What a difference a year had made. What a difference this journey was from the one Imagine once travelled with lightness of heart – herself and her grandfather clock and she coming here on her merry tippy-toes to celebrate her happy nuptials with Lord Plus-Fours. She would never recover from her grief and all her former beauty would disappear in the cloudy mists of a war-torn land.

Imagine spent the rest of her days in Rathlofty. Within a short time, she became a tired and withered old lady. Had it all been a dream, a nightmare? Who would have believed that her friends – the old Irish – would turn out to be so heartlessly cruel? Weeping a good deal each day, she could be seen gazing for long hours at a picture of her mother and her father on their wedding day where it hung on the dining room wall. Or else you'd find her sitting by the fire and pretending to read a newspaper though her disbelieving parents could see that the poor girl was plainly holding it upside-down.

But maybe she still remembered (as Dowager hoped and prayed she would) the sweet kindness that My-Son-Jack had once bestowed on her. Maybe she'd remember the day when he rescued her pony, Rosetta, in the lightning storm and how she looked up into the charm of his cornflower blue Irish eyes.

A day or two later the children were sitting near the stream. In their dreamy little heads, they began to compose a fairy-tale. They started to draw it on the flagstones with their pink and lavender stones from the river. They drew pictures of a princess. And her name was Imagine. Beside her they drew her handsome prince. And his name was My-Son-Jack. What came next? They said that the happy couple leaped up onto the back of Rosetta-the-Pony. They said that My-Son-Jack clung onto her creamy mane. They said that Imagine clung onto her prince's waist. Then together they rode away at top speed, up passed Sheep's Cross and off into the red sunset and out over Chieftain Hill and away into the fluffy clouds.

They would draw these same pictures in their copybooks when they got to the schoolhouse. But, being young, they'd ask their master, Dang-the-skin-of-it, to write down their exact words for them. Yes, they would write of a poor Irish boy and a rich English lady. It would be a good fairy-tale, if only they could get the words down from their heads and into their hands and written down properly on paper.

Oh, imagine it! Imagine the thought!

BIG RED

1

Sorrow came upon Big Red when, armed with his new satchel, a few apples and a slice of brac-and-butter, he trudged his boots into the schoolhouse of Dang-the-skin-of-it. Instead of the master's wife (*Biddy,* who was now retired) he found himself greeted by a new and cantankerous mistress in the form of *Briary*, a lady from Clare, already anxious to make a name for herself.

Though his body was growing like a beanstalk, over the next few years the child found himself left behind at the bottom of the schoolroom alongside the six-year-old children, who had just started school. Even before the class had time to bless themselves the poor lad was seen cringing in the far corner, unable to get to grips with the new learning and his brain was all a-fumble. It was as though he had the flaps of his ears closed and never opened and he had a permanent frown stamped across his forehead. Of course, he wasn't born to be a donkey or a gatepost. But no matter how hard he tried he couldn't read and he couldn't spell the simplest of words like the rest of the children – even though his mother (*Halfpenny-Gret*) could spell rocks of words from here to the bridge across the river ('twas said). Nor could he write his name or copy out the daily news from the blackboard. What a terrible thing it was to be straddled with the label of *numbskull* on one day and *leatherhead* the very next. And as a result, Briary was often seen putting the hay-sougan ring around his neck and standing him on a chair in the corner as though he were some stray rabbit at the edge of a cornfield. To the other children this was a very strange thing to behold, for within a year or two Big Red had grown higher not only than the sour little mistress but a good deal higher than the master, Dang-the-skin-of-it.

Each day he became the victim of Briary and her squints of black temper. At the best of times she was not a delicate lady to be seen wasting seconds on morning pleasantries and you'd hear the tremor of her silk dress vibrating as she puffed and panted all around the room as though she was an old bellows. And then she'd go to work on Big Red, whaling into him with her savage point-to-the-map stick.

At other times the children saw the poor child frog-marched out the door, armed with the black-handled knife and the commands of Briary ringing in his ears, 'Go down to the river and cut yeerself a sally-switch – a good one that's bendable and a yard long.'

Dutifully Big Red brought back his new sally-switch. Briary would then inspect it, giving it a bit of thought as though it were some sort of rare beast. She'd make a few dainty twists and turns like a practising sword-fighter, swishing it threateningly round over her head in front of the children's awestruck faces. After that little escapade she proceeded to teach Big Red his lessons by belting him a good few times across his extended hands or (if the humour was on her) battering him on the seat of his britches.

How sad it was to see Big Red – his dangling arms and his sombre-looking eyes and not a single twitch out of him as he took the belts she proudly bestowed on him. He collected more and more of these belts each day and the marks on his legs were often as big as a duck-egg.

However, to see Briary laying into Big Red and bringing him down to size helped make the day go smoothly enough – the rest of the children having escaped the lash. The sound of her switch on the seat of his britches was to become a regular bit of entertainment – a distraction from the otherwise dreary monotony of the school lessons. You might well ask yourself, what cruel witnesses these children had become as they looked on in amusement at Big Red's pain. When they thought of it in later years they must have bowed their heads in shame.

As soon as she heard of these chastisements, Dowager had the answer. it wasn't Big Red's dull wits that were causing Briary to beat him so often and mercilessly. It was his sheer size. At the dinner table she'd point her fork at the table, 'And who – tell me this – can blame our lively little schoolmistress for being so ungracious with her switch? God (it can be seen by us all) has given this woman a mere four and a half feet of height in her stocking-vamps. To Big Red he has given more than 6ft of height – and the lad's not yet fully grown.' Such an unfair distribution of heights was Dowager's excuse for Briary's acts of cruelty to the child. Wouldn't such unfairness in the distribution of heights anger The Devil himself and cause him to leap round the classroom and go whaling the arse off of Big Red each morning the very minute the school-prayers were said?' My-Son-Jack had to nod his head in agreement with his mother' subtle explanation and we were all left wholeheartedly bemoaning the loss of Biddy and her musical piano.

When it came to answering the two times table (a simple task, since every child recited it on their way to school) Big Red got into a sweaty panic all over again. His dry mouth was so uninspired that he was unable to give even the simplest of answers. As a consequence of this supposed outrage the little vixen could be seen dancing a set of jig-steps round the huge child.

In a fit of frustration, she took upon herself a new means of teaching him wisdom – one that she had learnt back in her own schooldays in the far west country, namely a few tidy cuffs to the poor boy's jaw. So unusual a tactic was this that some children thought it might do the trick and bring the two times table spilling out from Big Red's mouth. Their wise old parents could have told them that it'd knock far more sense out of his brain than into it.

From her own schooldays, even Dowager had heard of other masters and mistresses attempting to provide the feeblest of scholars with extra brains by giving their jaws a few similar cuffs with an upturned fist. Indeed, Briary was becoming such an expert in the use of this method of teaching that she added a few little trimmings to it that were all her own. For when Big Red went cowering back to his bench she made a rush after him like a hissing snake and administered a well-aimed kick to the seat of his britches to help him on his way, driving him headlong in amongst the startled six-year-olds on the bench.

Poor Big Red – he lacked even the smallest morsel of tact for, had he howled with the pain of his chastisements, he might have seen the intervention of Dang-the-skin-of-it from the room next door. But, like any boxer in a scrap, he wouldn't give in to this mad new teacher and uttered not one cry of pain. This was enough to incense Briary all the more and to such an extent that she'd stop only to get herself a drink of water from the bucket before getting at him with her sally-switch all over again. By this time the entire classroom had begun to marvel at the antics of her. If she – a small frail woman of four and a half feet in height – could belt this huge giant-of-a-child like this, what wonderful powers she must have been given by her Heavenly Maker the time she was born.

However, enough was enough. It was clear that the schoolmistress had her own well-defined brand of intelligence. Big Red was to find his own intelligence too. He'd grown sick-and-tired of the daily beatings from this little beauty-of-a-schoolmistress. And then – one fine morning after the children had drunk their mugs of cocoa the lively one made a singular mistake. It was a fatal one. She insulted Big Red's saintly mother for having been such a born fool as to have given birth to a numbskull like this giant-of-a-child and bring shame on herself, on her family and race, on the entire schoolhouse, on the whole of Tipperary – on the world. It was a long list.

Through the mists in his feeble brain Big Red could see that such an insult was unbearable. The recent kicking from Briary's boots – these he'd been able to withstand. When she'd prodded him up against the wall and kicked at him till the soles of her boots were exhausted – this too he had been able to withstand. Even her cuffs to his jaw and the sally-switch on his arse – whatever the shape and size of the delivery – these too he could bear. But the sudden insult to his mother – this was to put an end to one brief chapter in his life and start another one.

For the first time in their history the children saw Big Red blinking back his tears and wiping them away from his jaw. To see him crying was a new one on the class. More was to follow when they witnessed his particular new brand of intelligence. It was as though a big drum had started to beat a tattoo inside in his head, as though the blood had suddenly started to boil inside in his veins. He walked blindly to the front of the room and snapped Briary's sally-switch into several pieces. Then he caught hold of her and wrapped his big fist around her dainty wrist – almost gently like any gentleman would do. Then, dropping his own wrist, he took hold of her by the seat of her black dress and held onto the heel of her left boot so there'd be not an inch of room left for her to start kicking out at him. After that (remember how later in life he was able to carry a sixteen-stone sack of cow dung on his back across the yard) he gingerly lifted the coy little mistress into the air as though she was a bird's feather. He took her out into the yard where the children heard the squeals of her ('Put me down, put me down – you little fecker!') – so loud you'd think a pig was being killed. And with the strength of our previous blacksmith (*Old Titan, Hammer-the-Smith's father*) he then let a roar out of him that could surely be heard above in heaven. After that he pelted her fair and square ('ye ould bitch' said he) into the middle of the dung heap at the end of the schoolhouse where you could see nothing more than her neck and chin sticking out from the dung. Would she ever rise up again? The children wondered.

Poor Dang-the-skin-of-it – he who had always bemoaned the use of a teacher's fists on a scholar's jaw – was next to receive the wrath of Big Red. For this was to be a day when he'd not be parting the flaps of his coat and warming his gable-end at the fire. There was a six-foot-high locker where he kept his greatcoat and his silver-handled walking-cane for the lunchtime parade with Briary up and down the avenue. Big Red rushed in the door and before the master could blink an eye he lifted him up, as though he were a cabbage, and placed him on top of the locker. There sat Dang-the-skin-of-it – himself and his stiff white collar, looking down on his pupils like an ass staring out over a wall. He'd never be able to get down. The children would never forget the sight – the mistress in the middle of the dung heap, the master sitting cosily on top of his locker. It was a dream of pure delight – a dream that they'd never forget for the rest of their lives. There and then they beatified – almost canonised – Big Red for the job he'd done that day.

Suddenly it dawned on them what had happened and they began to feel a great fear. After all, they had all been sniggering and jeering at the stupidity of Big Red not being able to read his letters, not being able to write his name, not being able to do the sums. Would he turn on them next? Might he take it into his head to take them out one-at-a-time and kill them all? For the remainder of the morning, however, they went unscathed (thank God).

That was only for a short while. The afternoon came around before anyone knew it and a fine drizzle began to fall mournfully on the schoolhouse. The children knew their weather. This was a bad sign – almost prophetic. For that was when they found themselves lucky to escape with their lives, realising that Big Red hadn't quite finished the job he'd started. He made a smart excursion over to the nearby Yellowstone Quarry and hurried back with a wheelbarrow full of rocks. By that time the children had somehow managed to drag Dang-the-skin-of-it down from his embarrassing perch on top of the locker. They had wiped the dung fairly well from Briary's black dress. Both of them had recovered a little of their previous composure.

All of a sudden, the entire building shook. The Sacred Heart picture on the wall was sent dancing about from a new and unreal vibration as Big Red took an armful of rocks and sent them *(boom! boom! boom!)* hopping off of the slate roof. 'Mee mother! Ye basthards from hell! Oh, mee mother! How could ye do such a thing as to call her a fool?' Listening to the hammering of the rocks and almost dead with fright, the master and his dainty-toed mistress were getting the worst of it all over again. At home time would they ever be able to get to their pony 'n' trap under the trees and get back alive to their house above the school?

The two of them cowered behind their desks, "Get down, lads! For the love of sweet Jesus on his cross, get down!' and bade everyone hide themselves behind the benches. There they all crouched like a flock of sheep beneath a ditch when the rain comes on. It was now as though a jeep-load of Tan soldiers were entering the fray - open warfare between Big Red and his captives inside in the schoolhouse. Decades later many of the children could still conjure up the immense scenario that was to remain stamped on their minds forever. If only one of them was a painter in oils – to capture the animal rage of Big Red and the sight of the terrified master and mistress cowering behind their desks – what a museum piece it would have been. And to conclude this lively little sketch, Big Red broke every goddamn window in the two schoolrooms and with a battered look and his nose flattened from all his tears, he cast the school aside forever and wiped his eyes and jaws and went home and put his arms around his tearful mother. What need had he of meeting the bishop in May and getting his Confirmation-ticket (said he). 'Give me a reins, mother,' he sobbed, 'till I go back and hang Briary from the rafters for calling ye nothing but an old fool.'

7 1

Later that evening the weary lad took a pile of furze bushes from the cowshed. He laid them at Briary's front door in a vain attempt to set fire to her. However, in a week or two matters began to cool down a good bit and the rest of us wore a great heap of happy smiles on hearing of Big Red's rage and his own particular method of punishing anyone who transgressed against his saintly mother. Before the summer was over he was the hero-of-the-hour and (as with the children) he was almost canonised in everybody's eyes, for we all hated the dastardly punishments often handed out inside school walls up and down the country.

2

Two years later and Big Red was living on feeds of good beef and plates of mutton-stew together with raw steak and milk. His mother couldn't take her eyes off of him. Father Sensibly summoned him to attend the hurling training-session with the men's team (*The Abbey Rovers*). You can imagine the big lad's excitement as he cleaned his boots with his mother's black polish the night before training and went about inspecting his togs and oiling his hurley-stick with the drop of paraffin.

The peak of his stardom came in the very first match against *The Mountainy Streamers*. The evening before the match was a stormy event and everybody stayed indoors by the side of their fire. Big Red stayed indoors too, inside in Lepping-Guinness's drinking-shop where he lowered half a dozen *twins* – a well-known combination of whiskey followed by a glass of stout. Though just 16 he was well able to handle all the drinks that came his way. That stormy night proved a bit of a problem for next day's match as the ground would be as heavy as lead and a bad day for the hurlers. There were parts of the field that would be turned into oozy mud before the match was well into the second half and, worse still, the ball would be nothing but a wet rag, thanks to the heaviness of the water sinking into it as the match wore on.

Big Red felt on top of the world as he cycled towards the ground, his hurling-boots proudly tied to his hurley-stick, which was belted onto the bike's crossbar. He was at one with the world, the blue-coloured mountains mistily ahead of him and the bog's solitude over to his left and it covered in windy heather and scarce a bush to be seen.

The ground was soon well-packed with the tricolour flag rippling in the breeze as out stepped the two teams, their coloured jerseys embroidering the green of the grass in a dazzling patchwork. Then the priest threw the ball in between the hurlers' legs and ran like a hare for the side of the pitch as though he was expecting a shower of hailstones to follow after him. The battle commenced and the field soon turned as lively as a beehive.

At halftime the players dug into their oranges and listened to a thousand pieces of conflicting advice, which left them more confused than ever when they came out for the second half. And then the match re-commenced before we knew it had started, both teams again attacking like gnats and setting the grass aflame. The game spun along nice and handy till it reached the die-away minutes. Up until then both teams had been evenly matched and no-one could foretell which team was going to walk home with the laurels. Some of the men started looking at their pocket-watches when a side-line puck was given in favour of our own team – the Abbey Rovers.

Among the spectators there were some grand and respected hurlers (real ones and imagined ones). Brilliance also burned in the wrists of our own man, the Meddler, who had scored many great points for us in recent years. He was as elusive as a wizard on wheels and you might as well try stopping Rambling Jack's runaway pig when you saw him gliding down the touchline with the ball stuck to his hurley-stick on one of his famed solo-runs. Best of all, he would often send the ball curling over the crossbar from the narrowest of angles with the crisp beauty of his side-line strokes. All eyes were now on him to see what he would do. But he was too far away from the Mountainy Streamer's goalmouth – three-quarters the length of the pitch and there was devil-a-fear his puck would reach such an immense distance and bring home the winning score. Once more men began looking at their pocket-watches. The referee too began looking at his own watch and it seemed as though he was about to blow his whistle and that the game would end in a draw.

The Meddler stepped up to take his puck, swinging his hurley-stick threateningly round and round above his head and eyeing the forwards of his own team lurking around the rival goalmouth. The crowd trained their eyes on the great man and a breathless suspense settled over the field. All of a sudden, the crafty rogue gave Big Red the wink and slipped the ball squarely across the field and into the young lad's outstretched fist.

There followed an inspired moment, forever captured in our minds - as though our young giant had never forgotten the insult of Briary to his saintly mother. There and then, he turned himself into the biblical Samson and an unnatural energy found its way into his huge body – a creeping sensation that went right down his spine, far greater than anything else he'd ever felt before (he'd later tell us). You know it yourself – in every man's life there comes a high point, a peak and a glory from somewhere on high and this was to prove the most sublime moment in Big Red's life – a joy that could never again be matched anywhere, that would shine his name into the annals of all the mighty Tipperary hurlers. In front of him he could see only the goalposts, the breadth of a church door. And that's when the fairy godmother of the High Winds flew down and sang sweetly into his ear, *'Come to me, Red! Come to me, Red!'* He tossed the ball (the greasy ball that was soggy and heavy as lead) into the air and raised his hurley-stick as though it were a weapon of war before sending it rasping across the sky with the speed of a hawk - not only over The Mountainy Streamers' crossbar but clean out of the hurling-field.

We weren't blind - we all saw it - as if the clock had stood still. The ball hovered in the clouds for just a second before disappearing forever - or else by now it would have been enshrined inside the four walls of our church as a sight rarer than wintertime swallows. Big Red's score was the winning score and it was said by the smartest men among us that he'd struck the ball not only the unbelievable distance of ninety yards but a further twenty yards in excess of it. The whimsical drinkers below at Curl 'n' Stripes' drinking-shop (weren't they always the wags) professed that when Big Red's ball finished its devastating journey it was completely covered in snow!

The sun's golden light now started turning to rust as the exhausted hurlers left the field and together with the crowd made their way into the drinking-shop of Joe Tornado – himself a once-great hurler, who ('twas said) would have sold his mother's boots for the price of good booze. Throats were now as dry as parchment from all the shouting – indeed, you'd think it was *the crowd* that had been doing all the fine hurling. The youngsters were as excited as hell and swallowed their whiskey in a single mouthful (*give us another shlug of yeer best whiskey*) or gulped their stout greedily, their lips full of frothy foam as they smacked them together. The older fellows puffed blissfully on their pipes, sipping their booze speculatively and many now were the tearstained eyes among them as they re-enacted Big Red's great puck time and time again. It was a sight to melt the heart of a stone when one of these old-timers made a quick run at Big Red and planted a wet slobbery kiss on his lips with a faraway look (*'I love you!'*) of admiration in his eyes.

The sun at last settled down and the hills lost their orange colour, turning themselves back into a mystery-land with only a small wedge of sunlight remained in the corner of the field that had offered us so much joy. We all made our weary way to our bikes, our ass-and-cars and our traps and went off down the hill - our hurlers too.

Crowds of happy-faced children ran up the road to welcome home their victorious team – as though they were storybook heroes that had come back down from the moon. They'd be talking about it for weeks to come.

Late that evening the true distance of the flight of Big Red's hurling-ball was discussed among the remaining drinkers.

It was the Meddler himself (and he still nuzzling his glass of stout), who found the answer that would close the argument for once and for all. He called the men out (*'follow me, lads, till I measure it'*) and put a dab of white paint on the wheel of his bike. He wheeled it in a straight line as though he were starting to plough a field - from the rivals' goalmouth to the spot near the side-line where Big Red's strike had been taken. Then he counted the spins of the painted wheel and confirmed the distance to be ninety yards to the inch.

What a bleddy marvellous man Big Red must have been (said everyone).

What a bleddy marvellous man too was the Medler (someone else laughed). He'd the brains of a pope, hadn't he?

That tale was told again and again and a bike with white paint became a central part of Dang-the-skin-of-it's Euclid lesson from that day forth. In days to come (indeed for the rest of his young life) Big Red was hailed as a raving genius. What did it matter if he couldn't read or couldn't write his name? The rawgut whiskey and the pints of stout were repeatedly poured down his throat as time after time he was led into one drinking-shop after another to recall the day of his gigantic ninety-yard puck. And soon this puck went into the annals of Tipperary's folklore – to be trotted out in our tales at winter firesides till (with the odd embellishment) Big Red became not only a saint but an entire god.

3

Such a huge attraction was Big Red – a man who could point a greasy ball from ninety yards outfield – that he was not going to be left without a final flourish to his bow. And it came sooner than any of us expected. A few years later his father (*Saddle-the-Pony*) went sadly to his grave, having died suddenly from an inward pain. Big Red was filled with a grief that was almost too much to bear. To escape from his sorrow, he took his big boots off to the Regatta at Kindy-Wells beside the River Shannon – a spot where a stretch of the river was known for its swift currents and squally storms.

Amongst the swimmers for the Challenge Cup there was a young priest fresh in from Clare. He had stripped off to race in the two-hundred-yard dash to the red marker out at the island. The saintly man was gifted above all other swimmers in the yearly regattas up and down the rivers of Ireland. His father (*Old Dinny*) had been a fine swimmer too – hadn't he outswam the great Billy Hayseeds? And now, huge crowds had come to see him put on a bit of a show. It was strange to see his lily-white body shivering alongside the other fellows on the bank, for it was unusual to see a holy man stripping off his togs and showing us his hairy chest and ignobly involving himself in a regatta swimming-race; priests as a rule were seen propping up the counter in the Big Tent of the Regatta – with a large brandy in the heel of their fist and another one at the ready beside their elbow.

From his perch on the spectators' bridge Big Red looked down at the colourful scene and the crowds gathering to see the start of the swimming-race. He took it all in – the fine swimmers in their costumes and the Clare priest among them.

He saw the combatants stepping out and lining up at the starting-tape. The expectations were high.

The swimmers looked up to the skies and blessed themselves. The starting-pistol was fired and the race was on. Big Red heard the freezing gasps as the swimmers splashed into the cold water like horses dashing across a river. He heard the mighty cheers of the excited crowd in the glory of it all. A minute later he saw the priest well out in front of the other swimmers and making a beeline for the red marker.

Suddenly – as though a huge black cloud had sailed in across the sun – he heard the groans of the crowd when they saw what was taking place in front of their eyes. Following the great man's early breakfast, a cramp came on him out of nowhere – freezing his legs and taking him down beneath the grasping waves.

There followed a split second of silence – a silence when a piece of our history was to be written down all over again. For in this singular moment Big Red was to be marked out for posterity a second time. He found himself in a strange dream-world amongst a thousand slowcoaches, whose brains were all too addled as to know what next to do. His father's recent ghost came down in a flutter from the clouds and poured his wraith into him. He whispered sharp words into his ear – father and son twinned into one. It was now up to Big Red to show the other poor scholars (the miserable Briary included) that he wasn't so dumb and slow-witted after all. He couldn't (whispered his father) stand there like a simpleton on the bridge – a bewildered spectator like the rest of the stupified crowd gazing out helplessly on the tragic scene unfolding before his eyes, could he?

His father's spirit was then accompanied by an army of spirits from Big Red's forebears, surrounding him like ivy to the oak, stifling him, breathing into the heart of him, urging him to do the right thing for the sake of his family – for the sake of his race. He hadn't a moment to contemplate the dangers to his life and limb and perhaps at this stage of his life – and with nothing better to think upon but those persistent images of a lonely old age in front of him – his every impulse was to take up this great challenge in the battle between his own life and the priest's cruel death.

He threw off his boots and coat and in a blur of speed burst out from the throng in a glorious effort to get to the holy man. Like the day of the long puck, an unearthly strength rushed into his every sinew. He took an aristocratic leap out into the air and down from the top of the bridge. He was seen thrashing around in the water and swimming far out. We didn't even know whether he had learnt to swim a stroke or two in the few years he'd been abroad in Wolverhampton. Maybe Big Red himself didn't know if he could swim so far out and then double up on the distance so as to get back in again.

The crowds craned their eyes down from the bridge and blessed themselves one and all. They saw Big Red attempting to frighten the life out of the river. They saw how he reached the side of the priest, how he held the priest's terrified head above the waters of the mighty river, how he brought him back into the land of the living. They saw him swimming back towards the bank with the holy man's head held high in his hands.

Nearer and nearer to the shore he came – all the way towards the spectators and the prayers being uttered on this side of the river. In one moment, Big Red's head appeared above the waters. The next minute he was down underneath them. The priest struggled away from his grip and, living another day to tell the tale of it, he forced himself as far as the outstretched arms on the bank and was dragged safely ashore.

It was Big Red's final hurrah and testament. He was never the man to earn his fame as a swimmer. Hurling in Tipperary? Yes, our young giant could do that. Whoring when he'd been abroad in Wolverhampton? -Yes, that too. And now, exhausted and to the everlasting groans of us all when we saw what was happening to him, he sank beneath the waves some 30 yards from our helpless eyes and drifted away with the current. And as with the beltings from the fists and sally-switch of Briary, the poor misfortunate lad never gave so much as a cry or a cough but was swept away by the force of the river – all the way downstream (ah, no!) towards the ocean and oblivion.

Next morning – even before the sun had risen in the sky – bishop High-Hat came running from his palace in Ennis to do the ceremony. The dismal crowd followed him along the bridge. He solemnly blessed the waters and informed his flock that Big Red was finally at peace at the bottom of the River Shannon. He called for a bale of straw. He blessed the straw. He threw it over the bridge and into the river. The bale of straw swam away downstream towards the river's right-hand bend. The crowd ran along the bank. The straw came to the bend in the river and there it stopped. 'A man's body will follow certain currents,' said the worthy bishop. 'Even so, will the bale of straw if given an equal weight.'

Bishop High-Hat was not only a holy man, he was also a wise man. The bale of straw was trapped in a mass of underwater briars at the bend of the river. The men and their excitement ('*down here, lads*! *down here*!') all rallied round. They found Big Red and his puffy face trapped in those same underwater briars – with two fists of weeds in his grasp.

His mother, Halfpenny-Gret, went and brought him home in the horse-and-cart. There was no wake. There'd be no complacency. She'd let nobody near him. After the recent death of Saddle-the-Pony her sorrow was far too great and she locked herself in the bedroom and stretched herself out beside the once-athletic form of Big Red's corpse for the next day and a half.

A day later, the cold rainclouds blotted out the sunlight from the snivelling sky. We heard the church bells ring as we crunched our boots into the graveyard. Our hearts leapt up in our throats as we vividly reflected on our giant and poured out our sobs of farewell to him. Then we took him in the hearse

EDWARD FORDE HICKEY

and we buried him in his early grave (his mother always knew he'd die early) below in Abbey Acres graveyard alongside Saddle-the-Pony. We gave him full honours with the hurley-stick and the blue-and-gold colours of Tipperary wrapped around his coffin. He had been a man that in the end proved he could hurl a ball as good as any man in Ireland. At sixteen years of age he had brought himself fame with his ninety yards puck of a greasy ball on a wet day above in the mountains. He had tested and tasted the charms of many a Wolverhampton temptress (if only the rest of us had had the fine chance) – lying all night in their dusky arms. But now, at two-and-twenty the poor lad was dead and gone forever to the Beyond – just the bright stars of the night and the cold midnight airs to guard his spirit. One and all, we thank our God for the gift of our only true giant. May the Lord have mercy on your soul, Big Red, for as long as our rivers flow out to the ocean your name will be remembered with pride. Rest assured of that.

SADIE

1

Sadie was the only daughter of Deed'n-be-Chrysht and Tickle-mee-Fancy. They lived on the lush green hills behind Hammer-the-Smith's forge. She was the apple of her mother's eye and her father called her his little sunbeam. Sadie was a lovely young girl of 18 with cheeks as soft as a rose. She had a beautiful head of unusual sandy hair. It fell down in a shiny rope along the broad of her back. We were all the time admiring her, at which she'd blush up abruptly all through her young face and run away from us, leaving us all looking after her like a pack of asses without a bit of clover. Wouldn't you give your two good eyes to see a sight such as her?

When Tickle-mee-Fancy sent her down from the Valley-of-the-Pig on the 2-mile journey to warm the bed of Black Neddy on his farm, this old lad had everything that a man could possibly wish for. You should have seen the crafty smile on his hairy old jaw as he got ready to welcome the tearful young soul into his Welcoming Room. It seemed like only yesterday that she had been a child wearing her ankle-socks to The Platform Dance-in-the-Fields. It was 30 years and more since Black Neddy had been able to run after a chicken, let alone chase around the bedroom after a fair young damsel like Sadie. She was as thin as a rake and as hardy as any snipe from the sound training that her father and mother had given her at both the milking of the cows and the bringing home of the turf. There wasn't a thing that she couldn't or wouldn't turn her hand to. And so (like her three sisters before her) she had become the object of her father's need to match her off with this old fellow and thereby secure her lifelong future and well-being. After all, what else could a young girl do these times?

EDWARD FORDE HICKEY

The alternative was to get herself a vision-from-God and take herself off into some hidden convent – that is if the nuns would let her in the door. If your face didn't fit, there'd be no welcome in those places either. So, if your heart wasn't truly set on a life of knee-breaking devotion to God, your next best option was always this one – to set up home with a tried and tested old farmer (in this case, Black Neddy) knowing that he had a few pounds in the bank and that he could buy you a new suit of clothes for Sunday Mass and a brooch and a black hat to go with it.

It was no use a damsel trying to get herself matched off with one of the younger men since their fathers never gave those fellows an inch of land till they themselves had one foot in the grave. Black Neddy's own father had died the previous year and he was now the inheritor of what was a fair-sized farm. Sadie, therefore, had to get her skates on quickly and go down and get hitched to this old obstacle before any other young madam got her thieving hands on him. 'He's a fine catch,' said Tickle-mee-Fancy. 'And he's only 52,' said Deed'n-be-Chrysht. After all the sobbing and crying there wasn't a tear left in poor Sadie's red eyes and she shuddered throughout the sleepless nights when she thought of being cast off and latched into the arms of this hairy old yoke.

It was now June and the corn would be getting yellower by the day. The sky had been robbed of its charcoal and there was now a motleyed series of ribbed purple 'n' blue clouds as the sun started hitting the hill. It threw a bright bar across the ass-and-car whilst the flies danced around like rushing stars. This was the day of poor Sadie's departure – the saddest day in all her young life and she was trembling like a little bird that was lost. Deed'n-be-Chrysht tackled up the faithful ass to the jambs of the cart. Still idling in her bedroom, Sadie smoothed down her sandy ropes of hair and gazed at herself in front of the looking-glass: 'I'll be different from now on – forever different,' she told herself. There would be no bridal gown in white for her, no rich bouquets of flowers, no jewels in her

8 6

ears, no rings on her fingers, no ribbons in her hair – just a black veil to cover her face and modesty. She came out into the yard with her father's brown suitcase and her mother's hatbox. The ancient ass (*Tiger*)had seen it all before. Together with her father (a separate bedroom having been arranged for her, prior to the wedding) she was heading off for Black Neddy and the Road-to-The-Hollows.

Off they went. The sunny day led them on. Sadie's heart was broken in two. Her mother's heart was damaged too. She hadn't had the courage to come out into the yard and wave her handkerchief over Sadie and give her the dash of holy water. She hadn't even peeped out over the windowsill geraniums to give her that last little smile but had sloped off to her bed and collapsed in a heap of grief. How sad the place would be without her daughter's light laughter. Between herself and Sadie they could have filled the mighty Shannon River this day with the anguish of their tears.

'Wipe away yeer tears, mee good woman,' said Deed'n-be-Chrysht to his daughter. There wasn't even the comfort of a kindly word, let alone a fatherly hug. It was unknown for men to be slobbering over their daughters with that sort of tomfoolery. 'It'll all be for the best in the end, ye'll see.' We shall later recall how prophetic were his words.

Sadie took a dreary last look back down the lane at her old homestead where she had played as a child with the four kittens on the upturned ass-and-car. What must have been the thoughts going through her mind, piercing her young heart and puncturing her soul? She was young enough still to be wearing her best dress which she had worn to Sunday Mass when she was 14. Until that very day she had slept with her mother's favourite doll beside her under the blankets. It would be a far different bed that now awaited her after her wedding took place and Father Sensibly had dealt with the officiating of the sacramental ceremonies in a fortnight's time.

As the two of them and their ass stumbled along towards Black Neddy's farm Sadie was as silent as the grave. Rather than talk to her father she preoccupied herself with listening to the buzzing of the bees in the honeysuckle and foxglove, to the sudden hum of the horse-bees in the cattle-dung in the centre of the lane behind her. In the back of the cart her father had folded a blanket over the traditional dowry, the half-grandfather clock. At the last cattle Fair Day, he had placed a purseful of silver dollars (the gift from his sister in far-off Yonkers in the Land of the Silver Dollar) into the fist of Black Neddy.

They pulled up the ass (*Sight, blasht* ye!) at the flagstones of the old farmer. Sadie stepped down from the cart. It was one fatal step and she was very much afraid. She was turning her back on the past and was about to spend the rest of her days with a man she had never before laid eyes on.

Black Neddy shuffled across the yard to meet her. He gazed at her with his drivelling gawk-eye. Ah, what a lovely sight – a young girl with all her own teeth on her and they all in a row (he thought). He hadn't a leg left on him strong enough to give a kick (she thought). She stepped across the yard towards him and her heart beat fast. Good God-in-heaven! Black Neddy was as wrinkled as a dead leaf and old enough to be her grandfather.

In spite of her understanding of the bull and the business with the cow (how often had she helped a small bull to mount towards his joy!) Sadie had no real knowledge of what was expected of her in the bedroom during the weeks that were to follow. She'd be fine in respects of the daily farm-work alongside Black Neddy - feeding the hens and the geese, giving the calves their buckets of skimmed milk, milking the seven cows, collecting the eggs, chopping the logs with the axe for the fire, fetching the six buckets of water from the well, and so on. There was no more industrious soul than Sadie. She would wash and mend his shirts as her mother had taught her – as good as any wife in the hills She'd ensure that he looked decent when he took out the pony-and-trap for Sunday Mass. His boots would be polished asunder and she'd put the dab of butter on his toecaps. But for the murky business of churning out a new little baby every year as any good wife worth her salt would do, Sadie was completely flummoxed. The bull – yes. The stallion – yes. The boar – yes. She had even taken Uncle Danno's goat up the hill for his annual performances amongst the fortunate she-goats. But now it was her turn to be at the whim and the will of Black Neddy. She was caught in a birdcage. She took out her rosary beads on the first night. She prayed as hard as Saint Teresa of the Little Flower – asking God to make Black Neddy treat her decently and not bring any shameful acts upon her. She would offer up her prayers each Sunday at Mass. She would make the nine first Friday visits to the church in Copperstone Hollow and receive Holy Communion at the rails. She would offer further prayers to Saint Jude the patron saint of all lost causes so that he would stand by her and not let her be disgraced.

Fears and uncertainties had visited her before, a common enough state of affairs for all our growing girls who were often plagued with the nerves. She recalled when she was 14 and had found herself (like the rest of the girls) bleeding in under her skirts. She thought that she was about to die from a burst pipe in her belly. She came to know what fear was on that day. She had fled like a young greyhound across the fields but had the good fortune to land in the arms of Father Sensibly as he was on his way out from Fat Nora's establishment with his basket of eggs.

At 18, however, there were many secrets yet to be learned. She had tried to force all thoughts of the coming nuptials to the back of her mind. And to stomach the marrying-acts of Black Neddy she would have to close her eyes. But she promised herself that, as ordered by Holy Mother Church, she would give her new husband her heart if not her soul. And wouldn't that surely be enough for the old man?

2

In the days that followed the house of Black Neddy was cold.
The fire-grate was a mean little spark with no trace of a log on
it. The man himself was a mean old yoke. There was little true
welcome in his Welcoming Room. The bed in the black night
was colder still and he himself had the smell of farmyard
manure wafting round her. She kept her soft linen shift
wrapped tightly round her chin and in the silent bedroom she
hugged herself to sleep with only the crickets to serenade her.
But thank the Virgin-in-Heaven! – she soon realised that the
hairy old man was just as shy and ignorant as herself when it
came to the removal of the secret night shirt and the business
of rattling the bedsprings and injecting her with a child.

In a few months the frown lines on her father's forehead
doubled. He began to see that there was no child being born
from this union. What had his family done to deserve this? He
was as embarrassed as hell in front of the other farmers. What
on earth could be wrong with his daughter? Soon his
embarrassment turned into something like rage. He couldn't
set his foot inside the doors of Curl 'n' Stripes' drinking-shop.
The men were forever making a laugh and a joke at the weak
state of himself and his breed. 'The old breed is beginning to
shrink away,' they sniggered. 'It's worn out like a cabbage-
stump.' It was true - he knew it. What good was a daughter if
she couldn't perform her nightly duties, if she couldn't deliver
at least half-a-dozen sons and daughters in her first six years of
marriage? One fine evening Deed'n-be-Chrysht called at the
door of Father Sensibly. He gave the knocker a loud rap.
Following their conversation, the priest drove his motorcar
out along the creamery road to Black Neddy's half-door in

order to carry out his priestly investigations. In his hip-pocket he was carrying (a useful introduction) a naggin of whiskey. In his overcoat he had another small bottle of potheen. A mixture of these two drinks would surely do the trick. He would need a drop or two of it himself so as to get up the courage to approach the subject of a man's use of his private equipment underneath his night-time shirt. As for Black Neddy, not a drop of drink had ever passed his lips before this time (the mean old bugger).

Father Sensibly soon put the life into him by pouring a few drops of it into his teacup – and then a few more drops until Black Neddy was getting a liking for it. And so, the afternoon rolled along, merrier and merrier by the minute. The holy man advised Black Neddy as to the nature of a young maiden's charms, the feelings she might have in her young breasts and lower down (ahem!) elsewhere. He talked in detail about the need for bodily coercions and the detailed arrangements that now had to be acquired by Black Neddy when it came to the bedroom cosiness. The potheen and the whiskey worked their way rapidly all the way down through Black Neddy's burning throat and on into his gizzard, making his eyes look red and bloody-looking. But, alas, they never made their way down into the private regalia resting lamely between his thighs for him to perform his joys!

3

Isn't Time a wonderful healer, a wonderful bringer of good news? In the course of the summer, when the heat was almost oppressive and the meadows were the purest of colours, Sadie leapt into the arms of Hammer-the-Smith's youngest son (*Sweet William*) a lad of 16. She saw him lightly stepping down the steps after Sunday Mass. She had never noticed him this way before. From being a young boy, he had suddenly turned into a handsome swan with an almost-demure look on his face and a bit of hairy fluff on his chin and the trace of a moustache on him. He displayed a flock of wavy ginger hair and a snow-white linen shirt. He was wearing a tweed sports jacket with the collar of the shirt out over the jacket. He seemed gentle and well-mannered with a smile on his lips and a sparkle in his boyish blue eyes. He was more than a dash amongst the young men – like a gift from out of heaven amongst the young ladies. And another thing – he was wearing his first new cap. He had put it on over his wavy locks at a rakish angle. And afterwards it was said: it wasn't so much that Sadie fell into his arms as that he fell into hers.

It all happened on the following Saturday when Sweet William was riding the rickety old bike that his farming employer had given him the use of so as to visit his ailing mother. Like all young men the lad was mad for speed. What a sight he was as he tore round the bend of the road near the gateway of Black Neddy's haggart. You could see how anxious he was to get to the bedside of his poor mother, whom he missed so much?

After Mass the very next day the news sped as fast as a jig-step. Some said that it was the drink (the lad had never tasted it before now, they said), which had caused his accident. He had fallen off his bike at the very bend of the road where Sadie had just been driving her cattle into the field. There she was – dallying in her yard, which was situated a bit underneath the side of the roadway. The little dreamer was admiring the sunset and hoping (the romantic little fool that she was) that one fine day a gate would open in her heart and a Prince Charming like the one in her schoolday storybooks would come speeding along the highway – that he would rescue his princess (her own good self) and whisk her away on his white stallion to some faraway Fairyland palace beyond the clouds. Oh, how she had prayed that God would lighten her burden and let a young man land in her arms. 'Dear God-in-heaven, if only a handsome young man (*'please! please! please!'*) would fall in the door to me and speed me away from this hairy old man and his cold old arse in the midnight bed!' Incredible as it may seem, her wish was granted quicker than she could ever have imagined. For, while she was standing there at the half-door, she heard the *tingaling-tingaling* song of a bicycle bell and the rattling of the speeding wheels as Sweet William tore along on his runaway bike.

The next thing that happened was like a visitation from the Angel Gabriel. A vision of youthfulness appeared in front of her eyes as Sweet William was hurtled out over the handlebars of his bike. Into the air he flew before landing in her arms. And there he lay – senseless. The good God-in-heaven had indeed listened to her cries of anguish. A man had come down from the skies and (wonder of wonders) had fallen straight into her arms! In future years, as they sat across from each other at the evening fireside, men and women would wonder what infernal magician had worked the magic on Sadie and Sweet William so that they should have met in such a very strange manner.

Sadie brought the damaged youngster in the half-door and put him down on a blanket near the heat of the fire. For a short while everything was black night for him. But she tended and nursed his wounds with the delicacy of her fingers, which (in spite of the harshness of her daily work) were still soft and tender. When he awoke, she smiled down at him and Sweet William saw in that clandestine moment the charm of Sadie's features and that she had a pair of striking china-blue eyes, which were fast now glittering their dovelike charms into his previously-untroubled soul. For a minute it was as though he were struck dumb – as though a merry fire had lit up inside him and his young heart started to melt away on him. In simple terms – Sadie had struck a love-note that soon turned from merry to smouldering for she had firmly trapped him in her clutches and he'd be hers for now and forevermore.

That Saturday was a Fair Day in town and Black Neddy had driven his cattle into the market square. He'd be there all day with the drinking and carousing that always followed a sale. The time now came for some youthful lovemaking and in his absence the hungry young lovers withdrew to the bedroom and there they played out their enchantment like two turtledoves, throwing their steaming bodies into jostling and tussling till the room began to tingle and jingle with the sweaty tumbles of these two little savages. Their dizzy antics continued throughout the afternoon till they almost jumped out of their skins and were exhausted from it.

Following the activities that were Sadie's natural birth-right a child was conceived in her and the birth of a son followed nine months later. Would you credit it! In the eyes of us all the fame of Black Neddy went soaring up to the moon. 'Why, the lecherous old bugger!' said some. 'What miracle cure did Father Sensibly bring up to Black Neddy's door in the motorcar that the magic of love should take such a hold of him? said others.

Father Sensibly stuck out his chest like a turkeycock. Whatever secrets he had imparted to Black Neddy it was now seen to have done the trick. At the next Saturday's confessions where there were usually a dozen rows of sibilant women kneeling outside the confession-box (all anxious to fill the priest's ears with their own scarcely impure thoughts and those secret emotions which they were far too timid to pour into the ears of their own men) they were joined by a similar number of old men. All of these hairy old schemers had come shoving one another in through the church door, wanting to be the first in the queue and their hearts as light as a bit of paper. Once inside in the confession-box they hoped they'd get hold of the secret, which the holy man had in his powers to give them, so that they could acquire for themselves a bit of Black Neddy's brute joys. Yes, Father Sensibly (he who was the receiver of the parish's confessions and had enough knowledge of the bodily goings-on of the entire population to fill a book) was going to be the answer to the prayers of every man-jack of them.

In the weeks that followed, we proclaimed the fame of Black Neddy as never before. It even went into our rhymes and our songs and the children themselves sang it on the way to school: '*Fair play to you, Neddy, you gave her the blast – you gave her the old injection, at last*!' But only Sweet William and Sadie knew about the bedroom frolics that were the real source of Black Neddy having apparently fathered so fine a child.

As for Black Neddy, he was now in a terrible fix. The rage, which he was forced to keep inside his chest, had no bounds. He knew that since the first day of his marriage he had never been able to raise so much as a cough in the marriage bed. And from that day onwards his mind was made up: if ever he found out the dirty little whoor, who had been giving Sadie her pleasures, he would cut off his danglers and stretch him out dead with a belt of his pickaxe handle.

Days moved on into weeks and the weeks moved on into months and thence into years. The two young lovebirds met in secret trysts whenever and wherever they could, behind the haystack, in under the shelter of the woodland trees, along hidden riverbanks where only the spirits of nature could behold their hot bodies and their discarded heaps of clothes.

But these sharp and irregular volleys of lovemaking were in no way enough to satisfy the youthful desires that they had for each other.

Sweet William could contain himself no longer. The Devil now came along on velvet feet and got a firm hold of the young lad's soul and then came and took a grip of his fair damsel as well. In the coming days the two young lovers began to plot and scheme and to whisper unheard of thoughts into one another's ears – devilish thoughts. And such were the powers of their love for each other, even the fear of hell's flames couldn't stop the wickedness that eventually fixed itself inside in their wild heads. Sweet William was so urged on and inspired by the beauty of Sadie that the moral restraints taught him by the priests and at his mother's knee fell away from him like a pair of horse-chains.

It was a starless night with no moon when the villain crept into Black Neddy's Welcoming Room. From there he tiptoed up to the bedroom door. At the last minute, Sadie herself was not nearly as sure as her lover of the steps about to be taken and she (the little heathen who had goaded Sweet William on) stood in her shift outside the bedroom door, shivering far more from fear than from the midnight cold. She had never dreamed (she kept telling herself) that matters would have gone this far. And yet, as she listened to Sweet William sidling his way towards the side of Black Neddy's bed, she didn't lift a finger to hold back the wicked hand of her lover.

What were the thoughts inside the head of Sweet William? Had he no father of his own on this earth? Had he never heard tell of hell and heaven? For a moment there was no sound in the room – only his intake of breath. He took the bolster in his fists and placed it over the snoring face of Black Neddy. And in spite of the poor man's thrashing around on the mattress, he held it pressed down tightly until he was sure he had choked the old man and there was no further quiver out of him. And then, when he was sure that Black Neddy was as dead as a fly, he crept out the creaking door of the bedroom. No one had seen him come in. No one saw him going out. No one had witnessed the dark and deadly deed. No one except the hundreds of ghostly ancestors of Black Neddy who forever had been his trusty companions in the days before Sadie had come to greet him. And without so much as a backward look at Sadie, Sweet William whispered his stealthy feet out across the dark haggart (the trees gazing down sadly on him) to where he had stowed his bike. What on earth had he done? The angels looked out pitifully at him from behind every twig and leaf and, with the hounds of persecution running fast after him, he rode his terrified way home with a speed that outmatched even the wind.

The equally terrified Sadie, realising what Sweet William had finally plucked up courage to do, now found herself in a damp cold sweat and she took Black Neddy's greatcoat from the back of the door. He wouldn't need it anymore. Then she stirred up the tiny embers in the black grate with a few hawthorn twigs and a few small bits of turf till the blaze was yellow and red once more. Wrapped in the greatcoat she spent the rest of the night huddled near the fire, dreading what the outcome would be when next day's light came in. The coat would keep her warm and free from the cold of the night. But free from the stain of such wickedness she never again would be.

Next day when she ran down the road and raised the alarm there wasn't so much as a raised eyebrow. Neither did Doctor Glasses have any questions to ask when he came to sign the death certificate the day after this sad event. Along with him came Father Sensibly to pray for Black Neddy's soul. They could see for themselves the sad state of the old man's yellow face and his grotesquely twisted mouth lying there in the bed. Doctor Glasses came out quietly into the yard to meet the crowd of old keening women, who had come to light the death-candles and to cry over Black Neddy and help prepare his corpse for burial. He told them that it was not only his old age that had beaten the aging farmer but (he tapped his nose and gave a discreet little cough) his unusually exertive practices in the bedroom that had proved too much for a delicate old man like him and he warned them to be sure and tell nobody.

By this time Father Sensibly was feeling as miserable as a tree without water. There was no need for him to speculate about the death for it was he himself and no-one else who had encouraged Black Neddy to put a bit of a spring in his legs in the nightly bedroom tumblings and jostlings. In spite of Doctor Glasses' instructions, the whole of the countryside (wouldn't you know it?) soon recognised the reason for Black Neddy's death and they raised a great big shout of approval. Indeed, there wasn't a man that didn't envy the dead man the powers of his fierce lovemaking. Thanks to Father Sensibly's original visit they knew that the old fellow had died in utter ecstasy and gone up to heaven in a blaze of glory. The following day Sadie buried him in haste below in the graveyard.

It was May next year when Sweet William and Sadie called out their marriage banns inside in the church. Wouldn't you think that the little heathen would have kept to her honour and worn her black widow's weeds for the full duration of the customary twelve months? Free at last and anxious to bury the recent dark deed firmly in the past, the two of them were now in their absolute heaven. They couldn't get enough of the lovemaking and in the next few years children and more children followed. There was one, then two, then three and four. 'Doesn't the love-making flog all!' said the two cosy ones.

BALARAGGIN

1

Balaraggin was the one and only son of Sally. He was such a little rag-bag of a baby that she could think of nothing else to call him only Balaraggin. She was forty-five and would have you know that she had never so much as kissed a man on his whiskery lips. At the time of his birth it seemed to her and to others amongst the women as though she was having *A Virgin Birth*. Maybe future pilgrimages would be made to her door? Maybe the townies would come out in their hundreds and scrape their knees round her spring-well and ask her for a blessing or two. Sally's mother (*Lena*) knew better – in fact she knew the whole truth. And though this daughter of hers was old enough to have a stem of sense in her head, Lena was sorely tempted when she heard of the imminent delivery of this baby (this special virginal birth), to give Sally a few belts of her broken chair-leg across her skinny pagan arse.

How had this birth happened? It was just when the sun was rising that Sally would be visited by half a dozen poachers on their way back from their nightly visits, lamp-lighting the rabbits above on the Little Bald Pain. Tired but proud, they were on their way home to spend the rest of the day in bed. They passed by Sally's back window (it was her bedroom), swinging their rhythmical bikes and they full-to-the-gills with floppy rabbits and their necks broken. From time to time Sally looked out shyly at them from behind the geranium box. She marvelled at the huge pile of dead rabbits hanging down from the handlebars and crossbars of their bikes and she was a jumble of emotions as she started counting them.

At first, for the price of a shy little kiss or two, the sly townie rascals gave her one or two small rabbits for the pot.

The summer was growing hotter – very hot – and the evenings lurched heavily onwards that little bit longer. We found ourselves melting with sweat and it was often hard to catch one's breath. It was then that the poachers on their way up into the evening hills began to tease poor innocent Sally, to give her the odd little wink or a bit of the glad eye and to praise her comely face and the curves of her plump body. And in time (the brazen heathens) they were asking her to raise her skirts so that they could get a little peep at her knickers.

Gradually they began to introduce her to new and unheard-of refinements so that she followed them out into the dusky fields and into the forest where she quickly learnt about those earth-shaking bodily pleasures – so much so that it frightened the life out of her. The *woodland fairies* heard her crying out in terror and then (almost at the same time) cackling with fits of outlandish laughter. As a result of her playful battles with these townie wildcats she mysteriously found herself nine months later gazing down at her one and only offspring - Balaraggin, this little rag-bag of a-child.

2

In the years that followed, whenever Balaraggin was on his way to Sunday Mass, it was his habit to keep away from the lanes and take the shortcut, walking across the fields with his best leather boots well-buttered and laced across his shoulders. Like our children, he preferred to be in the bare feet when making his speedy 5-mile journey amidst the cows and sheep so as to catch the dew of the morning grasses in between his frozen toes. His mother, Sally, had always told him this was a sure cure for any bunions or corns that might be troubling him.

A mile or two into his journey a fog of steam would rise up on his sweaty forehead and could be seen some distance away. As soon as he reached the road it looked as though he had dipped his face into a barrel of rainwater. In the meantime, our own journey to Mass was less than half Balaraggin's mammoth distance in search of his God. One or two of us could hold their chins up high, being the proud owners of bikes instead of walking along with the rest of us. Weren't they the lucky rascals (you'd think) since they could snugly fit on their crossbar the flowery dress of a comely damsel later in the evening before throwing their bike in across the ditch for an evening's dancing at the Platform-Dance-in-the-Fields. The older folk (the majority) came to Mass on their ass-and-car or even the horse-and-cart if they had a big family. If anyone was the cousin of a priest or (better still) a bishop, he could lay hold of a pony-and-trap and then he was indeed the swank of all swanks! Amen to that.

By the time Balarggin reached the Blue Gates, there were only one or two lads left walking and he was now in a tearing hurry and moving at the speed of a well-tuned jinnet with the worry of death stamped on his face. Would he be early for Mass? Would he be late? Would he be in church before the bell rang and the priest stepped out on the altar? Maybe he'd be the last one in the church door, meeting the rest of the sniggerers as the priest wound up his sermon or began washing up the Communion vessels. It was always the same puzzle for him and he was damned if he'd ever learn to fathom out which way the sun was heading across the hill so that he'd know the time.

Why should he worry? Hadn't he his grandfather's watch in his waistcoat-pocket – the one he was always taking out and gallantly swinging round on its chain like a pendulum and showing off to anyone he might meet on the way? Everyone knew about his watch. We were always talking about it. Indeed, we were all a bit jealous of it, since none of us had one of our own and knew the time only by looking at the grandfather clock on the dresser back home. But there was one thing that none of us knew – Balaraggin didn't have a clue how to tell the time and (worse still) his watch was no longer in working order.

He hopped out over the ditch to join his few fellow-walkers and without so much as a *good-day, byze* he hurried on ahead of them. One or two go-byze shouted after him, 'Balaraggin 'Balaraggin! Make yeer watch tell us the true time. Coom on, blasht ye! Stop fooling us – don't keep it all to yeerself!' They were ready for a cruel fit of ribald laughter as they hoped that a poor scholar like him couldn't really tell them the time or understand the hands on his watch.

Balaraggin suddenly stopped and took out his watch and gave it a studied look. It was a beautiful little scene as he then gave the watch a few impatient shakes, holding it up close to his ear to see if it was ticking. Then he looked at it again and gave a gasp of horror before hastily re-pocketing it. 'Cripes, byze,' he yelled back, 'we'll be late for Mass if we don't hurry on – look at the time - would ye ever think it was so late?'

Then we saw him take to his heels and speed on towards the church, leaving us stunned and with only one thing on our minds - Balaraggin could tell the time. Wasn't he the cute little actor – the way he'd made fools of us? The news would spread like wildfire and his star would rise to the sky for being able to read the hands on a watch – at least for the next few weeks until the old gossips thought of something new and more useful to be spouting about. Oh, the frustration - just when a few walkers were on the verge of seeing him put out of his stride by their slyness in asking him to tell them the time. Yes, a clever one was that Balaraggin, realising that few (if any of us) understood the workings of a watch. And after Mass we were all asking ourselves: was ever anything so truly wonderful as the gift of a watch to Balaraggin from a grandfather's dying hands when the only watch any of us knew about was the rise and fall of the blessed sun?

3

There is a turning point in any man's fortunes and Balaraggin's moment finally came when he was to prove himself a man among pygmies. Not one of us had ever dared enter a Protestant church and we wouldn't do so for many years to come – not until that miserable day came to knock down the Protestant church in Copperstone Hollow and leave it in smithereens so that we could put up a new one to take its place.

But Balaraggin was always a strange fellow and he refused to join in others' fears and hatred of the so-called heathen Protestants. He knew that God wouldn't condemn him if he entered their foreign church and he made this known to all the cowardly souls he came across. Not for a minute did he believe it a shrine to Impiety or to some estranged God and, as a result, his neighbours quickly began whispering their malice and poison against him.

How did it all begin? The news had spread that Lady Posh-Frock, after choking on a wishbone, had given up the ghost in the middle of a February night when the landscape everywhere was streaked with snow. Being one of the few foreign settlers left among us (and also a Protestant) she had no one to dig her grave and besides, the ground was as hard as a shovel. This was indeed a very sad case and there was a profound silence among all of us.

That's when Balaraggin put up his hand and stepped forward to do the honest thing. The very next night he made whatever religious preparations were needed for Lady Posh-Frock's burial and the washing of her corpse in readiness for her last journey across the fields and into the Protestant

Church. It was the middle of a dark night and the moon and stars were hidden in the mist. He fetched the wheelbarrow from Lady Posh-Frock's shed. He was not alone, however. To help him he had three handy-sized men (I think it was Taedspaddy, Bunnyfoot and Tommy's Tim), armed with several pints of stout, and they now helped him to load up the poor soul's coffin onto the wheelbarrow.

As soon as they got near the Protestant Church they proved to be the brave little fellows and helped Balaraggin carry the coffin from the wheelbarrow and onto their shoulders and up to the very front door of the church. But suddenly, just when they were laying the old lady's coffin down reverently on the church steps, a haunting fear came over their manly hearts. They thought they'd now be struck down dead by lightning and they kept on blessing themselves. In the following weeks they would relate how they saw a black serpent running across the moon, how the hair had stood up on their heads, how there was an eerie silence all around the foreigners' church, how they saw the eyes of God looking scornfully down on them and Jesus weeping (the bleddy liars). The hush and the expectations of God's wrath - as though they were back in Eden - made them think the gates of hell were opening up beneath their feet (they said).

Balaraggin told us the rest of the story. He saw them take to their heels in scattered flight, tripping over each other as they leapt out over the ditch – as though the Devil was trying to catch hold of their heels, how they had turned into frightened little bunny-rabbits with the sparks flying out of their arse. Would he ever forget it? He had had to hold his sides (he said) from the pain of his laughter at the spectacle of their heels disappearing from view.

Of course, he had had other things on his mind and had turned back towards the Protestant Church, taking off his cap. With the help of the wheelbarrow he pushed Lady Posh-Frock's coffin quietly down the aisle and loaded the dead woman up onto the wooden trestles. Then he knelt down reverently in the Protestant Church (was there ever so great a sin?) and said a silent prayer for the repose of her soul – that she might find an everlasting home for herself in the Beyond. A day later he went to bury her decently with his pick and shovel behind the church wall. Not a shilling payment did he take from the good woman's brother (Lord Elegance).

4

In the harsh wintertime it was not surprising that a single son would occupy his mother's bed (he at one end and she at the other) and that they'd keep each other's cold bodies warm and spare the need for going out in the stormy weather for a bag of logs. It was at times such as this that the souls of Sally and Balaraggin were as close as two sides of a window-glass. Sally (no matter what others might now be saying) had the utmost faith in the actions of her son. She had turned his soul towards heaven and was the inspiration for all his acts of kindness (as in the case of Lady Posh-Frock). By now he had captured the soft spot in her heart. A son and a mother - a love from her eye into his eye and a love from his eye back into her eye. Enough said.

But, sad to say, this love story was soon to come to an end for the sky was not always virginal blue and even the beautiful sun was able to forego her brilliance amongst us. There came a grey and dismal day when Sally found herself alone at her work abroad in the bog. She loved nothing better than to be out in the fresh air, her nose sniffing at the breeze and she plunging her spade into the soft boggy earth. The lonely wilderness lay around her as far as the eye could see. There was nothing to listen to but the mournful song of the curlew. She was working like blazes and had built up a fine sweat on her forehead while planking up the last of her turf from the dried-out footings. Before she knew it, an unbelievable tiredness came into her bones and she fell into a deep sleep. The song of the weary day continued its way into the silent evening and the customary damp dews came down from Chieftain Hill. Sally was soon covered in the evening mists.

Miserable, cold and lonesome, she awoke to see nothing but the eeriness and the ghostliness of it all. Like many before her time she began to be afraid. She knew those old stories – how the wilderness fairies came alive at these indescribable times of the day when the light was neither daytime nor night-time, how these same fairies in the days of old had removed from this earth the souls of good women, taking them with them out beyond the rowan trees. Dark dirty clouds continued to waft round her and she felt these same spirits straddling over her. She heard their voices calling her unto the other world, 'Sally! Sally! Sally!' She walked off into the darkness of the bog.

Next morning, when no-one had heard from her, a great crowd gave the entire day searching for her. The demented Balaraggin led the pack, 'Mother-mother-dearest mother!' he kept calling. 'Sally-Sally-Sally!' the crowds kept bawling. By this time the hearts of the neighbours had turned upside-down and some feared the worst. All the old backbiters (such is human nature) had forgotten their bitterness against Balaraggin and his trip to the Protestant church and were full of anxiety for him. They began to mutter to each other, 'Didn't we always know that Sally was too good for this world? The wilderness fairies must have taken her.'

They heard the shaky voice of Pat-the-Hat calling from the bog hole where Taedspaddy had been within an inch of getting himself drowned after going for the kettle of water for the tea and sandwiches - the day his uncle (the Gog) and White Snow had found his flailing arms sticking up frantically out of the bog hole, the kettle close by. Almost rupturing their guts, they had pulled his bruised body out with the ass in the nick of time. And now the giddy crowd rushed across the heather to where Pat-the-Hat was standing, his father's hat reverently in his fists.

Balaraggin was the first one to get there. All he saw were the two sad wellingtons of Sally sticking up out of Taedspaddy's bog hole and a giant sob rattled round in his throat. Men came running up with a rope the way they'd often done before so as to drag out a belly-deep horse. It was too late! Sally was gone, snatched down by Sergeant Death into the peaceful purity of the fairyland kingdom, to appear again as a fairy-child in years to come.

Next day a fierce woe took hold of Balaraggin's soul and left him trembling and sobbing like an ass in the rain. The day's light was nothing but a knife in his chest and he passed his hand over his eyes. He was dull-eyed with fatigue, as though he'd been wrestling with the Devil the whole blessed night, not knowing which of them had won the battle. There was no more warmth in his bed, no mother's arms to comfort him. He was entirely alone - himself and his sad thoughts, himself and the empty fire grate, himself and the mice in the rafters. The house-ghosts and spirits of his ancestors that had once been so friendly to himself and Sally now seemed oppressive.

In the night-time when there was no-one to spy on him he went out and began collecting wildflowers. With these he covered the floor around his mother's bed. He took the Sacred Heart picture off of the wall and placed it in the centre of the flowers. He gathered together his mother's few possessions and placed them in a drawer in the chest. He knew she'd be coming back for them and spent the following night talking foolishly to her, a strange smile on his lips. The talk was friendly and good-humoured, almost a laugh. 'Mother, do ye remember when we took the white calf out into the field for the first time? Do ye remember how he frightened all the cows with his newfound freedom and how they ran headlong down into the river?' The talk of the deranged man went on and on like this. 'Mother, do ye remember when the gander turned on the sow and pecked his two eyes asunder and he ran into the Welcoming Room and buried his head in the sack of flour?' He imagined he saw the poor dead soul lying in the bed beside him with the rosary beads in her fist. But as he talked away to her ghost, no answer was given back to him.

In the middle of the next night (the day after Sally had been taken away to hospital in Black Bess's truck) he woke up and sat upright in the bed. He listened and he listened. He could hear the moaning of the wailing wind, as though it were a child. He could hear a few scattered raindrops and then he heard the rattle of the phantom ass-and-car pulling in across the stream's flagstones and on across the moonlit cobblestones. He heard the mystical ass being tied at the singletree. He heard the clink of the ass's chains. His mother had come back and he felt a great fear as he listened to the well-known click of Sally's boots and felt the spectre of her flitting across the yard towards him. Sally paused at the front door. She stood there a long time. Balaraggin held his breath, his ears on edge. He heard the latch of the door being lifted and the door creaking. His mother's ghost had entered the Welcoming Room. It was pitch black and Balaraggin was in a river of sweat. He could hear a pinprick. His mother's boots scraped back and forth around the floor as she jerked open the drawers in the tall press. She began to fling out the piles of saucepans and the boot-polish, the boot-last and the river jug. She was looking not for her few priceless bits of finery, her rosary beads or her holy books but for her one and only cardigan. He knew it: all women wanted the cardigan to keep them warm on the journey to the Beyond – the best one, their Sunday one. The poor man was terrified and could smell the pungent scent of her ghost – a warm pissy scent mixed up with mothballs and the ache was killing him and his heart was about to stop beating. Sally would be back the next night – he knew it. She'd be wanting the rest of her possessions to be loaded onto the ass-and-car so as to get her soul into heaven.

In the morning he got all the clothes and bits of trinkets that his mother might need for the journey and placed them in a heap on the floor. When his mother would come back she'd have no hardship loading up her ass-and-car. Then, leaving the heap behind him, he ran out and closed the door. At full pelt he ran down the hill to Dowager's half-door and in a strange gibberish told her that his mother's ghost had come back and that he was too frightened to return to his cabin, that Dowager had to give him the loan of one of her sons to keep his body warm throughout the night – at least till after the funeral.

Dowager feared that madness was about to catch hold of the poor man. Her son (*Stylish*) was young at the time, barely 6, and she sent him up home with the lonely man. That night when Stylish got into the bed alongside him, Balaraggin placed the head of the little child against his own chest so that they both could share in the warmth and drive away the feeling of loneliness. But Stylish couldn't sleep. And then he heard the phantom ass-and-car coming across the yard-stream. 'What is it?' he cried. In the bright moonlight he heard the chains and axle rattling round the yard. 'Who is it? Tell me, Balaraggin!' he cried again.

'Whisht, child! Keep quiet – 'tis mee mother,' said Balaraggin. Stylish heard the door opening and Sally's ghost loading up her ass-and-car with her possessions and setting off across the yard-stream. A mere child of 6, he was scared to death and couldn't escape from the clutching arms of Balaraggin for the poor man was himself terrified out of his mind and was holding him in a grip as tight as death. The two of them began to kick the mattress asunder and Stylish pissed in the bed.

Next morning – and long before the cockerels had peeped out their heads or had started to crow – the little fellow broke all speed records in flying home to his startled mother and never again did he return to share the bed of Balaraggin or to help him keep off the loneliness that was turning the poor man into a deranged lunatic. Enough said.

5

A night came when there was a frost that would cut off your nose and ears. The loneliness of Balaraggin's cabin was choking him. He put on his thick coat and scalf and crammed his pockets with boiled crab-apples from the fire's heat to keep his hands and belly warm. Then, in an effort to escape from the company of Sally's ghost, he wandered blindly out the lane and headed towards the drinking-shop of Curl 'n' Stripes in search of forgetfulness. It was many years since he had darkened the doors or sat on the barrel-planks – in the days when there was just himself and Batty-the-Cripple and his mouth organ alongside Cleverly-the-Cattle-Drover. Somewhat guiltily, he reached for his first pint of stout. 'Couldn't ye have waited a little longer, at least till I was well dead and buried?' Sally's ghost whispered in his ear.

He hunched himself down on the barrel-planks, the crackling logs on the fire illuminating his sad face. He took a few furtive sips of his drink and tried to hide the glass from view in under his coat as though he was some imaginary tinker running away with an egg. For a short while he seemed to derive a bit of solace as he looked into the bottom of his glass. But soon it was glass after glass, the whiskey as well as the pints of stout. And though he felt that these drinks were doing him a power of good they soon began to turn him from sad to morose, and finally to being bad-tempered with the rest of the world. 'Throw me out a pair of yeer twins and be quick about it,' he roared as he swallowed yet another pint of stout, twinning it with a glass of whiskey. Eyeing the bottles of raw-gut potheen on the top shelf, he added, 'And give me some of yeer top shelf, mee good man – top shelf is the drink for me.'

Soon his voice became papery thin and his eyes began to look fiercely tragic. Every man has a soft heart at times and reluctantly Curl 'n' Stripes poured Balaraggin yet another drink. Somehow it felt good for the shopkeeper to be filling the poor demented man's gizzard with strong drink – it'd help him stave off the ensuing madness which (if he wasn't careful) would carry Balaraggin off in a month or two to the sombre grave after his mother.

Midnight struck and Din-Din-Dinny was sent for. He carried the drunken Balaraggin out from the artificial light of the shop and helped him up onto his cart. He drove him home and put him into his damp bed – a bed in which there'd be no peace for his poor demented soul. The ghost of Sally rose up out of the grave, then came and stood before Balaraggin. She called him out of his drunken sleep. Balaraggin! Balaraggin! Her ghost was utterly powerful in its calling.

His eyes blinded with forlorn tears, he sat up in the bed and an unmerciful impulse took hold of him. He was sick to death of wrestling with sorrow. Sad and angry, he crawled out on his unsteady hands and knees and followed the ghostly voice that was beckoning him. Out the door and into the black night he staggered in answer to her call. He crossed the haggart singletree where the steely moon and the millions of sharp stars perched above his yard and blinked down on him. The ass and the seven cows from across the ditch looked on bemusedly.

He stood for a moment. He cast a confused look back at his life and felt the frozen universe whipping rapidly passed him. He took from his pocket the sharp cut-throat razor, which was always reserved for shaving himself for Sunday Mass. There under the cover of the lonesome sky he felt for the soft spot beneath the stubble of his chin. He knelt beside the hay-reek and said his last farewell prayers, speaking silently into his mother's ears. 'Mother-Mother-Mother! I am coming . . . I am coming . . . can't ye see. . . that I am coming home to ye?' And there in the quiet of the secret night the black branches of the pine trees gathered closely in round him as (laughing sardonically) he cut his throat from ear to ear. He managed to stagger to his pig house and spread the blood all over the cross-lats of the pig house door. From there he swayed a little further and came to the green door of his cabin before floating away above the clouds to the Land of Sunshine in the Beyond where his mother was waiting to greet him. The ruby red of his blood was a fitting match for the red of the geraniums in his window boxes, wedded together as closely as himself and his mother in death.

The Guards and Father Sensibly came next morning and took his body away before the foxes or carrion crows could get at it. Despite all of Balaraggin's previous charitable works, the fact that he had killed himself meant that on this saddest of all occasions Holy Mother Church didn't even give him the Last Sacramental Rites or bury him in the graveyard and his bones would lie forever under a heap of rocks in God-knows-where.

From that day to this it became a sacred part of every child's initiation into the realms of adolescent fascination and adventuring to be taken up to see the ruins of Balaraggin's cabin – to see where the demented man had cut his throat. On dark evenings and with the early moonlight guiding them it was a journey known only to children and to see if they had finally become brave little men. The older children would lead the younger ones by their trembling hands – up along the green lanes before trudging on passed the Little Bald Plain. They'd put the blindfolds on the mouse-hearted little ones as soon as they got close enough to the edge of Balaraggin's haggart. The place was deserted these days. No cockerel had ever been heard crowing there since the death of the unhappy man. The little procession would tiptoe cautiously to the green bloodstained door of Balaraggins' pig house and cabin.

The blindfolds were taken off and the bigger boys took over the ritual. 'Can ye hear the rattle of Sally's ass-and-car? Can ye see Balaraggin's ghost behind the hen house? Can ye see the immense quantities of blood that he shed? He must have had a barrel of it inside him.' The list went on. The little ones saw the bloody streaks across the green door of the cabin. Rather than feel frightened or sad, they became as excited as a cow on heat. They had witnessed (though they didn't understand its depth till much later in life) a terrible mystery – a manifestation - a revelation of a truly tremendous love – the absolute devotion of a son for his mother. They had been privileged (though this too they didn't yet know) to see into the heart of Balaraggin, into the blood of Balaraggin, whose grief and lonesomeness, after Sally had drowned and gone away from him, was so utterly unbearable that he cut his throat from ear to ear. May God spare you, Balaraggin. You meant no harm.

BOHORLODY

1

The men were coming home from the creamery. A short distance behind him Bohorlody could see the hooves of the little red mule of God-be-with-the-times belting along the road and the merry old soul slapping the reins gently against the mule's back and filling the road with his singing – the latest homespun tales brought back to us from the Land of the Silver Dollar by Toby-from-the-Hill.

But (ah and alas) a distance ahead of him and about to disturb his beautiful reveries was Hannyways (bad cess to him) and his white jinnet (*Raggity*) - the product of a skilful union between the jack-donkey of Ducks-and-Drakes and the draft-horse mare of Rambling Jack. He could see the dainty strides of Hannyways' little black-and-white terrier (*Crack-Jaw*) – a dog that had gotten his name thanks to a kick in the head from Raggity last May. Crack-Jaw was on his tippy-toes as usual, daintily strutting along between the wheels of the ass-and-car in the rhythm of the jinnet's hooves and the rattling creamery-tanks.

Hannyways was a raw-boned sort of fellow with a few red veins in his nose and a pair of glassy eyes from his love of Irish whiskey. He was not the most popular of men and everyone was sick to their stomachs from the political sermons he drew down whenever he met any of us who were simple enough to stop and listen to him. Three weeks ago, the self-same fellow had had the misfortune to be twisting his neck round and laying into Red Buckles in a terrifying argument about the virtues of that redoubtable politician, De Valera. Of course, the rest of us knew that Michael Collins (De Valera's arch rival) was the next best thing to Jesus-on-the-cross and a national hero - even our women knew that as a solid fact and revered his gallantry.

The row and the ruction got so hot and heavy that Red Buckles stopped his ass (*Sammy*) and leapt down from the cart. With a face as cold as ice he took off his jacket and then took off his waistcoat. It was time (he felt) to administer a firm bit of his own homespun diplomacy and give Hannyways a smack of his fists in order to resolve this particular debate. 'We're here at the Blue Gates, Hannyways,' he shouted. 'Let me and you step in over the gate and settle this matter once and for all. Coom on, blasht ye – spit on yeer fists and be a man – show me the mettle of yeer knuckles as well as yeer miserable gob!'

Red Buckles then proceeded to give Hannyways a few tidy jabs to the jaw and into the belly and leave him with his legs cocked up in the air, a pure rake of himself. It was good enough for him (we all said) and he was left to crawl home, sulking like a bear with a sick head. The matter had been settled, the law had been delivered.

But that was three weeks ago. And the same incautious old fool was here again and as bold as a cockerel – turning around in the cart and wrangling with the same old provocative argument. The sight of him was enough to make Bohorlody sick – the old eejit's godforsaken nose pointing up towards the sky and the runny candle of snot hanging down from it. A few more *H-H-H-H-Hannyways* and the ears of the rest of the men finally heard this would-be politician in full flow as he prodded at the sky with his pipeful of spitty tobacco so as to emphasize his latest argument.

'No matter what the rest of ye simpletons say about yeer brave Michael Collins, didn't he hike himself across to John Bull and do the traitor on the rest of us, didn't he sell the souls of us all to the rotten British and hand them on a plate six of our precious counties above in the north? Of course, he did, the bleddy whoor!' And that's the way he went on and on.

You'd have to put your hands to your ears. What other hero was there on earth that could disguise himself as a spy and parade round the streets of the Big City on his bike, exchanging pleasantries with the Tans outside their very own barracks? Those young eejits, who were supposed to be out looking for him and putting a gun to his forehead, didn't have a notion whom they were speaking to. Why, the man was a pure miracle-of-a-man – a patriot if ever there was one. That's what men and women alike would have said had they a chance to meet up with Hannyways this morning and educate his gob for him - that was the reason (they'd tell him) why their hero's picture was hanging almost sacredly on our walls alongside the pope and the Blessed Virgin and the Sacred Heart and the first thing to greet you when you set foot in the Welcoming Room. Enough said.

With the sun shining and it being a grand bit of a day until then, the antics of Hannyways proved too much for Bohorlody and he gave him an answer that he knew would boil the inside of his chest. 'And what is that prime upstart of yeers – De Valera? Tell me this – what is he only a half-breed Spanish basthard!'

At Bohorlody's cruel jibe we were beginning to enjoy the morning's bit of sport tremendously – especially the change that suddenly appeared on Hannyways' face. These harsh words had almost knocked the pipe clean out of his impudent gob and he appeared to swoon in an utter faint on top of his ass-and-car. Indeed, for a minute or two Bohorlody thought it likely that the old goat was going to fall down out of the cart and hit his brazen head off of the road.

Of course, we all knew that Bohorlody himself could be every bit as big a reprobate as Hannyways, that he was always looking for a good long-winded argument like this one, that the two of them were evenly matched with one another when it came to politics and a good bit more stubborn than the animals leading their carts.

2

Bohorlody was about to step down from his horse-and-cart and let fly at Hanniways with his fists when he realized he'd already reached his own flagstones. By this time the impudent fellow had gone up past Cheerful Nan's and was still standing up defiantly in his cart.

'That thundering eejit, Hannyways, (cried Bohorlody) – would somebody hand me a rope till I go back and hang him – or at least give me a rock to put hopping off of his brazen skull the next time I see him?' He unwound the reins from the creamery tanks and threw himself down from the lace of the cart, tying the pony to the singletree. He could still hear Hannyways singing like a morning cockerel and before he set foot inside the haggart he said a silent little prayer to the Blessed Virgin – that the Devil might come along during the night and snuggle up close beside Hannyways, that he might chastise his gobby tongue for him and ask him to come and sit beside him in the burning corner of hell before the month was out.

He felt awfully dry after listening to Hannyways and was about to go in the half-door and get a mug of water from the bucket before taking up the tanks of Easy-does-it and Red Scissors. However, he hadn't time to draw his breath when (damn the bit) he was confronted by a galaxy of his children, their faces a picture of mournfulness. He was already in a foul humour from the insults of Hannyways and this was a sad way to be welcoming their own father back home.

'Father-father-father!' they all began to bawl, led on by his eldest son (*Barbaha*): 'Listen-listen! Please listen to us! We have been out in the yard all morning, waiting for you to come home and give us the law.'

'Fair play to ye,' said Bohorlody, nodding his head. And again, he reminded himself that when things went astray – whenever an argument rose up between any of the household members – it was his job to address the rest of them and give them the law.

'Right, byze, get the chairs out, let ye, and we'll go to law.' He would listen to all the arguments and (wise man that he was) he'd give his children his verdict. Himself and his wife (*the Dainty Woman*) would administer justice fair-and-square for each of their children to clearly contemplate. It had always been like this - they knew it. There had been times in the past when the law said that the guilty child had to get himself a belting with the razor-strop, times when one of them had to be pelted into the stream, times when another one of them had to get himself the full contents of the bucket of water down on top of his condemned head.

Then up spoke the brave Barbaha. 'Father, ye know how we've always needed yeer advice. After trying out our own bouts of the law this morning, we find ourselves well and truly beaten and there's nothing for it but to go to law with yeer own good self. Ye'll surely give us yeer verdict like ye've done in the past for there's no better man on this earth than yeerself.'

In all his born days this was the biggest mouthful of words that Bohorlody had ever heard pouring out of Barbaha's mouth. 'Grand to ye!' said he. He was secretly delighted with the high praise that Barbaha had just heaped on him as the leader of the house and his good humour was now restored.

However, he still had one or two little doubts nagging at him about his children's ability to refer to the law in his absence. He recalled the last time they had gone to law before he'd had a chance to get home and give them his own final verdict. The misery of it haunted him to this day – how could he forget it? It was no laughing-matter. The hens from Timmy Bellow's ragwort field had found themselves a small hole in the briars near his ash-pit. 'Why shouldn't we come in here (they thought) and lay a little egg or two for ourselves in the ash-pit?' And in through the gap they came, more than a dozen of them at a time.

'Why shouldn't we eat a little grain in here, while we're at it (they thought)? Then the little trespassers found their way into Bohorlody's yard and were in the act of eating the oats and spuds from the galvanized tray near the ass-and-car when the children spotted them. They shushed them up the yard with their hands until they had trapped them inside in the Welcoming Room.

What were they going to do about these thieving hens? Their father wasn't yet home. There was no time to waste. There and then they decided they'd have to go to law by themselves and hold a family trial. Barbaha kept watch over the hens with the yard-brush and kept them imprisoned inside the half-door. The brothers and sisters sat in a circle on a bench and then solemnly went to law. It was the first time they had done this sort of thing and they felt a little bit uncomfortable. However, it didn't take them long before they reached a unanimous verdict and found the hens guilty of trespassing. Though they were none too certain what the penalty for this crime should be, they made themselves a ramshackle gallows. Then they strung up and hanged every damned one of those chickens before throwing them back into Timmy's field.

As with Adam and Eve, there followed a good deal of shame – a kind of nakedness to their spirits. So, they kept themselves away from the yard and the chastising dishcloth of the Dainty Woman. When evening came they were even more ashamed of having hanged Timmy's chickens and they wondered whether it had been right to do so. 'We'll have a second bite at the law as soon as father cooms home,' they said and they each nodded their heads and waited in silence for Bohorlody to come home and be their judge. Whatever it would be, it'd be acceptable to all.

But an hour later – as soon as he came back into the yard after setting his traps and snares on the edge of the Bog Wood – Bohorlody had the rage of a pure madman on him. 'That the Devil may shit on top of ye, ye little ninny-hammers.' They'd never seen him in such a fury and he stamped his big boots almost through the floor and hastened for the sallyswitch to redden their legs. Then he raised his voice and let a roar out of him. 'I'll now give ye a lengthy epistle, indeed I will - one that ye'll remember for a long while to coom' – and he whaled into them with the sallyswitch till they were black and blue and banned them from ever again carrying out the law without reporting first to him for his approval or disapproval – whatever the case might be. After that he kicked out from under them the bench on which they'd been sitting and left them in a tearful pile on top of one another abroad in the yard. Then he stormed out across the stream and went off to drink six pints of stout so as to wash the taste of his children out of his mouth.

3

Eggs. Eggs. Eggs. The Dainty Woman was all the time thinking about her eggs. Seemingly no-one had a single egg in the place, thanks to the thievery of Bohorlody's dog (*Rapper*). There wasn't a soul these days, who wasn't pressing hard to get rid of this wretched dog – as much as he loved him. In the back of every farmer's head was the hanging rope or the gun or the sack for drowning him.

The lack of eggs had thrown the Dainty Woman's mind back to those earlier days during the Civil Strife when there wasn't an egg to be got. It was a most shameful period (she reflected) in our history. May God forgive the fighting men. Families were going to war against each other the length and breadth of our countryside, families who had lived amicably enough all their lives. Suddenly they'd become bent on killing one another and the smell of cordite from their guns was everywhere, some taking up the gun for De Valera and others the gun for Michael Collins.

It was in those days that the present high-faluting Hannyways had become a bit of a hero and also a bit of a clown in one and the same week - a sort of miracle. He had put on his wife's apron and gone off to the hayshed where for the last three mornings his wife's favourite little guinea-hen (*Rosie*) was deliriously cackling as she laid her eggs. Hannyways climbed the ladder and was delighted to find six newly-laid eggs, which he put into his apron.

He was coming down the ladder and making his way very carefully – eggs being so precious. Blast the bit – at that precise moment didn't the guns start blazing away at full force. To his eternal credit (and we talked about it for months to come)

Hannyways pelted his body off of the last few rungs of the ladder and dived towards the ditch. Mindful of his precious apron-load of eggs, he had the good sense at the very last minute to twist his body away from the metal stanchion of the hayshed whilst he was falling out into space. In that moment of glory, he was better than a tomcat in the air and not a single one of the six eggs was smashed. It's sad to say, however, that he collided with the upright stanchion of the iron hayshed and was knocked out cold. When the firing of the guns was finished and we all rose up from the ground we found the poor fellow still lying unconscious (if not dead entirely) on a sop of hay. The news spread quick as fork lightning. 'Hannyways has broken his skull in two places but has not broken a single one of his eggs'. He was the hero of the hour – indeed he was.

A few days later, however, these words of praise were to be rubbed off of his slate for the same fellow had utterly disgraced himself by putting his soot-cleaning rods up the chimney with a white sheet on top of them for his enemies to see. Again, the news spread fast and this time the old gossips were in full pursuit to bring home to us the truth of the matter. 'Hannyways has shown the white feather – he has shown the white feather! Yes, he has! He has played the craven coward!' And from that day onwards, (at least for the next month and a half and until the rest of us had the heart to forgive him) Hannyways was given the royal name of *Captain Shun-the-Battle*.

4

Bohorlody had had the rearing of Rapper ever since Moll-the-Man brought him down as a puppy. He had gone up to her house to play the forty-five-hand-wheel game of cards and recalled the evening well. It was during the magical hour of twilight that Rapper was born on a heap of hay in the brilliant green light of Moll's summertime haggart. The wind in the sunshot leaves was rustling delicately above the little puppy's new life. The geese and the hens were marching majestically up to see what all the fuss was about. It was a grand and special occasion.

Bohorlody took the little puppy home under his warm jacket and started to feed him on a bran-mash of bread-and-milk with a dash of pepper to keep him trim and healthy. Very soon the two of them became as close to each other as two sides of a sheet, always gazing trustingly into each other's dreamy eyes, the little fellow with those lugubrious looks that'd break your heart and he all the time wagging his cute little tail.

And as the next year wore on, whichever way Bohorlody came home from Curl 'n' Stripes' drinking-shop with his package of biscuits – be it the Old Road, the New Road or the creamery road – Rapper was sure to come scampering along to meet him, leaping up on him when he was halfways home and his tail thrashing joyfully and his tongue lolling out. Bohorlody couldn't believe it. None of us could. It was enough to make you doubt your own senses - as if Rapper had been pulled towards Bohorlody through the air by some sort of supernatural magnet, as if witchcraft had caused him to come flying through space and time itself – to travel the correctly chosen road and come trotting home gaily by his master's side. None of us had the brains to fathom out how he, a mere youngster, knew which of these roads his master would be taking home from the shop.

Nor was Rapper like any of Bohorlody's other previous dogs – silly little fools, all of them. They would go scampering hare-like ahead of him across the Pool Field whenever they saw a rabbit. You'd see them cannonading (oh, the frustration) into each other (the hysterical little squeaks out of them) – allowing their quarry to escape and vanish. In contrast, Rapper always had the good sense to follow at Bohorlody's heels. He had always been like his very shadow, a perfect little dog.

On those memorable days when Lord and Lady Elegance brought their dogcart out travelling to meet the wind coming down from the hills, he would perform acts of pure genius for them. He climbed up onto Easy-does-it's stile and, at Bohorlody's whistle, jumped down and landed on his master's shoulder. He leapt over his ashplant when he held it 3ft in the air. He rolled over at his command and would speak up with the loudest of barks. He'd sit on his haunches and then put his nose subserviently between his front paws to beg, his brown nose peeping out coyly and flirtingly. He was as good as the Daffy-Duck Circus. And oh, how he made the fine rich lord and his lady shake their dogcart asunder with their fits of polite yet hearty laughter.

At other times, Rapper went scurrying off down the yard and into the haggart, chasing the chickens and their little chicks good-humouredly all around the windy grasses. He almost blew the little creatures away with the harmless heat of his milky body. In between times he sneaked behind the hay-reek. Then he sprang out (oh, the prankster that was in him!) and terrorized the ladylike flock of geese as they went marching through the haggart and out as far as the potato-sack on the stick. He was laughter itself as he sent them flapping and squawking in a musical harmony to the top of the dung heap near the far ditch. They were enjoying these games of cat 'n' mouse every bit as much as himself. Of course, that was long before he took a liking to ripping open the bellies of lambs and devouring their carcasses.

Time flew by and as the seasons changed there came into Rapper the air of a young poet. For ages, it seemed, he would sit on the ass-and-car at the bottom of the yard. The children could see him watching those aimless fluffy clouds above him as they drifted across the sky on their way to Clare and Galway and on towards the ocean. In an almost dreamlike state he slid down from the cart and dazed himself across the yard, as though mimicking those very same cottony clouds. In and out he wafted amongst the brown and yellow chicks, through the green and rusty docks and the mallows he wafted – without ever hurting a single one of the hens and ignoring the charms of the sow.

But sadly, everything changed and the children knew it. It was as though Rapper had become an unquiet dog – a total stranger. Had he forgotten those days when he'd follow Bohorlody out by the pig house gap, his nostrils breathing in the raw air of the early morning, his ears listening to the twittering of the little birds in Timmy Bellow's Lane? Had he forgotten those days when just the clink of his master's spoon on his mug of tea, the ring of his knife against the kettle, were enough for him – telling him it was time for him to set off for the cows? Six times a day they had strolled together to the well inside Old Sam's grove for the buckets of spring-well water.

Those days were now gone. In his heart – in his soul – Rapper had developed an inexplicable exhilaration awaiting to be satisfied, had become intoxicated by the harping of the wind and the sunlight and rain. Like any young poet (the simpleton that he was) he was no longer content to sit moping by the fire with his nose twitching, no longer content to watch the uneven flames flickering up the chimney and listen to the crickets serenading him. He began to run races with imaginary dogs and shadows round and round in the thistle field and fought with the scintillating gleams of the sunlight. He danced with the shadows of the purple and yellow wildflowers.

Our hillslope had become too small a place to hold a soul like his and to bring him the everlasting happiness he desired. Like many a dog before him he craved for the fairy woods above the forge and its hidden pathways. He looked to the hills of the mountainy men and longed to be up there – up there where the wild dogs lived – dogs bigger than black lions. It was as though they were sending secret messages down the hill to him. He could see unaccountable possibilities for adventure, which we humans could never imagine with our limited eyesight.

And now as the lawmakers sat in the yard on their chairs Bohorlody found himself in a state of unhappy contemplation. Himself and the Dainty Woman were like any other household, who had lost a number of their dogs to the call of the wild and had to get rid of their dog in order to destroy the bad luck that such a dog might bring on their farm.

Boholody's own sister (*Dowager*) said it was an ancient curse, which had now come to Bohorlody's doorstep. Moll-the-Man talked of the curse of the *come-hither* having been put on him. Dowager herself called it *the evil eye*. She too had been given a curse when she once found a bag of cattle-bones down near the metal bridge. They had been thrown in over her ditch just below John's Gate, a well–known curse that she called *the pishogues*. Everyone had their suspicion at the time as to which precise fairyman among us had the power of the *come-hither*, *the evil eye* or *the pishogues*. But they feared to speak out in case the priest might damn them from the altar.

Bohorlody now found that Rapper had joined up with a pack of wild dogs that had recently arrived in the Valley-of-the-Pig. This was a new one on him. The dog was beginning to stay out the whole of the night. What was he thinking of (the simpleton)? At four o'clock in the morning hadn't he a warm nest for himself by the side of his own turf fire to warm his tail if he wanted to? Up on the Little Bald Plain two new lambs had been found frightened out of their lives and their bellies ripped open. Rapper's name was mentioned. Next day Red Buckles, on his way back from the creamery, reported that there had been a tremendous battle between Rapper and the father of the six young badgers below in the Bog Wood. From that moment on Rapper's right front paw would be crooked and he'd spend the rest of his days limping. He had barely escaped with his life. And yet there was no chastising him. He had lost all his nobility – all his previous goodness. It was clear that his relentless battles with sheep and badgers were not going to be enough for him, that the taste of their blood was not going to be sufficient to calm the bloodlust which had unfortunately risen up inside in his dog-soul.

It got worse. The old man (*Toes-Apart*) had two fine sons. They almost killed one another one Sunday afternoon in their efforts to shoot Rapper, who was killing their lambs faster than they could count them. They made an ambush for him at either end of Patsy-Mick's hayshed. They lay in wait, armed with Toes-Apart's two new guns.

Rapper climbed the five-barred gate. They saw him heading towards them up along the lane and from opposite sides of the ditch they let fly their enraged cartridges. They entirely missed killing Rapper but came within an inch of shooting the eyebrows off of one another. The Devil's father was in the soul of that blasted dog (they said). Some of the pellets had sprayed onto Toes-Apart's favourite hen, hitting her in her lower wing. From that day onwards, she was one of our comedy turns, having lost whatever sense of direction and balance she previously had. When the wind came roaring through Toes-Apart's haggart it blew this young hen off sideways as though she were performing an amusing ballet-step through the air. And when she landed on her feet she came dancing, dancing, dancing her little tippy-toe steps sideways towards the hen house, frightening every duck and goose in sight with her strange new dance-steps. Had you a piano, you could have waltzed the music to it.

As a rule, Toes-Apart was a very shy man like many of the mountainy men and we never heard a word out of him. But this time he needed no fire-bellows to fan the anger, which had risen up in him and which brought him down from his warm fireside above in the Valley-of-the-Pig. He marched straight into Bohorlody's Welcoming Room and without so much as taking a drop of holy water at the door he crossed the floor. 'Mee family is dacent, as ye well know,' said he, facing up to Bohorlody. 'But that renegade-of-a-dog must die and die he will'. There wasn't another word out of him, he being the very shy man. He snatched up his hat and turned back upon Bohorlody from the half-door. 'Either ye kill him or I'll do it for ye.' and he flung himself out of the yard and back up to the Valley-of-the-Black Cattle. Bohorlody was left looking after him and scratching his head. Enough said.

5

The Dainty Woman was full of sympathy for everyone and she called Arse-and-Pockets the stone that the builder rejected. 'Yes, he's a Jew,' said she, 'and does it mean that he's got to be an outcast all his life among the rest of us?' As you might have guessed, the Dainty Woman had been so called because of her daintiness of spirit and she always had this soft spot for the travelling-man, Arse-and-Pockets.

It was the same story every year. As soon as the heavy snows were gone and the new springtime was here, you could look out for Arse-and-Pockets trudging up the creamery road. This was the sign that the year had truly started and for these last 7 years this little scarecrow-of-a-man had been appearing amongst us as regular as clockwork. When little children saw him for the first time, they were frightened to death at the sight of him. Suddenly they'd see him standing in front of them on their flagstones, like a white-faced ghost from out of their storybook. But he was as harmless as the day he was born.

Where did he come from? Where was he going? Like the rivers all around us, we didn't know for sure. The truth (said By-Jiggery) was that he came from the back streets of Limerick, himself and his spanking new pony-and-trap, which he filled to the gills with all sorts of haberdasheries. The Widda-Widda-Woman inside in town had a spare room set aside for him above her stables where he could sleep and rest his tired legs. Each day he rose with the dawn and put on his gaberdine suit, which these days had a threadbare shine on it from constant wear. He drove his pony-and-trap and his two brown suitcases up the hill and into Din-Din-Dinny's barn and from there proceeded to walk the length and breadth of the hills – a timeless shade, who came and went, along with our uncertain weather.

The day was glorious, just like those recent days in April. Arse-and-Pockets had always loved the countryside. It reminded him of his warm homeland far away in the east. It had the smell of the new-mown grasses and the air was full of the greenfinches. The crab-trees around Easy-does-it's stile were beginning to bloom and the ditches were full of blossoms, especially the honeysuckle and the foxgloves on Cheerful Nan's Heights. He could hear the cattle bawling below Old Sam's wire-fence.

And now he was here on the flagstones, his red-raw hands stretched almost to the ground from the two heavy suitcases he was lugging at his sides with their secret contents. The Dainty Woman could see that he was a bit shakier in his limbs this time round, poor man. He smiled across the yard at her. She ran across the yard to meet him and see what he had in his suitcases. Barbaha and the other children ran out after her and marvelled at the sight of the two huge suitcases. They couldn't understand for the life of them how a small man like himself could carry such a heavy load.

'How are ye, Arse-and-Pockets? Ye're welcome at mee door,' said the Dainty Woman. He made her a polite little bow and produced a list of household goods as long as Tipperary. I have ribbons to sell for your fine hair. I have sewing stuffs for your man's socks. I have elastic for your knickers and your garters. I have hairpins for your chignons. I have ointments for the sore jaw. I have secret herbs for the piles on your arse and a few other seldom-mentioned country cures.'

'Stop-stop-stop, will ye! Give us no more of yeer litanies,' said the Dainty Woman, holding her sides and laughing. 'But tell me this, have ye razorblades and have ye shaving soap?'

'I have, ma'am. I have that.'

'And have ye flypapers and have ye boot polish and have ye a scrub-brush?'

'That too, ma'am. And I have cheap watches, in case you might be making the price of a pig!'

'That'll do, that'll do,' said the Dainty Woman good-naturedly and she gave him a wink and a little one of her glowing smiles.

Until this day, passers-by had had the good fortune to escape the savage jaws of Rapper but no-one knew when he'd attack either child or man and on this sad day the fates were to forsake poor Arse-and-Pockets To this very day children awake from their dreams some nights and they hear his horrified screams ringing off of the flagstones out at the stream.

And what were the men doing while this was going on? They certainly didn't come hopping over the ditches to see what was happening. Whereas the women always blessed themselves against harm coming to anyone, our fine men (without so much as a blink-of-an-eye) were usually praying that their dog would do his work and tear a chunk out of some tinker's arse, even the arse of a poor innocent man like Arse-and-Pockets would please them. Ah, the cruelty in them – to see the dance-steps of one of their travelling visitors as he went scorching up the road, holding onto his britches for dear life – and they laughing their sides off. Ah, how different their hearts were from those of our gentle women. Wouldn't you like to put a match to their own britches!

As if to answer our men's prayers Rapper came out of nowhere and leapt clean over the half-door. He levelled the misfortunate Arse-and-Pockets to the ground and (ah, this evil wretch-of-a-dog) set his teeth firmly into the poor man's britches. He then began to taste the foreign blood of the Jew in earnest. What a terrible sight! Would it ever be forgotten?

With the screams of Arse-and-Pockets ringing in her ears the Dainty Woman ran out into the yard. Barbaha was beside her with the speed of light. Armed with the metal tongs he brought out a burning sod of turf from the Welcoming Room and, toasting the villainous creature's tail, he relieved Arse-and-Pockets from the dog's teeth. His mother picked up the poor misfortunate man and cradled him in her arms. His cheeks were sunken and yellow, his pained expression as vacant as death itself. 'Mercy on us!' screamed the Dainty Woman, 'that basthard-of-a-dog has taken a chunk out of the poor man's arse!'

She lay poor Arse-and-Pockets gingerly on the settle-bed and boiled up the kettle of water to tend to his wounds. She got down her best goose-wing and poured out the iodine liberally from her bottle onto it. After she had hushed the children away, who were all gaping at the poor man's agonizing tears, she carefully let down his britches and gently eased the iodine onto his upper thigh where the dog had drawn his blood. She dressed his wounds and soon had him back into middling good shape. She removed his britches from round his boots and sat him next to the heat of the fire. With her needle and thread she mended the legs of his britches before giving him a cup of tea and some soda-bread with jam and sugar on it. Arse-and-Pockets, minus his trousers, drew in the blaze from the fire onto his painful thighs and began to feel more or less comfortable after that.

To lighten his burden even more, the Dainty Woman took out her purse and bought from the pile of goods in his suitcases, countless little items, which she had no need of and which (worse still) she couldn't afford. She finished off by giving him a dinner fit for bishop High-Hat himself and put a bottle of milk in his sack ('for the journey') after skimming off the top of the cream in case he should run away with her good luck as well. Wasn't she the noble Samaritan!

Abroad in the yard this little scenario came to an end when Arse-and-Pockets gave her his best and most sincere bow before showering down innumerable blessings on her and the rest of the household and on the whole of the Irish race, past and present and to come.

'Stop, will ye!' said the Dainty Woman, her eyes full of merry laughter and tears. She couldn't get rid of him out of the yard – so grateful was he as he backed away and kept giving her a string of his foreign blessings. He turned back one more time from the flagstones, 'And may the Lord grant you this, Missus, that you never button an empty arse-pocket from this day till the day you die!'

That same evening there was a great deal of commotion at the dinner-table as the children were leathering into their spuds, onions, milk and butter, together with the cabbages and fresh rabbit. They begged their mother to lighten the curiosity of them all – the boys as well as the girls. They were getting on her nerves and, dainty though she was, she had a voice that could sometimes cut like a rasp. 'Ye give me the sick, the whole crew of ye! What in God's holy name is the matter with ye? It's Arse-and-Pockets this ... and it's Arse-and-Pockets that with ye.'

She threw her fork into the potato-champ, which she was stirring onto her plate. 'I'll tell ye this and I'll tell ye no more: I saw his private credentials with mee own two eyes at the fireside. For once and for all, let me tell ye this: Arse-and-Pockets' little privacies are no bigger than an acorn,' and she put her thumb through her middle and forefinger to show the size of it. There was a roar of laughter out of her daughters. Indeed, Bohorlody too – as well as The Dainty Woman and their sons – joined in and they all soon forgot the recent carnage of the poor man's body. And as they golloped down their steaming heap of spuds with their competing forks they were constantly interrupted by one or the other of them making the thumb-and-finger gesture and this was followed by yet another bout of good-natured giggling and laughter all over the Welcoming Room.

However, when the dinner was over, the hilarious mood suddenly turned sombre and black. They could see the look on Bohorlody's face. It told them that before the week was out there'd be no more Rapper left on this earth – that his hour of execution had arrived.

6

Just outside the haggart and on this side of the thistle field there was a well-known spot of execution for savage dogs. It was a green hollow where strange eyes couldn't see a man performing the dirty deed of killing. It was called The Sin. Over the years, five noble dogs had already met their death at the hands of Bohorlody. It was not the hanging-tree behind the cowshed but the place for the bullet in the brain. Bohorlody's body shuddered when he thought of the dogs he had killed. Of all the ungracious and savage acts a man could do, this deed – the snatching away of a young dog's life - was always dark and dirty. At the moment of death Bohorlody felt an icy misery coming up from the spirit world and entering into the dying dog's soul.

From the time the children had agreed on Rapper's execution during family law, he had befriended his dog like never before. In the planning and the scheming for his coming execution he gave Rapper his sop of milk and bread and his bran-mash whenever his hungry eyes looked into his own eyes – anything to keep him inside in the Welcoming Room and keep him close by him. At other times he took him out into the yard and playfully rolled him around amongst the geese and the hens before the two of them came back in again to the turf-fire. He had the entire trust of Rapper now more than ever. Without a bit of cunning, the planned execution would all come to nothing. He knew that Rapper had four fine legs on him – faster than the legs of the tinker (*Swallytails*) who ran from the pelted tongs of Dowager after he'd spat his tobacco-juice misguidedly into the burner on her hearthstone.

He looked at his dog and he thought to himself, 'Rapper, ye'll never get a chance to throw yeer fine legs away from me. It's ye that is practically blind in yeer left eye where ye got the fine kicking from Big Blue, the rogue cow. It's at the left side I'll be sliding up to make a grab for yeer head.'

Tell me, my fine friend-of-a-dog, what is this new occupation of yeers? There ye lie, squatting sleepily in under the table, yeer nose tucked comfortably between yeer paws and yeer eyes squinting serenely in front of the steady flames of the fire. To look at ye there – a young dog – passing yeer daylight hours the same as an old man of seventy, ye lazy little article. It's no wonder that ye're so languid during the sunlit hours when we find ye in the dead of night changing from yeer coat of laziness into newly-sprung life, going off hunting in the hills and murdering the geese and hens of Toes-Apart.'

'I could have saved yeer life before it came to this, before the new law introduced by Barbaha and the rest of them. I should have given ye a few tidy kicks up the arse and sent ye high-jumping over the half-door. But now, ye'll be sent for a far higher high-jump than the half-door, sent this blessed afternoon. It's too late – far too late. Up till now patience hasn't always been my greatest virtue. Ask Hannyways! But I know a trick or two and this is the time for me to be patience itself. Ye're snoring by the fireside now. But the sky is grey and the dusk will soon be here. I can already smell yeer blood on mee hands.

The fire held everything in its spell and warmth. Fairyland dreams were leaping around inside in the snoring head of Rapper – in behind his eyebrows. Memories of his puppyhood days were filling his brain. But then a cautious frown crossed his face, an unearthly feeling of fear, of depression, began to fill his dreams and an utter loneliness came into him. It was a fear of something intangible from far back in his memory – a fear of something his mother had once taught him during those golden days in the green haggart whilst he was still a puppy. In the depths of his dog-soul came an awareness of the forthcoming confrontation with death. The light of the sun seemed to be dying – or was it the searching light from the fire that was fading, giving up the ghost? Pictures of his whole life came up before him. Some of them happy, but most of them festered.

The latch of the door opened. 'Here come those big boots of my master, Bohorlody (thought Rapper) – his tall man-shadow shouldering itself across my tail.' Rapper opened one eye, then two and gave a peep. The drowsy stillness of an early summer's evening was still hanging onto a yellow square of light reflected from the front window. He closed his eyes again and went back to his delightful dreams. In spite of himself his ropey tail wagged. The sunlight continued to filter vaguely in through the geraniums on the front windowsill. It surrounded him in a tinsel-like haze – a haze of sadness for the day that would soon be going away into evening. Its glow made a long shadow of the big man coming across the Welcoming Room. Fresh wood smoke began to spiral up the chimney. In his dog's life's dreaming he listened to the delicate sounds of the crackling logs on the fire. His wet nose twitched once more as he smelt the pungency of the burnt logs.

Behold Bohorlody, sitting on his chair, rocking to and fro. He sat there a long time, listening to the clock ticking. He looked at the dog – at the dog he had loved so well. There was an anger and there was a love – both fighting each other inside in his chest. 'By the power of the bellows (said he to himself) the clock is ticking, it's true. It's ticking for you, my lad.'

He got up stealthily, anxious now to begin his dirty work. He took down the double-barrel gun from the ledge where the horse's collar and haymes were thrown. He took down the box of cartridges from behind the broken jug of sour milk on the press cupboard. He knelt down beside the sleeping dog. For a long time, he knelt there, whistling silently – sadly – under his breath, stroking the dog's fur as if to remember it well. He could smell the milkiness of Rapper's breath. 'Ye'll be dead in a minute or two, in less time than it takes to skin a cat.'

He took the belt from his britches and slowly, ever so slowly, tied it round the neck of Rapper. The mind inside in the dog was clearly at work now. 'I have been expecting you, even before I saw you,' thought Rapper. 'Here comes Man. Here comes his gun. I must run – I must run faster than the bullets of Man.'

It all happened so quickly. Rapper cast about him frantically in his mind for an answer to what was happening. Between the man and the dog – between the two palpitating bodies – there was a violent heat, an inexplicable hammering of their feverish hearts.

It gave Bohorlody no pleasure. 'How often have we two strayed and hunted in yon greenery,' he thought. He loved his dog, even now, in those fleeting seconds. He shook his head lugubriously. His twisted sweaty face had a pained look to it – as if his boots were pinching his toes. He coughed harshly to clear the lump from his throat, trying not to work himself up into anger. He dragged the frantic dog out backwards through the half-door and onto the flagstones, knowing he would not be returning with him. He hauled him out by the pig house gap. A little procession of ducks and geese followed them to the place of execution – the Sin.

Rapper began to howl. This was what his mother had warned him about when he was a puppy. The fragile hens, not sure of their own fate, ran for cover in beneath the ass-and-car. They set up a tremendous chatter ('*Look at Rapper! Look at Rapper*! *Look at Rapper*!') as if aware of the dog's fate. From the glassy docks and the haggart parsley the guttural crows flew away to the thistle field.

Rapper was whimpering now – dragging at the belt, turning his thin body in sudden jerks. There wasn't a puff of air, not a puff of a cloud – only the shrouding trees and the hidden place of execution behind the haggart, only the threshold of death and the sinister whisperings of conspiratorial breezes in the dusty gloom and the strange obscure shapes in the black trees.

Bohorlody, his hands sweaty and clammy, was breathing heavily, gritting his teeth and cursing his dog ('get it over with') who wouldn't die gracefully. He tied him to the stake of execution firmly and watched the dog's unseemly indignity as he sat in a pool of his own yellow piss and squinted sadly up at him. There'd be no second chance for him. 'Back! Back! Back ye must go! Back to eternity, back to the source of yeer life, with yeer solitary spirit. Ye're here today. Ye'll be here no longer.'

Bohorlody stepped back and took up his position. What was it, Rapper? What was it? The final realization of the upturned gun-barrel – rattling low to the temples – was the last you heard and the song that sang you into fleecy eternity. Your feet almost jumped out of your skin. A splintering flash of light - *CRACK! CRACK! CRACK!* - filled the dog's simple brain in the hazy afternoon. The last crimson sunset of evening turned shimmering red with his blood and his unsung death.

Bohorlody blew the smoke from his gun and looked at the ruby trappings of Rapper's blood. He looked into Rapper's terrified eyes – lying there outstretched and crumpled into nothing, no better than a dead chicken. In the dark pool of quietness, the big man shuddered. He felt rage. And then he felt sorrow.

Dimmed with weariness he went back across the haggart. He took the warm body of his dog down below the laurels. Near the home of the weasel and the rat he dug a mournful hole and threw Rapper into it. He covered him with the fine black earth from the side of the ashpit. And at each shovelful he whispered, 'The fine geese and the fine hens that ye ate, the lambs of Toes-Apart that ye ate, the fine eggs from my Dainty Woman that ye ate. Our eggs are all gone. The geese will soon be all gone. Why weren't ye a true dog?' The dirge for his dog went on and on as he tended the grave. 'Why couldn't ye save yeer fighting for those sly old foxes?'

He wiped the sweat from his brow and put away his shovel under the dripping trees. The sun sank into the mauve and amber sky and the breeze sighed sadly. A black ribbon of smoke came across the sky. The night would be cold and no longer beautiful. The treetops stirred to life as little birds ('We birds are not dead yet!') twittered and chirruped. You cannot see or hear the birds, Bohorlody. Your mind and your kindness are gone – fled elsewhere.

He went back into the house and closed the door behind him. He rubbed his back against it – for fear the ghost of Rapper might come in and destroy him. Night soon came to him and to his Dainty Woman. The curly black clouds showed where the silhouettes of the tree trunks were. Bohorlody sprinkled holy water on himself and the foreheads of his wife and family. The children hadn't a word to say – it was all too much for them and the younger ones felt like crying. The big man didn't even bother to light his pipe. He flicked the holy water round the centre of the floor – to guard against the boodeeman and the wicked spirits that might now bring evil on him. He threw a mug of water on the fire, quenching it and he raked out the last embers of the dancing firelight. The heavy stars swam fiercely above his cabin. The moon reflected its slender medals of light in the dark black waters of his yard-stream.

BEDAD-SEZ-I

1

Bedad-sez-I had been given his unusual name for always having the habit of prefacing any pronouncement of his by shaking his index finger so as to gain a man's attention and starting off with the words *Bedad-sez-I. . .*

'Bedad-sez-I . . . in all mee life I never saw him looking better,' he sighed while gazing down on the Gog's dead body at the wake above in Sheep's Cross.

'Bedad-sez-I . . . wouldn't ye think that the man-in-black would give his tongue a bit of a rest some Sundays,' he'd moan when the priest went on jawing for longer than twenty minutes.

As far back as anyone could remember Bedad-sez-I was something of a Go-Boy like his son (*Jimbo*) a few years later and whenever he burst out laughing the folds of his belly would wobble about like wet dung on a shovel. Though he hadn't the fanciful cut of his son's later attire he was still able to win his own bit of fame. It happened on the day of his wedding and would never be forgotten. A few days earlier he had the good fortune to find a pair of discarded wellingtons in old Tim Bellow's dyke. They'd come in handy for the journey to his imminent wedding (he thought) and he could spare his shiny black brogues till the moment came for him to parade up the church aisle. He'd keep the old wellingtons on his feet till the very last minute and ride his bike right up to the back door of the church before changing into the new shiny brogues.

The wedding-day came along and the yard and the bushes were shimmering beneath a passionate sky. Bedad-sez-I's mother (*Tongue-of-all-Tongues*) dressed him up in a smart sports-jacket and grey flannels and for this special occasion a white shirt with the open-buttoned collar flared out over the coat's own collar. He had a high quiff in his hair as well as his father's best boots to wear (not the wellingtons). He was as shiny going out the door as a fine general and his father (*old Tom Jibberish*) stood back to take a long look at him. Puffing on his pipe, he asked him (wasn't the old fellow the whimsical wag) how many soldiers he had at his command on the battlefield – so proud was he of his son stepping out to go and get himself married.

It was the season when new flowers were shouldering their way up through the weeds in the fields. The ditches were already swaying with them and the birds all round him were singing cheerily. The meadows were getting into full bloom and the sun was shining down on top of his head. Bedad-sez-I was the soul of merriment as he cycled his way on through the pine trees and down along the hillslopes. His heart was ablaze like the sun.

Shortly after leaving the yard he had changed into the wellingtons, wrapping his father's boots neatly in a paper bag and strapped onto the handlebars of his bike. I need hardly tell you that his father had stolen these same boots from Red Scissors's grandfather whilst the latter gentleman was having a sleep for himself abroad in the bog.

Apart from his First Holy Communion Day his wedding-day was going to be the happiest day in his life. He was on his way to get himself hitched up to Lizzie-the-Herd ('*mee little bit of comfort*') and his mind was full of the little squeezes he'd be getting out of her stout arms when he got close up to her in the night and the bedroom tumblings and jostlings would begin to shake the house.

He had started out early enough on the road. Whistling like a boy, he sped along till he reached the stream across the Road-to-the-Hollows. It had never been anything other than a harmless trickle. He suddenly realised that the recent rains had raised the level of the water by something like a foot and a half. Damn the bit – didn't his right-foot wellington have a few small holes in it and it let stream of icy water into his sock, soaking it.

'Bedad-sez-I . . . I'll have to deal with this confoundedly extraordinary situation,' said Bedad-sez-I, who (like his later son Jimbo) was inclined to use a few big words now and then. He hopped down from the bike and put on one of the new boots in place of the leaky wellington. He took a hurried glance at his pocket-watch and found that he had less time to spare than he'd have wished and so, he pedalled on at top speed until he reached the church door.

By then Lizzie-the-Herd and her entire pack of cousins (and what looked like half of Tipperary) were all seated snugly up at the front and they decked out in their finest fashion. They were beginning to get a bit fidgety. Where on earth was Bedad-sez-I? Was he coming or was he not coming to his own wedding? And in between praying for a satisfactory outcome to the day's wedding one or two of them had begun to curse the poor fellow into the depths of hell.

Meanwhile what was Bedad-sez-I to do? He was going to be late. He'd be the talk of the whole church – of the entire parish. He reached the churchyard and without giving himself a minute to think he rode his rusty old bike straight through the front door of the church. By this time a few of the sleepy congregation had started to have the odd little romantic dream about the future love-nest of Lizzie and Bedad-sez-I. However, they woke up in an instant when (horror-of-horrors) they beheld the intended groom and his bike cycling furiously up the main aisle – up towards the very altar steps, a wellington full of holes on his right leg and a shiny boot on his left leg. They gasped. They groaned and confusion hit them like a rock. This was a pure disgrace (the likes of it never having been seen before) – to be seen cycling a bike around inside the House of God and a man dressed out in such outrageous footwear. Breathlessly Bedad-sez-I threw his bike in a heap next to his bride-to-be and, giving her a sly little wink and a nudge, he cast his merry old soul next to his *little bit of comfort*.

Suddenly the congregation could see a cheerful smile on Father Sensibly's face. It was as though a dark cloud had just flown out the church window. Relieved at last, they got back their senses and the previous hush and their sighs of distaste now turned into bursts of thunderous laughter. Its echoes might well have ruined the dignified composure of the holy place (where such laughter was clearly forbidden) if Father Sensibly hadn't already filled his pockets with a pile of green pound notes from Lizzie-the-Herd's father. And for days thereafter Bedad-sez-I with his one wellington and his one shiny black boot (and he riding his rusty old bike up along the church aisle) made a laughable story that kept us all in fine form. It travelled not only the length of north Tipperary but (we're told) back as far as Father Sensibly's birthplace in Clare. It had been an exceptional privilege (he told his ancient mother) to marry a man in a wellington and a boot – a privilege that would never again be witnessed in the whole of Ireland.

2

After rabbiting successfully for a few nights with his ferret and nets Bedad-sez-I would sometimes take himself off on a little drinking-spree with his best friend (*Lowry*). It was just for a few days (no more than this) that he'd leave his mother and the farm unattended behind him. On his return Tongue-of-all-Tongues would meet him in the haggart even before he tumbled in the door and had time to pelt off his jacket. For a woman with little or no schooling the scornful words she then spat out of her mouth were enough to fill a bible as she leathered him with the list of his sins. 'Most rakish of all the unsaintly rakes in Ireland, ye're the talk of the whole wide world. Where is yeer decency? Have ye no shame in ye?'

It was the last straw – the one that finally put an end to the patience of Bedad-sez-I, the thousandth time that he'd asked himself the same old question: was she hoping to conquer a grown man like himself and make him bawl like a child and sue her for mercy? He looked away from her and in spite of himself his eyes filled up with painful tears.

Without so much as going to the bucket for a mug of water he turned on his heel, leaving the ghost of his mother to swallow her words back down her throat and stand at the door like a damned fool. He belted up the road to meet Lowry and the two of them sat for a while on the ditch. There and then they laid out plans for a new and unheard-of journey into The Unknown. Yes (he told himself) he'd give his old crone-of-a-mother plenty of reason to be wagging her filthy tongue at him the next time she saw him crossing the haggart. Yes (he again told himself) he'd finally get her wicked words out of his hair and shake the dust of the yard from off of his boots. He'd leave her to rot at the doorstep, leave her to milk her own cows and fight with their shitty tails, leave her to chop her own logs and take the splinters out of her eyes. When he finally came back home she'd be good and ready (said he) to kiss his arse. With dreams of adventure filling their heads, both himself and Lowry would spend a whole month in Galway. They'd see and breathe into their lungs the heart and soul of the great big ocean. Lowry then put his two arms round his friend's sad shoulders and gradually brought the smile back onto his face and the life back into his heart until Bedad-sez-I began to feel a good deal better.

The next morning when the dawn sky was just turning white and aware of the sun's arrival, Lowry went into town early and sold his mother's best cow. He had the price of it stuffed teasingly in his hip-pocket. It was a soft mid-summer's day and the two brave byze went off over the fields with the reins and blinkers to fetch their horses. They didn't take with them so much as a drop of holy water (the heathens!). Bedad-sez-I was in an unforgiving mood. Nor did he go back to give a wave of the handkerchief to Tongue-of-all-Tongues.

Those dreams and those spirit that made the great seafarers and past explorers sail out over the seven seas now saw our two heroes disappearing out of Tipperary and into the early morning sunrise. Ah, the honeysweet life! Their hearts were full of the brightness of the new fields and hedgerows and not long afterwards they could be seen rattling their way along the road leading towards Galway. It was going to take them weeks of wild carousing along the way before they'd reach Galway itself. In the meantime, they were going to help themselves to the Drink in every drinking-shop that stood in their way.

Though they had given themselves a good feed of rabbit-stew with oceans of turnips, carrots and spuds thrown in, they soon found themselves with their bellies hanging out of them and craving with hunger. However, they kept themselves going with a few stolen apples and a pocketful of hazelnuts along the riverbanks. At last they came to a lonely Protestant church in the middle of God-knows-where. They sneaked in through the back door where they found a welcome bottle of altar-wine and a sack of dry communion-wafers. Then the two unholy blackguards (may God forgive them their sin) kept their merry old souls alive by eating half the sack of wafers and feasting on the wine till the bottle ran dry. Had all saintliness faded from the rascals' brains? When the two heathens came home a month later and told yarns about the great adventures they had given themselves it would be hard for anyone (even the old gossips) to believe such damned lies as theirs. Didn't every-one know that to step inside the door of a Protestant church was a sure way of getting yourself struck down by a bolt of God's lightning?

They finally arrived at the side of the ocean. The poetry of their schoolbooks *(the white-crested foamy sea-horses, the ancient wine-dark waves, the storm-tossed mountainous snarls of the angry salty main)* filled the mind of Bedad-sez-I and his love of the long words. The two of them hadn't put a razor to their jaw all the time they were on the road and by now Bedad-sez-I *(the gingery hairy one* the Galway girls were later to call him) had a beard that reached down to his waist if not all the ways down to his ankles.

With anxious eyes some of the Galway men came down to look at the two wild men and to ask them what part of the world they came from for they looked a very strange couple. Galway had never seen the likes of two such hairy apes as these two coming to greet them and they asked them if all men elsewhere were now wearing their beards this way. Was it a new kind of fashion that had come down the road from Dublin? Of course, this was said with a bit of a smirk. The children ran down and hid behind the men's wellingtons. As always, these little ones wanted to know the truth and in their own way they were just as inquisitive about the two new arrivals. In their eyes the two doughty heroes looked the very same as Saint Peter and Saint Paul in their picture-prayer-books.

Next morning, even before the first cockerel had begun its crow, Bedad-sez-I and Lowry went down to greet the mighty waves – waves that they knew they'd never see again. They were delighted to be the centre of such gay old times. They stripped off their togs (shifts and all) the way they would do when taking their yearly washing in the sally-hole abroad in the bog. They went leaping into the freezing waters of the great ocean. Oh, the joy of it! They could scarcely believe it. Tipperary's rivers could go hang!

This was the life for a real man! They soon felt like two young sheepdogs prancing around in the snows of a January field. They spread out their legs and fired their piss all around the great ocean. They challenged her to put up a bit of a fight and attack them. 'Coom on! Blasht ye! We're here from Tipperary and ready to test yeer mettle.'

You'd have liked to get inside their heads there and then – for the two fainthearts were in dread of their natural lives lest they got themselves drowned and never got home to their own warm fireside. Nobody in our part of the world could swim a stroke barring Spare-Ribs and Matt-with-the-Machinery. Of course, they couldn't let on to one another their dread. So, to give themselves a bit of a lift they continued to curse the great ocean and to threaten her destruction and to kick her waves up to the heavens. The roars that came out of their mouths must have startled the sleepy sea-nymphs in the depths of the waves! Horses couldn't have done a better job of it.

It was fortunate that their two beards were long enough to cover their bellies and their private credentials – else the bemused Galway girls would have been put to the blush at the sight of their manly private bits. For, on hearing the early morning roars of the two new arrivals, both girls and boys had come down to the edge of the sea to witness such unheard-of commotion:

'A box-camera! Quick! Quick! A box-camera!' shouted one of the Galway men. It was a chance for history to be written down as never before – two strange men from

Tipperary and they standing in their pelts (*'glory to ye, byze!'*) without a stitch of clothes on them, without even a coy, little blush – and they entertaining the eyes of the whole of Galway. It would be a remarkable photo, a sight never to be seen or heard tell of in Galway again, a sight that even our own Father Sensibly would soon have the privilege to lay his eyes on. As though the one lewd photo wasn't bad enough, there was a second photo taken – with Bedad-sez-I and Lowry turning their brazen bare arses up at the camera for a photo that would have shocked the holy pope in his palace back in Rome.

Of course, our women later on never got so much as a glimpse at these unseemly photos for there was a limit to what the eyes of our prim damsels could be let look at. However, when both sets of photos found their way back to Tipperary a few weeks later and were shown in Curl 'n' Stripes' drinking-shop, the steam could be seen coming out of the heads of our old crones (the old gossips). Wouldn't you know it – they were more than a bit envious of all the attention showered on our two manly specimens. Always wanting themselves to be at the centre of the news, these old sour-pusses told everyone that the photos had been selling like hot cakes right across Galway, that they were bringing in a tidy sum of money for the man with the box-camera, that it was a shame that poor old Lowry and Bedad-sez-I couldn't make a brass farthing out of it. Wouldn't you know how these jealous wretches would make hay out of the two adventurers' lost opportunity, how they'd get in the last gleeful word! Women and their gossiping, I ask you.

When he got back home, Bedad-sez-I was in the worst possible wear and even his own mother kept herself and her tongue a safe distance away from him for his clothes stank to high heavens. Silently she'd have wished she had an eagle's wings and could fly back to Galway with him strapped to her back and pelt him straight into the middle of the great ocean in order to scrub the dirt off of him.

As for Lowry, so fierce was his mother's tongue that he didn't dare bring his boots into the yard but crept secretly in over the back ditch of the haggart. He was met, however, with a beautiful surprise – namely the battle for his very life. For his mother had picked out her best few sods of turf from the shed. They were rock-hard and with these she greeted his head. Before he could blink his eyes shut, she had blinded him with the first few fine volleys. This she followed up by chastising his two shins with the broken leg of the chair when the poor man (groping his way round the edge of the haystack) was in no fit state to defend himself. The yard-brush on this occasion was not thought fit enough to kill a miserable son (*mee little shitty-arse*) for running away with the price of her best cow in his pocket.

Yet when Lowry had mended his wounds and when Bedad-sez-I had been converted (for a short while) to drinking from the bucket of spring-water and when the two of them had washed away their sins in the depths of the river, not one of us could deny that they were the two best men on the planet and there was laughter and smiles galore as we raised them (almost) to the status of sainthood – heroes above all other heroes – established forever as an unassailable piece of our history. And from that day on, as children sat and smoked their stolen fag butts on the logs in Old Sam's orchard, the magical journey of Lowry and Bedad-sez-I to see the great ocean and get their pictures taken without a stitch of clothes on them would often cheer up a sad and rainy afternoon – the way those two brave explorers had stepped into the waves to challenge and frighten the life out of the great ocean - 90 bleddy miles from home. In the children's minds it was as good as having travelled to the moon and back.

JIMBO

1

We all knew Jimbo – he was a merry old soul and full of character, what we called a Go-Boy. When Samson witnessed the antics of him, his own ardour for the life of a Go-Boy got the better of him. His calling, however, wasn't as pure and honest as Jimbo's. But, to be fair to him, with his mane of long dark hair he sometimes had the stance and gymp of a Go-Boy. He walked with the hayfork horizontally across the broad of his back and in under his armpits – hoping to advance the upright stance of his manly carriage whenever he came striding through the Valley of the Pig to catch a mouthful of mountainy air. But, being a farmer (at least for half the day), he didn't fit the true nature of a Go-Boy – namely a landless entertainer. And try as he might, it was to prove no use for him.

The dance in Gibbet Hill came around. The rage of life was rising up in him. He stood before the looking-glass, admiring his newly-shaven face. He oiled and frizzed up his new pair of whiskers. He was wearing his best brown suit and his father's ginger topcoat. It reached down to his boots. He put the soapy water on his long dark locks to stiffen them into a fashionably wavy quiff. He caressed his hobnail boots with half a tin of blacking. He felt he was spotless and ready to demolish any fair damsel who came within his sights. He would entertain her with his style and comely wit. He'd tear the wooden floor of the platform to bits with his fine dance-steps as soon as he reached the Dance-in-the-Fields.

The amorous lad set out. It was a cool evening and the sun was still faintly glowing. He felt almost serene and threw his chest out challengingly. It would be a magnificent occasion. Wouldn't any Go-Boy envy the style of him? Like a young turkeycock he entered the field's gateway where the stewards (big towering lads) were collecting in the fourpence entrance-money from each of the dancers. He threw his coat and jacket in under the first bench he came across. He was stripped down to his shirt and was ready to tear the women apart.

He strolled round the edge of the platform, spitting on his fists and rubbing the palms of his hands together. 'Mee time has come,' he said. 'I'm about to chastise one or two fine young women in their flouncy skirts and lay them in mee clutches'. He was suitably oiled not only in his hair and his red cheeks but also on the inside of his chest with a good few mouthfuls of his father's raw-gut whiskey.

He made a few sidesteps across the floor towards the women seated in a colourful line at the far end of the floor. 'Will ye dance, missee? Will ye dance, mee dearest?' Was there something wrong with their hearing? He heard not a word back from the giggly girls. 'Will ye dance, blasht ye?' he repeated.

'No, kind sir,' said they in mock imitation of one of their former schoolday rhymes, 'we will not dance with ye.' Then one of the little hussies put paid to any chance of further conversation: 'We'll not dance with a farmer's son and the smell of cow-shit on his clothes.' And the rest of the girls took a fit of laughing at him.

Samson felt as though he'd been struck by lightning. He gave way to a tearful fit of anger and stamped his big boots on the wooden floor, sending splinters into the air. Oh, to be the victim of a bunch of silly women! Like a chastised schoolboy his cheeks turned red and he made up his mind to abandon any further attempts to dance. He'd seek out the bottom of a few glasses of stout in Merrymouth's drinking-shop across the road. But before he left the dancefloor he cursed the laughing *mee-damsels* straight into hell. 'At home in the hills, ye saucy young sour-pusses,' said he, 'I've women of mee own and plenty.'

It was then that the little madams took an even greater fit of laughing, almost doubling themselves in two. It was the best bit of sport they'd had all evening. Little did they know – an even better bout of sport was next to follow.

Samson staggered across the dancefloor, his shoulders now slumped. He felt humbler and less sure of his stride than before. He started looking for his coat and his jacket, trying to remember where he'd put them. These damned women had distracted the brains out of his head. Ah-ha – he found them, in underneath the bench at the entrance to the field. But the bench was no longer empty. It was thronged with a new array of apple-cheeked women, their hair tidily half-plaited and half-loose and they all dressed up in their gaily-printed frills and flounces. Like the previous bunch of women, they were having the time of their lives – laughing and giggling in the shiny light of the dancefloor. The older ones were giving the wink and little smiles of invitation from their wet lips to the men seated on benches the other side of the platform. They in turn were giving the glad-eye back to them good-naturedly. A bit of the Devil's brazenness had found its way into one or two of the more experienced young madams. They whispered encouragement to their younger sisters, who still had their hands clasped coyly between their knees. The immodest heathens had crossed their legs and began to show the young men more than a bit of their white thighs and their stocking suspenders – causing uncomfortable embarrassment to the younger lads by revealing also a shade of their mauve knickers and the elastic.

Poor innocent Samson! What an inauspicious end to a night's dancing was about to follow. He reached for his coat and jacket underneath the women's legs, his fingers grasping about in search of them. He made a sudden grab and roughly pulled out his coat, anxious to get away from the women and the smell of their perfume and face powder and still cursing their entire race under his breath. But they, thinking that he was about to molest them and make a raid on their thighs (*'the dirty little whoor'*), frightened the stars round the field with sudden squeals and shrieks. You'd have heard them at the fireside in Merrymouth's drinking-shop across in the village. 'Help! He's making a raid on our legs! Go 'way, ye dirty little devil!' could be heard all round the dancefloor.

In front of them stood the startled Samson with the coat and the jacket in his fists. From out of nowhere stormed the two, sturdy gate-stewards to confront this rascal from the mountains and keep some sort of calm and orderliness in the dance. They knew what to do: they'd give him a taste of their medicine. They made a rush at him from behind his back and whipped the two legs out from under him. 'Is this the way ye do things above on the mountains?' said one of them. 'Looking up with yeer gawk-eyes to see if ye can spot the colour of a young girl's knickers, is it?' said the other one.

They dragged the poor lad ferociously to his feet and over as far as the door. Some of the dancers said they overplayed their part in order to impress the girls and maybe get a jostle or two from them in the bushes later on. Others said that they were hoping to raise the temper of the mountainy man and hear the profanity of his curses so that they'd have good reason to belt the jaw off of him when they got him outside. Poor artless Samson – with neither a dance for his feet this unholy evening nor the feel of a woman's legs later behind the ditch – was spirited out through the gateway. The stewards pelted him into the darkness – into oblivion, you might say. His entertainment was not to be got at the Platform Dance in Gibbet Hill. Enough said.

2

And now we come to Jimbo. A Go-Boy's life was a rare vocation. A Go-boy has a certain air of capriciousness to his name – a style that few could ever emulate. There is an unfathomable joy (*play! play! play your life away*) in the heart of a Go-Boy. Indeed, Playfulness is his true calling – the very centre of his existence. You'd be sitting on your ass-and-car and see him running at speed a stone-throw from the creamery gates. You'd see him an hour later entering the town at a similar gallop and then coming back over the railway bridge with a pound of mutton – that's if you were travelling at the speed of a greyhound. How on earth did he do it?

To keep us on our toes we awoke one morning to see poor Samson's hat and britches (*where did mee britches go to?*) perched on top of the church steeple – stolen by Jimbo, placed up there by the same fellow. It was a puzzle that left us scratching our heads for a week and a half. The commotion caused Father Sensibly such a shock that he caught an unusual bout of flu and took to his bed. Even the little birds stopped singing as if they were in mourning over him.

By mid-morning the usual crew of women were outside the confession-box and (unaware of Father Sensibly's illness) were hellbent as usual on telling him their small sins and getting themselves saved from hell. Who was the scoundrel (a needless question), who crept unnoticed into the sacristy and togged himself out in the holy man's cassock and soutan (the mitre and the stoll as well)? Who was it that beat them all to the door of the confession-box? Yes – it was Jimbo, admirably dressed for his new role as a visiting priest (the heathen). In his most syrupy voice he gently prodded these poor old dames to tell him their harmless few sins. 'Yes, my child! Go on! Go on! That little sin of yours isn't nearly enough of a sin to get you into hell. Come now, don't be shy – you must have a few more serious sins for me to absolve you from.'

For a finish he wheedled out a cartload of intimacies and misdemeanours not only from the shy women but also from two of his own uncles. By midday he had been given such a shock to his system that he could fill an entire book. Of course, when his blasphemous rascality was discovered he didn't dare set foot in the parish for a month and a half as there was an army of four-grained forks waiting for him – to do untold damage to his rear quarters.

The anger of our men and women, however, was short-lived and we were soon laughing when we heard of Jimbo's next endeavour – his battle with Old Sam's fierce terrier (*Bassy*). He was heading to the church to buy a heap of religious medals to pin on his jacket as a reminder of his wartime bravery when Bassy (that devil of a dog) leapt out over the ditch and bit him so severely on the seat of his britches that he couldn't sit down at the table and have his dinner. Later that evening he marched into Old Sam's yard. Letting a mighty roar out of him, he ran at the terrier and caught him by the tail and his leg. Mindless of Bassy's countless fleas, he proceeded to bend his hind leg back as far as it would go – until the poor creature roared blue murder. Then he sank his savage teeth into the squealing animal's ear till he had it nearly torn off. It's a sure cure (said he) for any dog that likes to bite humans.

In the snowy winter Jimbo was the first to arrive at the top of Easy-does-it's hillslope – the first to start the downhill sliding on his belly-board. He won the hearts of us all as he took the wooden board down the slope at an unmerciful speed unnatural to man. Without a thought of stopping he hurled himself and his sledge (what we half-expecting) straight into Simon-not-so-simple's ditch, bouncing clean out over it and landing in the briars in a leg-wriggling heap of mock rage. We were left in stitches.

As if that weren't enough – on his next slide he risked breaking his skull altogether as he sped down the course only to end up somersaulting through the air and landing on top of Dowager's cowshed. The talk of Jimbo and his sledging filled us with bouts of amusement that lasted throughout the winter.

August came around. It was the time when most of us were worked off of our feet – what with the mowing and harvesting of the hay – and yet we found time to do a little bit of celebrating now and then. Jimbo managed to keep us on our tippy-toes with more of his whirling antics. It was a Sunday evening and the smoky twilight would soon be arriving on the skyline above the church in Copperstone Hollow. A good crowd of us were out and about in the fresh mountainy air – watching the final of the handball between Towser and Joe Soap in the ball-alley next to the church. Others were sitting inside in Merrymouth's drinking-shop and already well down into the second and third pint of stout. Jimbo had been up at the counter with a few old cronies, carousing his gizzard for the past hour at least. But now he was gone out.

Suddenly we heard a commotion down near the Shrine of the Blessed Virgin. It was Jimbo – and he roaring and pawing at the ground like an enraged bull. The news ('come and see Jimbo!') went quickly round. We were bristling with anticipation. The handballers stopped their play and the rest of us emptied the drinking-shop without bothering to finish our drinks.

Thirty yards down from the shrine we saw a telegraph-pole propped up against the side of Jimmy Lamplighter's hayshed. There was a rope wrapped round it. Jimbo was about to make a run at this treacherous obstacle in an effort to knock it down with a belt of his forehead. We looked at the pole. We looked at Jimbo. Were our eyes deceiving us? One of them (the pole or Jimbo) was about to meet its doom and we roared on our encouragement. The suspense was killing us. Shouts of joy rose from the children.

'Hush, let ye!'

'Be quiet yeer mouths!' Jimbo positioned his arms and legs. He clenched his fists. He was about to make another bit of history – about to make a mad dash at the telegraph-pole and destroy it.

'The heavens to you, Jimbo!' He was off and away. We kept a safe distance from the hayshed in case Jimbo had doctored the pole and it'd fall down on top of our heads and kill a pile of us. 'Molly, avic, will ye look at the whoor!' shouted Towser to his sister. Such a feat had never been seen before – a duel between a man and a telegraph-pole. Ah, the vanity of the man! 'Ah – me and mee mother,' groaned one or two women and they prayed silently for Jimbo's head and they rattled their rosary beads.

A minute later we saw that Jimbo had smashed his forehead off of the pole. The Guards and the nurse (*Black Bess*) came quickly on the scene and carried him away to the hospital. Who were the filthy blackguards who had mixed the potheen and the whiskey – mixed the brandy and rum – into Jimbo's half-empty glass when he was out making his poolie? Didn't they know there'd be no fun in it – that Jimbo would get the thought fixedly into his head that he could fly to the moon, that he could swim the mighty Shannon River – not that he'd be sure to damn near kill himself?

3

Were ye at the Regatta in Windy-View or were ye sick?' asked the old gossips. Of course, we were all there. Jimbo was once more on show – him and his haughty swaggering after his historic row with the telegraph-pole. The stewards had a roll of chicken-wire rigged up around a stretched-out track. By special invitation there was to be a handicap-race between the great man and a broken-legged hare. The crowd gathered round. They stretched out their necks like a pile of young ganders. Several penny-bets were thrown down as to which one would win the race – Jimbo or the hare.

It would soon be time for the race to start.

Jimbo had been drinking a good few drops of the black stuff throughout the morning. He tore off his shirt (the one his father left him) and proceeded to rub a few handfuls of spearmint across his chest. 'A sure cure for the fleas,' he laughed.

He began preening his puny body and strutting back and forth, showing us the great man that he was. The steward called him to the starting-line. He suddenly turned and glared at us. 'Take a good look at me now. I'm the Star-of-Paradise, that's who I am – as fine a man as ever blew froth from a pint of stout.' What the startled hare thought of this sort of speechifying as he wriggled about in the hands of the starter we dread to think.

Jimbo spat on his fists. He stared glassy-eyed at the finishing-tape. He raised his leg and held it a moment in the air. He made a few scurrilous gestures with his backside and let rip one or two squeaky farts before positioning himself alongside the hare. And then they were off.

To help him on his way the hare had been given a savage dart of a pin up under his tail. Jimbo and the crippled creature made an earnest attempt to get away down the track. Soon enough our Go-Boy was out in front.

That's when the real buffoonery took hold. A visiting curate from Clare had a cute little terrier cradled in his arms and was stroking it thoughtfully. He could see Jimbo heading for the finishing-line where the prize of a pound of tea was waiting for him. And then he had a vision that would add to the sport. He threw the terrier in over the wire. In the confusion and excitement (if not terror) the eejit-of-a-dog ran straight across Jimbo's path, entangling itself in his wellingtons and leaving him outstretched on the grass with a dent in his nose. It was nothing less than a disgrace. And to the angry shouts of the gamblers (blasht it!) the race had to be abandoned there and then. The hare had already reached the finishing-tape – only to be disqualified on the spot and deprived of his one bit of fame, poor thing. Some wily wags said that the exhausted creature was subsequently arrested and thrown into the lock-up and that Father Sensibly had the finest hare-soup ladled out to him from his maidservant the very next evening.

The following week was a major event when the Munster County Hurling-Final was to take place in the Showground. Long before any of us came alive or the sun had embraced the mountains, Jimbo reached the sleepy town. Taking part in the hurling for us would be the blue-and-gold jerseys of our Tipperary stone-throwers. Hurling against them would be their mortal enemy – the cherry-shirted Cork hurlers from the River Lee. There was already a festive air to the day. 'It's a good year when we have Cork bate and the hay saved,' would be the phrase on all our lips.

Jimbo with his white linen shirt and his yellow cross-sash was like the conductor of a Dublin orchestra. With his glistening walking-cane and his white surgeon's gloves he was a man of consummate importance if you didn't know who he was and if you'd come from as far afield as Cork. Today he was about to confront the unsuspecting visitors and bring out the finest notes of his creative madness. They had travelled in droves – what appeared to be the whole population of Cork. He could see them from over the ditch as they came bowling towards him from the railway station. He smiled to himself and placed himself at the crossroads. They'd be sure to pass his way in order to get to the hurling-ground.

'Here they come! Here they come! Stand back!' With their red rosettes and the screech of their silver whistles and all the hurly-burly that went with it – here was a spectacle for our sore eyes. The visitors stopped at the crossroads, unsure of their direction. Should they take the left road? Should they take the right road?

That's when *the wily fairies*, who always lived on the edge of hell, sped up under Jimbo's feet and lodged themselves deep in his brain. With his raised cane and his officious pair of white gloves he stepped out to greet the Cork men. With a proud wave of his hand he instructed them (*coom on! coom on!*) to follow on behind him. They turned and followed him like a herd of sheep. Graciously brandishing his cane and waving at the amused townies who had come out to see this exciting pilgrimage, he proceeded to lead them off towards the right, stamping his boots down along Bell Alley and around the corner passed Tom Slappity's Barber Shop.

From there he proceeded to lead them off to the left. Building up steam and raising his voice into something like a military bellow, he escorted his Cork guests back along Sky Street. You'd never think he'd have the nerve as he trailed them around the blessed circumference of the town – in along one side and back out the other side. After marching them all over the blessed neighbourhood, he finally led the poor misfortunates to within a stone-throw of where they'd started out – back to the crossroads. And there they parted company.

A moment of confusion (a moment of untold mystery) followed and then sheer panic and pandemonium took over.

The bedraggled Cork men turned into a swarm of angry bees. 'The bleddy little fecker!' roared their leader, 'let me get at him till I break every tooth in his head.' They'd not be seen dead in Tipperary again: 'Why – the little shitty-arse!' screeched others, 'wait till I get my hands on him – he'll not have a testicle to his name when I'm finished with him. The match'll be as good as over by the time we get to see the action.'

Their repeated misuse of poor Christ's name outmatched even our own inventive oaths and swearwords as they heaped curses on Jimbo and his father and mother. Their nostrils flared – sniffing here and sniffing there to see if they could smell out Jimbo anywhere. But our agile hero had fled like a ghost in the night, missing all the commotion. By now he was safe and sound at the lower end of Bell Alley, his heart chuckling merrily and fit to burst. This day had been the finest of outings for Jimbo - a magnificent climax, a day of purest merriment and fun-making – ending up (unlike Samson) in his complete getaway. Lest we forget – it had been very cruel indeed to lead our Cork guests astray the way he did – and in such a time-wasting exercise. But the humour of a Go-Boy was always going to be different from everyone else's – a humour all of its own making. Nevertheless, Jimbo's mother must have slept uneasily in her bed that night when the men from Cork continually questioned her son's parentage (*the basthard! the basthard!*) long into the evening.

4

Two weeks later the sun was again strong in the sky and driving us all delirious with sweat. Jimbo went to the Daffy-Duck Circus where he entered the Donkey Derby on a very emaciated ass (*Ragamuffin*). Some lads had cleverly oiled up our hero with a drop or two of the rawgut potheen.

The race would soon begin. The pranksters (urged on by Jimbo) stood at either side of Ragamuffin. Jimbo got them to heave him up on the ass's back and sat there like a delicate egg on a horse's saddle. A moment later we saw his arms flailing the air (the actor that he was) and heard the screams of him as he hung onto the ass's ears for grim life. We saw him wobbling about hysterically – his lungs gasping and his eyes glaring dizzily and his legs jiggling in the air (*help me! help me! I'm getting killed!*) till you'd think his bodily appendages were about to fall off of him.

At his behest the juggling pranksters pelted him up (time and time again) on one side of the bemused Ragamuffin – only for Jimbo to bounce off at the other side and down onto the grass. The rapturous shouts of the men – the radiant faces of the women – defied all description (but fulfilled the dreams of Jimbo). After each bit of pitching and pelting there followed a hush – a hush that'd break your heart from trying to stifle the laughter rising up in you. Finally, however, our hero (*no better man! no better man!*) was seated firmly on his saddle and the race could then get properly underway.

By now Jimbo's face was as red as a lobster with the sweat dropping off of his nose. The best entertainment was yet to follow when just as the race was about to commence he persuaded one of the women to take the hatpin from her coat and stick it in under the fidgetty ass's tail.

WHOOOOOOOOSH!

Away stormed the frightened ass (*make way, lads! make way*!) as though he were a zebra fresh in from Africa. Indeed, he almost went out from underneath Jimbo's legs altogether – followed by our flurries of laughter at the sight of our Go-Boy seated firmly back-to-front and his nose up close to the ass's smelly tail and the two of them in sweaty harmony. A second later they were seen levelling to the ground three furious tinkers and two blind pensioners as Jimbo and Ragamuffin headed for the finishing-line and the award of the Big Prize Cup. Fair play to you again, Jimbo!

With the Donkey Derby now behind him and the Daffy-Duck Circus put away till next year, it was time for the Show Fair. Apart from hurling the slither ball into the upturned milk-tank from twenty yards out and the Carrying-the-squealing-piggy-race and the Blindfold-handbarrow-race, there was going to be the famed Mad-Ass-Race.

Jimbo's recent ass-racing accomplishment had given him a bit of an edge and he was anxious to visit Moll-the-Man and get her help and encouragement for so famous a race. In due course the sympathetic Moll gave him her wise advice. He'd be well prepared (she said) when he got to the starting-line.

There were other lads (mere schoolboys, he thought) ready for the jolting gallop. There was Ned Nettles (*the son of Big Horse)* and Freckles (*the son of Eyeless-Tom*, who was half-blind from a fall in the Yellowstone Quarry). There was Batty (*The Water Diviner's son* from Goat's Cross whose grandfather had been a jockey of some fame). 'Why not enter the race and keep up the ould name?' said his proud father. And then there was Bad Organization's one and only son (*Handlebars* – with his new moustache and not a bit of his mouth in sight). These brave boys were standing up in their stirrups and ready to whip hell out of their skinny old asses, who were already steaming in fear as they staggered their way down the field towards the starting-line. It would not be long before the real sport began.

With a piece of twine a few pranksters had fixed up a bit of a board on Jimbo's back. Across it was written in red rodden *The Derby Winner*.

'The Derby Winner? He is in mee arse,' scoffed some of the women. The day's high point was imminent. On Moll-the-Man's advice (wasn't she the wag) Jimbo called for a spud – a roasting hot spud from the tent. It had a good spiral of steam rising up from it. He then called for those two old sly-boots (*Clever Jack and Tenderfoot*) and whispered a few soft words in their ear. The devils didn't even raise a smile but produced a stocking and wrapped the hot spud inside it – a spud that was to prove the greatest spur that ever ruled an ass's hooves.

The whistle went for the race to start. Clever Jack and Tenderfoot stepped forward. 'By the time we're finished they'll think Jimbo's ass is running on electricity,' the two of them smirked. They quickly thrust the hot spud straight up into the ass's arse. It was just as Moll-the-Man had advised for she'd promised Jimbo that no arrow on earth would match the likes of Ragamuffin, that the poor devil would be out the gate like a bolt of lightning, clean out of the town, out over the top of Chieftain Hill and half-ways to the moon before the rest of the eejits had pranced their asses away from the starting-line.

The Derby Winner – his eyes ablaze and his hooves flashing like polished gold (and with Jimbo once more seated back-to-front on him) proved faster than the wheels of Doctor Glasses' motorcar ('twas said). A pack of mad dogs could not have set such a pace as this mighty ass. And when the crowd raced from the field to catch a hold of Jimbo and put a stop to the great creature, they came back and told how his iron shoes were so hot that you'd fry an egg upon them. Ah-ha – the bone and beauty of an ass and his master!

That's the way to do it, Jimbo! That's the way to do it! You have the blessings of every man-jack-of-us showered down on your head this day. You've earned yourself a handsome feast of stout as soon as the evening sun goes down, Fame like yours doesn't often fall on a man's shoulders – and on this memorable day we will drink Jimbo's health till our eyes start smouldering, till we're fuller than ticks on a cow's udder.

5

Later that afternoon there was more in store for us. Having been given a few mouthfuls of whiskey to revive his head and his heart, Jimbo stepped forth to make the day's final guest appearance. To help things along Clever Jack presented him with a charm to wear round his throat – his father's lucky rat's foot.

Jimbo called for a tar-barrel. He called for a bucket. The crowds were unwilling to leave for home and they gathered in around him. The same pranksters who'd pelted him onto the ass had been briefed to put Jimbo on top of the upturned tar-barrel as soon as it arrived so that his voice and gesture could he seen and heard all round the field and given their rightful due. We were in for a bout of rare entertainment from our host for the great man was about to deliver his famed *Election Speech*.

The bucket was finally produced from the nearby drinking-shop. It was hooked up as a makeshift microphone. Into its depths Jimbo was getting ready to say a few words of condescending wisdom to our own good selves and (if you were fool enough to believe him) to The Irish Nation at large. His two acolytes (Clever Jack and Tenderfoot again) tied the bucket onto a long rope and trailed the rope to some fencing-wire. They then entwined the fencing-wire to the telegraph-pole. The new-fangled electricity could now be let loose from the pole to the wire so as to reach Jimbo's mouth. After that, he'd be well and truly connected to The Irish Nation and in a position to give the world his famed broadcast.

We closed in around Jimbo. To hear the roars of the crowd – you'd think (at the very least) a king was being crowned.

Clever Jack and Tenderfoot (the sportsmen that they were) lowered the bucket and clamped it firmly on Jimbo's head. Then they belted it with their fists and sticks. Mercy-on-us – to hear the rackety din of the metal bucket. And all this – even before our hero had been given a chance to give out his wise words to The Irish Nation. One or two playful rascals were trying to get the bucket up over Jimbo's sore ears. Others were trying to keep it stuck fast on his head. We stood on tippy-toe (*be-mee-oath, is he still alive?*) to take a good look at him and his famed bucket. Wiping the tears from our eyes, we could scarcely stand up from our fits of laughing at the sight of the frantic Jimbo (the merry actor that he was) and he struggling above on the tar-barrel. At last – freeing his aching head - he got himself into a seemingly towering rage, the fog steaming out of his head and the froth flurrying from his lips. Though he hadn't yet started his Election Speech his cheeks were as shiny as a pair of buttercups.

One thing more was needed before Jimbo could broadcast his news to the rest of the world. A couple of women hurried back with an army-coat once worn in the Great War and put it round Jimbo. A couple of expectant men had trimmed the coat with a row of metal buttons – coupled with Jimbo's own religious medals and a few tin saucepan-circles to show how bravely our dapper hero had fought in a number of horrendous battles. Finally, they brought out a few coloured flags to hang round him by way of a platform. The scene was set for him to go speechifying full pelt. 'Give us the whole of yeer heart, Jimbo,' we roared.

With head erect he cleared his throat and got ready to give us the full benefit of his wisdom. 'I'll show these simpletons that I'm no sop of hay on the road,' said he to himself. 'I'll give them a deluge of words that they'll not forget in a hurry,' thought he again.

Maybe he'd tell us he'd been appointed the new minister for all the asses in Tipperary – and for asses like ourselves among them. We'd have to wait and see as our hero drove his head deep into the hollow bucket to test it for microphonical effect (himself and his big words again).

'I'm speaking to the Irish Nation this evening,' came the nasally voice out of the depths of the bucket. This was a fine start – better than a Mission – and soon there wasn't a dry eye among us.

'I have been elected as Chief Pig-Surgeon for this region of Tipperary. I tell ye, byze – the price of pigs has gone far too high. Yes – far too high. And worst of all – the hemline of our ladies' dresses has gone far too low. Yes – far too low.' His voice was already rising like a fountain. Such a hero could outmatch the speech of a priest on the altar, couldn't he?

We kept firing questions up at him. 'What about the Work?' we yelled. 'Coom on, blasht ye, what about the Work?'

'What we want is Fair Pay and Fair Play,' said Jimbo, quoting a well-chosen theme that was to become a household saying for days to come.

'We want to know about the Land,' we yelled back at him. 'Tell us about the Land, coom on – what's keeping ye?'

After that we wanted to know about the Water. Then we wanted to know about the Women. And several scurrilities were fired up at him for we wanted to know precisely what we should do with these women of ours. The filthy answer to this question was such that even Jimbo was too shy to give it to us. The ground resounded with stamping feet and echoing bouts of more and more tearful laughter. For it was clear to every man-jack-of-us what we'd like to be doing with *the women* and Jimbo didn't need to befoul the air with forbidden words.

Then came a little hush when a note of seriousness crept into the festivities. We wanted to know what we should do about the Black North. Heavens above – how Jimbo let us have the full flow of his wisdom!

For the next half-hour his name and his fame ruled over us as he frightened us to death with his fierce fighting talk – his two fists all the time cleaving the air. He asked us for our support, if he was elected. What he wanted (he declared) was

Freedom for the town. What he wanted was Liberty from John Bull's claim on the six counties in the Black North. He was getting himself more and more light-headed as the minutes went by. His body was full of contortions, his face full of twists, his neck swelling as he danced on the tar-barrel in mock rage. He could scarcely hide the laughter that was constantly rising up in him – not just this minute but throughout his whole life. But he hid this laughter and hammered his chest and roared out his challenging defiance.

'May God bless Ireland.'

'May we live for the day when our island will be free – all thirty-two counties of it.'

He was now inspired. We should (he said) rise up – one and all. We should (he said) head for the bleddy north. We should (he said) burn out the basthards as soon as we could – that's what we should do. This was met with thunderous applause ringing off of the bucket as we also (hysterical with joy) began to play our part in this make-believe election. Jimbo's rascally words were clearly the result of his long feast of booze following his horrendous race with the ass and the hot spud.

A blaze of patriotism had filled the entire field as we looked up at Jimbo. Yes (we said) – Jimbo's heart was in the right place. Yes (we said) – a quiver of light was shining out of him. We almost expected him to rise up to heaven. Was there ever a Go-Boy like Jimbo – a man that could fill a crowd with laughter and (better still) could laugh at himself and still be alive at the end of this great day? And as he hopped down from the tar-barrel and wiped the sweat from his brow, we agreed good-humouredly that our one-and-only Go-Boy should be elected as our next noble candidate and should continue broadcasting whenever the chance came up.

6

There was one amongst us, who was not to be amused by the gifted entertainment of Jimbo. And that was Bishop High-Hat. He'd been invited in from Clare to officiate at the next hurling-match in the Showgrounds. It'd be another day of rarity and festival – an honour to have a holy man like him in our midst, he having been invited to throw in the hurling-ball and start the scrimmage at the start of the match.

The day came on and it was time for the ceremony. He threw the ball in between the legs of the hurlers. Then – all hunched up like a hedgehog expecting a shower of rain – he scurried his fat little legs back to the side-line in case he got a belt of the ball on the back of his holy skull.

Shortly afterwards an unholy row was heard filling the air. 'Who is that old bagman at the side of the pitch?' roared the bishop. Why, it was our own Jimbo and he full to the gills with drink. He was running up and down the side-line, encouraging the players to shift themselves and put a bit of flogging into it and dent a few more of their opponents' heads.

'Sit down, you silly old fool!' thundered the bishop, his angry face reddened from the whiskey affecting him after his dinnertime reparations. In the eyes of everyone a holy bishop was an authoritative personage next to Almighty God. To be lectured to by a bishop was usually enough to shrivel the stoutest hearts amongst us. But Jimbo turned around and stared at the bishop and the other dignitaries that were grovelling round the holy man like a red rash.

'Go kiss mee arse,' he roared.

The crowd burst out laughing in pure delight. This was better than a circus. It was far more than that, however: it was a sore trial for any bishop – a trial that might well undermine his very power and authority. What was he to do?

Oh, Holy Virgin-in-heaven! To have heard such obscenities out of Jimbo's mouth – a perilous thing for you to have done, old friend. Ah, the power that the Drink can have on a man's befuddled mind – for our hero to say such a filthy thing to a bishop of Holy Mother Church.

And then Jimbo (were our eyes deceiving us?) lowered his britches in front of Bishop High-Hat – for the holy man and his crawling cronies to inspect his true colours, his yellow arse. The world had finally come to an end – surely it had.

Next Sunday we all arrived early for Mass, having got wind of the trouble ahead. Father Sensibly came out on the altar – even before it was time for him to start saying Mass. His mind was made up. There had to be a stop put to our Go-Boy's friskiness. He'd give Jimbo a bludgeoning he'd not forget in a hurry before he and his likes got a foothold over the Church. He'd give the rest of us an unrehearsed sermon we'd remember for the rest of our lives.

The holy priest stood between the tall candles and the vases of flowers. Slowly and solemnly he put on his black hat. He wheeled round and raised his hand, commanding our silence. We could see his stormy face. We could see the grimace round his mouth as his cold glacier eyes penetrated into us.

Then he spoke to us in a very loud and harsh voice and (ah, the noble man that he was) his words were savage indeed. 'I am ashamed – I am absolutely astounded – indeed out of my natural life – to have witnessed what went on at the Showground's hurling-match. Ye were all there and (mother-of-god) the bishop himself was honouring us with his presence. What will his holiness think of me now? Do ye know what he'll say? "Is this the unsaintly way (he'll say) that Father Sensibly has been training his congregation?" Then our priest wiped an imaginary tear from his eye: 'I can never again look him in the eye – never again sit down to tea and sandwiches with him.'

His fury knew no bounds and his face became as red as a beetroot. It was a fine and tragic performance – even outshining Jimbo's mock Election Speech for he'd worked himself up into a fine old fit – good enough for the Dublin stage. This was so unusual in his nature – so unlike his genial good self with that unctuous flute-like voice of his *(God bless my little lambs)* when we were giving him our fistfuls of coppers every Sunday.

He had to pause and give himself a breath before the torrent of words could start again. Finally, he pointed a riveting finger straight down at poor Jimbo as though he were looking at a distorted scarecrow-of-a-man. It was the holy finger of scorn. And with his eyes raised towards heaven and his arms lifted shoulder-high our dutiful priest cursed the now-bedraggled Jimbo from a great height – cursed him and all his descendants (should he ever be fortunate enough to get married and have any). It was nauseating for us to have to sit and listen to him and we bowed our heads. We knew something was wrong. Just like Jimbo – Father Sensibly had gone a step too far in showing off his almightiness in front of us poor scholars.

Jimbo had felt as safe as a nest on a Clare cliff – up until now. We were all mesmerised at Father Sensibly's vengeful words. It was time for our hero to fret. His previous manly confidence and self-composure had disappeared in an instant and he no longer felt one bit sure of himself. Instead, he had the look of a tragedian about him and a pair of sorry-looking eyes that we'd never seen before on him – burdensome eyes with not a ray of sunshine left in them.

The now-tainted hero of the Mad-Ass Race was never going to be a match for a man-of-the-cloth – especially here in the church and on foreign ground. He bowed his frightened head at the comeliness of Father Sensibly's refrain. Such a curse – such a priestly prophecy – might turn a man into a goat (his mother once told him), might even bring back his dead grandmother's ghost on an unsuspecting night to haunt him for his wickedness till the end of his days. He had always had a premonition that something like this might one day happen to him and mar his happy-go-lucky Go-Boy days here in Ireland.

For the next night or two Jimbo returned forlornly to the loneliness of his sad little cabin. Then came Monday with its cold dawn when the ear-kiss of the birds seemed nowhere to be heard and the gloomy clouds of the half-light seemed to sag heavily on his tired shoulders. 'Tis time (said he) to free meeself from the handles of mee plough.'

He put on a clean white shirt. He put on his best brown suit (his father's wedding-suit) and his father's hat. He took the ashplant from its leaning-place behind the door, not forgetting to pocket his mother's rosary beads and the lock of her hair that she had wrapped in a prayer-book for him before she died.

It didn't need the old gossips to tell us (we all knew) that the poor fellow had been well and truly humbled by the prophecies of Father Sensibly – that our priest had frightened him more than any wild sow could ever have done, that the path ahead had been firmly laid out in front of him, that our Go-Boy had lost the heart to remain a Go-Boy amongst us ever again. With a tear in his eye he shut the door behind him. Then his clattering boots bade farewell to the now-dead spirit of Playfulness and Fun and he shook hands with Droopiness and its attendant *dispirited fairies*. He took with him his portmanteau with a few bits of his possessions and a head of raw cabbage and a bit of bacon in case he should starve on his journey.

He headed for the train and the station. He had never in his life even seen a train. A withered crowd of us gathered on the platform. Our hearts were melting inside in us for the gossamer thread that had bound us to him was about to get broken. Some of us had oiled his throat with a fearful amount of whiskey and a few good glasses of stout. There wasn't a soul that didn't hate to see him going away – going away for an exciting life above in Dublin's city, a place where there wasn't a trace of cow dung to be seen – and taking with him his colourful life which would surely awaken the dead therein. Perhaps he was heading even further out across the Herring Pond and on towards the Land of John Bull and the city we called Pandemonium.

In an ominous cloud of smoke and steam the train from Limerick appeared round the bend and lumbered to a stop. Before he entered the carriage-door our hero stood on the step and there was a terrible sadness in him – as though we had all neglected him over the years. His heart was as heavy as the train itself as he tearfully gave us a wave of his ashplant. It was his last farewell, almost as though he were about to be executed. There he stood (would we ever forget it?) in his father's wedding-suit.

There came a hush. Would he give us a last Election Speech? He cleared his throat and gazed down at us. Then his voice rang out as clear as a blackbird's as he gave us his father's favourite old song – *Sydney Harbour*. He sang it from start to finish – every bit as good as Bedad-sez-I – and nobody left till he was done. The porter had lowered his whistle and had hidden his green flag under his jacket and had taken off his cap as though in memory of a great man.

Jimbo closed the door tightly (*good luk! good luk!*' we cried time and again) and the cadaverous old train began slowly to edge its rattling wheels away from the platform till it faded into a small pinhole and our hearts went down the track after him. Our Go-Boy was about to plunge through time and space – away (though we didn't know it then) to an uncertain existence in Liverpool, many miles from the rest of us. Never again would our eyes behold him and we waved our handkerchiefs after him and our red eyes wept bucketfuls of tears. For us, it was like a death or a wake, like going off to the faraway moon. We knew that Jimbo would never be coming back and we could only guess how much he'd miss us all and the woods and the hills and the rivers and everything else that made up his soul and the soul of all of us.

After trudging home, we spent that evening deep in our bereavement of him and wondering over his whereabouts and whether he'd be making piles of money – wondering in what manner or shape he had greeted his new surroundings.

We weren't kept waiting long for an answer and we soon heard the whole tale of it. For inside in the Widda-Widda's drinking-shop the old gossips had met up with Lowry, the former drinking partner of Bedad-sez-I – the wild man that had once appeared in the naked photographs that had enlivened the citizens of Galway. Though he had left us ten years earlier, Lowry was home for the burial (God be good to her) of his mother below in Abbey Acres graveyard.

Questions. Questions. Questions. Yes – Jimbo had indeed landed safe and sound in Liverpool. Yes – he had spent the journey entertaining the rest of the passengers with his yarns and his songs. And yes (we had all forgotten them) what about his mother's two pairs of red drawers – the ones he used to dress up in to entertain the schoolchildren with? As soon as he landed, he had thrown them to the four winds for the Liverpool children to fight over. Wisely he knew that his days of dressing up in a pair of red drawers were over and done with.

But there was a humorous twist to Lowry's tale. Jimbo had brought to Liverpool his very own Go-Boy's strides and charm. The minute he landed he could be seen marching up and down the side of the quayside in search of his good friend (Lowry himself), who had promised to welcome him but was lurking instead (the rascal) behind one of the luggage-vans.

'Blasht ye, lads, have any of ye seen mee ould comrade, Lowry? I've been missing him awfully,' shouted Jimbo to any of the passers-by whose coat he could grab a hold of. You can imagine the look on their faces as they hurried away from him. The desperation in him – you'd think he was taking a casual stroll round our market square in search of his last stray cow. It was then that we all held our two sides from the fits of laughter we took. Poor innocent Jimbo had no notion of the immense size of a city as big as Liverpool. Nor could he have known that the whereabouts of Lowry (whether he was alive or dead or had even come back down from the moon) was of no interest whatsoever to the minds and hearts of the millions of people living in an impersonal and soulless spot like Liverpool. Indeed, the workers on the quayside must have thought Jimbo was yet another one of those crazed old Irishmen, who came across the sea to annoy the hell out of them.

Seemingly Liverpool would be left scratching its head for a good while yet. Indeed Liverpool (whether it was ready or not) was about to see the rebirth of a true entertainer – a true hero in the shape of Jimbo-the-Go-Boy, the son of Lizzie-the-Herd and Bedad-sez-I. And although he had been cursed by Father Sensibly and had disgraced himself opposite Bishop High-Hat, we would always remember Jimbo as the purest bit-of-dazzle amongst the legions of Go-Boys who had ever lived here in our hills. Enough said.

I'LL DAZE-YE

1

Above in Sheep-Stealers' Lane lived a man with a strange name - I'll-Daze-Ye. One morning he was drying himself with the rough towel when three fine fellows (*the Malignities)* made a vile and scurrilous remark about big-chested men like himself – how it was a well-known fact that such men were found to be very small in other more intimate parts of their bodies. Ah, them and their wicked tongues. I'll-Daze-Ye didn't take their uncalled-for scurrilities too well – especially as it was on his own doorstep that this insult was given him. The row started up in earnest and got hot and heavy. The finish of it was that the Malignities ungraciously tipped over the milk from I'll-Daze-Ye's two creamery tanks and spilt it all over his yard. Then they and their merry laughter went gallivanting out through the gap in the haggart towards the field. The likes of this (the spilling of the milk) was never known before and such scandalous behaviour was bound to burn the anger in our fighting man and prompt him to make use of his mighty knuckles on their impudent skulls – big men though they thought themselves to be and safe in their numbers (three against one small man like himself, however broad his chest.)

It was a sorry situation. There'd be no milk to take to the creamery, no skimmed milk later for the feeding of his calves, no cream from the milk to bring home to his wife (*The Saintly Woman*) to shake into butter in her sweet-gallon tin. The poor man was fit to be tied and he thought his chest would burst asunder from the anger rising up in him. But (rest assured) he was a man of inborn cuteness and of sound self-discipline. He held tough for a short while and took his time shaving himself, leaving just a few cat-hairs here and there, which were always visible beneath his eyes as a sort of trademark. He took the soapy water and he groomed his wavy hair with it so that it stood up straight in a handsomely-curved quiff. He looked at himself in the broken bit of looking-glass and he stroked his jaw. His hair looked more remarkable than ever, giving a further twist to the unusual silver sheen in it, which (alone among our men) had been its colour since his twentieth year. He smiled to himself as he inspected his fine set of knuckles and he blew on them and polished them. Said he to himself, 'I'll eat the three of those Malignities alive, so help me God. I'll rattle their teeth for them and with mee flailing fists I'll make three horizontal sportsmen out of them as soon as I reach their yard – them and their playful antics, wait and see if I don't.'

He loved a good fight – loved the very challenge of it. However, had the ghost of his grandfather (the *Great Bear*) stepped out of his grave, he'd have shaken his wise old head sadly. For the thought of I'll-Daze-Ye's fierce desire to beat and chastise the lives of the Malignities would have sickened his stomach. Mighty prize-fighters such as the Great Bear had been the very shy men of old when it came to showing the drinking-shops and the rest of the countryside the size of their knuckles. Of course, I'll-Daze-Ye would have argued with his grandfather, 'Surely ye'd agree – a family's milk is a delicate matter, as precious as a family's snares or rabbit-traps.' He was going to put a finish to this evening's fun and games. He could see The Malignities stretched out before him in a forlorn heap – the blood from their noses and lips flowing along the yard like his own spilt milk. God would forgive him for the anger that was about to galvanise his fighting fists and help him beat the impudent scoundrels to within an inch of purgatory's gates.

He put on his best boots. He didn't even have time to shine them with the dab of butter. Then he put on a clean white shirt. He looked a fine specimen of a man. He headed for the haggart gap, his wife all the time clinging to his back and dragging at his coat in an attempt to prevent him from going to fight the three huge men and getting himself half-killed by them. I'll-Daze-Ye gently cast her aside and hopped out over the ditch. In a roaring thunderstorm he hurtled his hobnail boots up the field, tearing towards the Valley of the Pig to introduce his fists to the three Malignity gentlemen.

His boots rang on The Malignities' flagstones, echoed by *the wilful fairies*. He was bent on giving them the thorniest of introduction to his fists – a welcome they least expected from him, a welcome they were unlikely to forget. He invited the three mighty warriors to step outside their half-door and get the benefit of his knuckles. 'Coom on out, ye basthards! Coom on out to hell – till I nail ye to the yard!' he yelled, the sparks flying from him. His blistering voice would have frightened a priest out of his boots and you'd hear him like a bull below in Abbey Acres. He threw off his coat and rolled up his sleeves. He spat on his fists and wiped the spittle from his chin. 'Upon mee soul, I'll make a Devil's eyesight out of the three of ye and paste yeer two eyes into one – ye'll see if I don't before I leave yeer yard!' Then he did a few cartwheels around the yard and danced the finest of jig-steps over to their half-door, all the time promising to daze the three Malignities out of their senses.

They had to laugh and hold their sides at the notion of him. If he was anything at all, I'll-Daze-Ye was always true to the name he bore for he had proved more than once that he was able to daze even the mightiest of our brawlers. But to the three Malignities (with their superiority in numbers) to fight against I'll-Daze-Ye seemed a safe enough action to be taking. They took off their coats and swaggered across the yard to fight. They were the essence of contentment as they surrounded I'll-Daze-Ye, their fists held high and menacingly in front of his face – the face they felt sure they'd be pounding to smithereens in a moment's time.

But the laughter soon left their eyes and you'd pay good money to see what happened next, I'll-Daze-Ye (oh, the vitality of him) met them like a thrashing-machine whirling before a field of corn. He proceeded to paste their faces and clout the skin clean off of each of them till their ears were almost put out through their jaw, their blood bespangling the chicken-dung in the yard and terrifying the ducks, hens and geese. He threw the three of them, senseless and glassy-eyed, up onto the ass-and-car and not a twitch out of them. 'Lie there and rue the day ye crossed me, ye gob-shites,' he said. Then he turned on his heel and hopped back out the way he'd come in. It would be a while before the Malignities knew which day of the week it was. Peace and quietness once more filled his soul. The villains would keep themselves quiet for a good while now. He had taken the squeak clean out of their boots.

2

Little things had always started the row. It needn't be those age-old arguments about boundary fences or boundary streams. Nor was it always about the odd stray bull breaking loose from a man's field and trying to engender his neighbour's cows with his precious seed. Nor was it about the stealing of impudent glances at another man's saintly woman. It was often a much smaller thing – like the annoyances at Holy Mass when we were all on our scratched knees and praying like fair hell, saying one decade of the rosary after another for our departed ancestors or making a silent offering to the Blessed Virgin or to our Heavenly Maker to save us from perils and unexpected woes and to guard our cattle from falling into drains. Suddenly you'd hear an almighty yell, followed by a savage oath from someone at the back of the church as a poor unfortunate wretch felt the jaw cut off of him from a well-aimed bit of turf with its hard edge.

The irreligious Donie Baloney (a young man who liked nothing better than eating black-puddings raw) attended Mass regularly like the rest of us, not wanting to receive a mortal sin on his soul. But (God help him) the restless fellow was more often than not bored out of his mind by the constant jaw-jawing and Latin sing-songing of Father Abstemious, the eighty-year-old in-between priest (before the arrival of the new priest Father Honesty) .

To amuse himself he liked nothing better than to fill his pockets with half a dozen handy-sized sods of turf (just the rough corners of them) before setting out for church. Halfway through Mass, as we looked over our shoulders, what did we see? Donie Baloney (a squint in his eye and he twirling a lump of turf) slipping out from some shadowy corner at the back of the church and steadying the aim of his right fist in our direction before deciding which one of us to kill with the first pelt of one of his sharp bits of turf.

Across the back of the church skimmed his turf-bit like a flat stone on the waters of our river. Kneeling with one knee on our caps (as we always did), we quickly sought refuge and hid our ears behind our coat-collars. Some of us dived for cover to the ground so as to avoid a broken jaw in the face of the oncoming missile and our rosary beads became twisted round our fists. It was then you'd hear the row rising up and the sermon of the saintly priest being interrupted. 'Sweet suffering Jaysuz, if I ketch the little fecker who has damaged mee jaw I'll knock the shite out of his britches! Let me at him!'

But Donie was not the only devil working at the back of the church. Of course, all the saintly women were above in the front pews, sanctimoniously hitting their chests with belts of their fists and looking up adoringly at the statue of the Sacred Heart and the thorns around it and kissing the feet of the statue of Saint Francis opposite Jesus. This was something more than foreign for our men to be doing – kissing the toes of the man-statue of Francis when they had their own wives at home to slobber over if the need ever occurred to them.

What happened next was a pure sin. A man would find himself about to celebrate the anniversary of his mother's death by going to communion when some almighty eejit would stealthily tie the fellow's bootlaces together in an unbreakable knot. When the time came for the Holy Communion bell to be rung and for the good man to get up off of his knees and march down the aisle to the starched altar-cloth, he'd no sooner get to his feet than (bless the bit) he'd fall helplessly out on top of his nose. Once again, the sudden bursts of impious cursing (*wait'll I ketch the whoor!*) filled the holy church. What the children made out of all this, heaven alone knows. Was no-one able to live here in peace? Was nothing sacred among us? Ah, religion indeed!

3

The boy called Sammy was twelve and making his Confirmation when he was to become a stout-hearted soldier of Christ. However, at this stage the mighty fists that were to manifest themselves in later years as I'll-Daze-Ye's fists, with the strength of a mule's hooves in them, were nowhere yet to be seen.

In spite of his newly increased growth Sammy had the appearances of a gentle lad – a lad that was expected to stay that way in later life. He couldn't help having his father's handsome face and a pair of startling green eyes belonging to his mother and the delicate jaws of a pretty girl.

Throughout his schooldays the Malignities were his enemies and he continued to avoid them like the plague. But seasons can unexpectedly change and a day was to come, which would dramatically prove the truth of this. He was halfway home from school when the Malignity children caught up with him in the field that ran along the banks of the river. 'Aha! – mee little goose-of-a-man,' they cried as they surrounded him. They swore they'd cut off his two ears – if not worse. Sammy was trapped like a field-mouse crouching in a stubbled field and they stripped him of his clothes in front of the giggling girls and threw him into the icy waters of the river. It was a miracle that the heavens didn't fall down on top of these cruel heathens for so great a sin.

The despoiling of his body was later to prove not the end of Sammy's world. Instead (wonder of wonders), it was at this precise moment in his life that, almost like the good Saint Paul, an indescribable gift came down from heaven and filled his spirit. It was the gift of *Rage* – a rage that would stand him in good faith when the right time came.

A year or two later, Sammy had left the schoolhouse and was walking home from town. It was a bright evening with a little breeze rustling its way across the fields. The Malignities followed him out along the road and caught up with him near the pump at Yawn. By now Sammy and themselves were just about fully-grown. He himself was a good five and a half feet tall and had a fine curly head of hair on him like a wild cauliflower. What's more – he had filled out considerably across his backbone and chest.

His sour-faced enemies reached him, expecting to see the tears trickling down his jaws as he staggered to the side of the road. What could he do only shove his back up against the stony ditch to prepare himself for his inevitable fate – or at least try to save himself from their thudding fists by putting up a bit of a fight lest they again strip him to the skin.

They informed him of his imminent death. Sammy would appear to be doomed. He knew he wasn't fleet-footed enough to escape from them and that he was in for a cruel beating. It was no use calling on the ghosts of his ancestors to come down from the skies and give him the strength that he needed and the unhappy lad leaned in submissively against the ditch and awaited his inevitable fate.

But there comes a moment in life when everything inexplicably changes. He looked up to the clouds as once he had done at school when trying to find the answer to a difficult sum or catechism question. Desperately he called on Almighty God to come down and rescue him – if only this once in his life.

For many months thereafter, Sammy told this story around the drinking-shops in Copperstone Hollow and Abbey Cross. 'I called on mee Heavenly Maker to come down from the skies and rescue me from the brutal fists of the Malignities. Then the good God-in-Heaven came down to me in the blink of an eye.' By now all eyes and ears were on him as he went on.

'Do ye know what happened next? I saw a flash of light pouring down on top of mee head and heard Almighty God whispering in mee ear and telling me reach behind me with mee fingers along the stony ditch-wall.' It was hard to believe his story and there were one or two smirks from the older fellows.

'Lads, believe me when I tell ye - I found that God had given me the present of a lifetime - a mighty big rock from the top of the ditch – right behind mee right shoulder - and I shouted at the three Malignities, 'Run, run, let ye - run for yeer lives, ye mushrooms or I'll daze the three of ye, ye pack of shitty-arsed basthards!'

By now we were all in stitches, laughing. But Sammy wasn't yet finished. 'Ye should have seen the startled look on their faces as I struck out at them with mee big rock. Without a second to thank mee Blessed Saviour and with all the power in mee body I belted that big rock straight up into their impudent heads, putting the blood pumping out of their faces and left them there, dazed and almost dead – the beautiful imprint of the rock warming their foreheads and leaving its print on their sad faces.'

We all knew that this story of I'll-Daze-Ye was perfectly true. We remembered how the Malignities had staggered into Curl 'n' Stripes' drinking-shop a few minutes later and were welcomed with, 'I see ye have been warmed and reddened with a rock.' For the news had already gone on ahead of them. And from that day forth we saw the purple marks on the hooligans' foreheads from the belts of the famous God-given rock and saw the nonchalant Sammy walking the roads unchallenged, with his hands in his pockets. Gone forever was the timid lad of old, gone the weak and undergrown child with the piss-in-the-bed look on his face. In his place stood I'll-Daze-Ye, the man-of-the-hour, the man who had fought the Malignities with a big rock.

Before too long he was to become a living legend in our midst – his sad and lonesome boyhood a memory forgotten by us all. And from that day on, the three mighty Malignities were no longer guffawing at him and seemed to be half-in-dread of this erstwhile goose-of-a-man. And whenever he was coming their way, it was like a dismal cloud passing over a harvest-field and they kept to the far side of the ditch, never knowing when the inspiration of the Heavenly Maker (who had once placed a rock in the young man's fist) might again come down out of the clouds and give I'll-Daze-Ye another big rock with which to tear the skin off of their heads. And yet - these were the men, who (a few years later) were once again up to their antics of yore – manly enough to spill our hero's tanks of precious milk the length of his yard. That left us scratching our heads. Had the simpletons completely lost their reason?

4

Like I'll-Daze-Ye, the rest of us had every confidence in Hammer-the-Smith and we placed him almost alongside the priest who absolved us from our sins at Easter-time. The man was pure gifted and his bellows and anvil were never silent. He could shoe your cartwheels and fix up your plough and from the rim of a cartwheel he could make a Celtic cross as your grave-marker if you were unlucky enough to lose your life from the belt of a cudgel during a faction-fight. And so well did he use his rasp and pincers on the shoes of our horse or ass (as well as the knife for pairing their hooves) that they were no longer tripping over their feet but were seen dancing a fine jig-step next morning on even the most slippery of our roads.

Though his smithy was filled with sizzling smoke and grime, Hammer always wore a white shirt beneath his apron and went home at nightfall without a stain or a smudge on it. This was a mystery to us all. Even the old gossips couldn't fathom it out and gave half the day talking at the well about his fastidiousness. To put it simply, for a big rough-fisted man like himself, our smith was neatness, cleanliness and tidiness all rolled into one. His wife boasted that she never had to pick a sock up off the floor after him before he stepped into bed to join her. She knew (but she wouldn't tell you) that alone among us he wore a pair of inner white drawers and that, rather than give them to her, he'd first remove the little pissy stains with a stealthy washing of his own before giving them to her for the Monday washing. In later years (when he was dying) the last thing he did was call for a bowl of hot water and lay his feeble hands in it so as to get the imaginary bits of grime washed away from him.

Hammer was the only man who could repair your fighting blackthorn stick (the *loaded butt*) and at the same time fix you up more than decently with metal splints and plates in your arms or your knees or head, having been given the unusual blessing at his birth of the powers of bonesetter as well as smith. Indeed, the smith's own father had been known by everyone as our homemade body-physician and went by the name of *Bonesetter*, never having been given any other name for he had never been christened. It was he that could mend an animal's bones and fix them up even better than the Bearded Vet. With his mixture of laurel-leaf paste and oils he could cure the body-burns of a frail woman like Gentility when she fell into the fire. He could cure a broken thigh-bone with a heated poultice of cow dung and cream and could put a fistful of goose-grease round a man's aching muscles till the pain was gone. He could use cups of flour and herbs to free them from blood-poisoning – just like his grandfather (*the Cow Doctor*). And if that wasn't enough – he could reach his hand inside a man's jaw and pull out a tooth or a bit of loosely-growing bone before the fellow knew he had done it and without him feeling even one *shnig* of pain.

With all that history behind our smith, that was why our men preferred to test the hands of Hammer after a day's faction-fighting rather than run to the doctor's surgery. And, although they feared the wrath and rebukes of Doctor Glasses for their devilish love of these wild sporting battles, in reality, the reason for attending the smith was the fact that his fee was a good bit cheaper than the doctor's. Of course, they knew that Hammer-the-Smith was a man born of the same clay as themselves and not an old blow-in from Cork. They also knew that their beloved blacksmith (not having the great education of Doctor Glasses) would not be inclined to speak words of rebuke to them but would measure his praise of them by the bravery they'd shown in the most recent battle and the consequential seriousness of their injuries and loss of blood. And it was said that though his jowls were beardy and as rough as sandpaper Hammer's fingers and hands were as smooth as a child's. Even the old gossips had to admit that God must have come down and lodged in his hands since he was able to turn old Gentility into a racing greyhound within a week of her seeing him. And (they said) if the pope in the Holy City was a man to be sainted then Hammer-the-Smith should have been given a holy ring around his own head.

5

It was always the same routine. As soon as the faction-fight began, The Guards suddenly became very wise men and retreated to the far side of the town. What use would they be in curbing such savage men when their fighting mettle had risen to such an uncontrollable height? By the time these law-and-order boys had gone to the nearest town for reinforcements and the necessary refreshments, the faction-fighters would have ended their battle and long gone back to their homesteads to bathe their wounds in the wash-tub and see to the repair of their cudgels in preparation for the next big war. Indeed, some of them would already be getting themselves carried up to Hammer-the-Smith's forge to get their heads fixed before the daylight faded.

It was a shame (said the townie women) for all the hilarity and hysteria of faction-fighting to be coming to an end all over Ireland. What on earth was wrong with our men these days (they said)? Were their bodies getting worn out from all the cudgelling over the years? But behind all their moaning and groaning they were still happy enough since there was this one last gasp of faction-fighting here inside our town where men still had a bit of strength in them (thank God) for the odd battle or two like the one coming up between the Malignities and I'll-Daze-Ye's supporters.

Otherwise (said the townie women) there'd be no excitement left for anyone to celebrate up and down Jinnet Street – except looking at the tinker-women drunkenly brawling on the evening of a Fair Day. Of course, these same townie women wouldn't dream of letting their own men run out into the street and catch hold of a cudgel: it was enough to see the farming yokels belting the heads off of one another. They pretended to have forgotten a thing or two – that there had been one or two deaths from recent blows to the skull - sufficient reason for the farmer's wives and the priests to throw their hands up in the air and demand that all faction-fighting be stamped out for once and for all, the length and breadth of Tipperary.

On this memorable day no one was prepared to step in and forbid a fine afternoon's entertainment. We all knew that the recent spilling of I'll-Daze-Ye's milk had been a justified and righteous cause for a good old-fashioned bout of faction-fighting and not to be missed - a chance to test the strength of men's cudgels possibly for the last time in Tipperary since none of us knew if men would ever be let loose to use them again.

After he'd finished a fine feed of meat above at Bunty's Eating-House, I'll-Daze-Ye tapped his belly below his belt and put on his cap. Together with his cousins (*The Out-and-Outers*) he headed down the lane towards Jinnet Street and, at the sight of their cudgels, a lively bunch of townie children followed them. I'll-Daze-Ye looked at his pocket-watch. At this time of the day the streets would be less crowded. It was a good time for the use of a man's cudgel – three o'clock and The Lord's own hour of crucifixion.

Since ten in the morning there had been a good deal of heavy drinking (a mixture of the rawgut potheen and pints of stout). The Malignities and I'll-Daze-Ye's men had been sitting side-by-side on the barrel-planks inside in the Widda-Widda-Woman's drinking-shop, exchanging pleasantries and wiping their wet lips. They all seemed to be drinking friendly enough.

For the past hour, however, the calm and laughter had died down till it was replaced with more words than a priest's sermon as challenge and counter-challenge were offered by each opposing group. It was time for the coats and ties to be thrown off, time for the cudgel and the fray.

The two camps stepped outside earnestly and twirled their cudgels and wattles aloft. Danger lurked behind each man's eyes and you could tell that they were about to murder one another. They began to shout and scream and to send wolf-like yahoos to the heavens, enough to raise the dead from the graves 5 miles away.

Their recent complaints against each other seemed modest indeed for they had far more hateful memories going back beyond the cradle and now proceeded to curse each other's families with unprintable oaths – back to the fourth and fifth generation. They prayed to God to give strength and vigour to their cudgels – give strength to their boots and their fists. Their prayers (*hell and damnation to ye!*) were more imaginative than a first-rate poet's and any fair damsel who had been foolish enough to be driving her ass-and-car along Jinnet Street was now sent off, scattering and screaming, at a tidy speed, with a belt of a cudgel on her ass's old arse to save her pretty little head from the imminent battle. This gave the creature a set of legs that would do a racehorse credit.

The confrontation and the joy of the cudgel was about to begin as the warring factions positioned themselves – The Out-and-Outers at the south end of Jinnet Street and The Malignities at the north end. For a second or two there was a hush and a quietness and if ever the hair stood up on a fighting man like a cat's before conflict it was at this very moment – so tremendous was the fearsome energy in the hearts of the fighters as the war began.

I'll-Daze-Ye and the eldest of The Malignities approached the middle of the street and gave each other the customary gobful of spit on each other's boots. They pulled down each other's caps over one another's eyes. Then the caps were snatched off and pelted high in the air. This insult to one another's caps was the signal for the fight to begin. I'll-Daze-Ye had blessed his boots well with holy water this morning. He had also blessed his cudgel and fists with lashings of the same and with the first kick he almost destroyed the testicles of his enemy. The true beauty of a battle had well and truly started.

With the blood buzzing like a swarm of bees in their ears the warriors rushed wildly forward in a mass of cudgels and wattle-sticks and without a thought for their safety they hit out randomly at one another's ribs, arms and legs. Such was the noise. Such was the joy of the battle, you'd think a haystack was on fire.

'Success to yeer cudgels,' cried the townie women and 'Shove into yeer man and grind the basthard's bones into the ground,' they roared and they prayed to The Blessed Virgin to aid the men's cudgelling in the breaking of limbs.

In the meantime, the blanched-faced countrywomen set up a great wailing at the edge of town in case their men were getting killed on them for between all the knuckling of heads and the cracking of sticks on elbow and kneecap you'd think the end of the world had truly arrived. Furiously gnashing his teeth and all the time cursing (*Coom here, ye scarecrow till I nail ye to the street*) each man now guarded his face, chest and inner thighs and waited for a chance to do the utmost damage -leaping to the left and then to the right and fixing his eyes on the man in front of him. It was the same as a rushing river that couldn't make up its mind which way to flow - as now one side was driven back to the market square - and now the other side was forced to retreat to the railway bridge above the trains from Limerick.

And soon they were all in a ball of sweat, no man holding back. And as the war waged on, injured compatriots (their faces the colour of the rainbow) were nursed back to consciousness on the side of the road. The Widda-Widda-Woman was as busy as a gnat as she ran out dangerously from her drinking-shop and into the street with a jug of whiskey and ladled it into the staggering men with their livid bruises. After that she pelted them back into the front of the battle for another good leathering of the cudgel or a chance to go and crack a poll or two or break a few bones.

But, like the daylight itself, the warriors at last grew tired from looking for yet another head to purchase and break open with their cudgels. The clattering of their boots and cudgels finally came to an end, the fire of the battle having gone out of their bellies. The evening sun in its ball of redness began to go down beyond the woods and Chieftain Hill and the last men left standing amongst the fighters shook hands somewhat confusedly, almost sadly. And after doing the cockerel on it abroad in the street-battle, they now picked their way silently across the roadway. Arm-in-arm they went in to attack the Drink in the Widda-Widda-Woman's drinking-shop where they sat once more on the barrel planks, the broad flow of their voices blazing up to the rafters. They began to quench their thirst (*droothy work indeed, mee byze)* as they whipped their glasses of stout and their fiery rawgut whiskey down into their throats – so strong, it'd burn a hole in the wall.

Their heads were soon muzzy from all the fine drinking that they were doing. Both sides grew happier by the second and, so friendly were they to one another as they drank each other's health that you'd think they were brothers, good humour now taking over from their previous angry rage. And apart from a few broken teeth and damaged ribs no-one had gotten himself severely injured or killed in the battle.

'Thanks be to God,' said the women who had braved it in from the edge of town in order to follow their men as far as the drinking-shop door. It had been a grand fight and both sides came out of it equally balanced, complimenting one another with poetic little pleasantries for their bravery and for their fighting prowess. One thing was sure – they knew that their family honour had remained intact.

'No, blasht it, 'twas yeer fine fists that did the trick on mee cousin Mikey.'

'No, be-cripes, 'twas yeer two boots that were the tidier in sending the fatal blow to Patsy's danglers and got him taken away from the street.' For the following hour or two you'd hear the same old song again and again out of them.

It was seven o'clock and getting late. The drinking had been good but the merriment in the drinking-shop was beginning to die down and the place would soon be empty and spider-quiet. The sun had at last gone behind the rooftops and dark silhouettes began to creep in and the clouds in the west were already purple and pink. By this time, I'll-Daze-Ye (pale and jaded) was like a sleepwalker as he stumbled out the shop-door.

Before cycling out by the Sheep Field, he looked back to see the houses of the town being swallowed up in the mellow light. Then he looked in front of him towards the shoulders of the misty hills beckoning him home to his wife and his family. The wobbly bike and its frail lamplight crawled towards Abbey Cross, a faint breeze stabbing its way behind him. The only sound (apart from his puffing and panting) was the lonely sound of the last few blackbirds still awake.

He crossed the flagstones and his children ran out excitedly into the yard: 'Father-father-father!' they yelled, jumping all over him like young puppies. Great was their relief for to see that their father had not been killed. I'll-Daze-ye went in and sat near the crackling logs on the fire – almost on top of the flames, warming his hands and thighs. He lit a cigarette for himself. The yellow lamplight shone on his face across the flagged floor and made dark waves on the walls. His wife, the Saintly Woman, looked tenderly at him. She knew only too well that if she gave out to him with a lash of her tongue for endangering his life and the livelihood of his family, his humour might turn sour in a second and he might give her a few tidy taps on the seat of her skirts. For men were an odd mixture and didn't trouble the women too much in the bedroom. There was no 'coom-into-mee-arms, mee charmer' about them – even though their songs were full of such nonsense. Few were the stolen kisses, following the fear of tuberculosis sweeping the land and it was an absolute wonder how any of us came to be born at all - something that happened mysteriously (as in this case) between I'll-Daze-Ye and his good woman in the stealth of the night and beneath the dark sheets when only the fox was about and the rest of the ghostly house couldn't spy on the pair of them.

That evening I'll-Daze-Ye was in a splendid mood – back home in his little clot of gold and as happy as a king in a palace. He sang song after song for his children. He sang them *Little Nell*. He sang them *The Black Sheep*. He sang them *The Jacket so Blue*. He sang songs he'd learnt when he was a young ploughboy below in Travellers Rest – songs from the lips of the men who had come to plough from the Land-beyond-the-water. He got down the concertina from the bacon-box and the children danced step-for-step across the floor with the same vigour that had been seen in their father this bloodstained afternoon. The big man finally knelt down and carried each of them around the Welcoming Room on his back, swinging this way and that way so as to topple them off. He was like a young horse as he skinned the knees out of his britches. Then he carried the youngest of them up the ladder on the broad of his back to the loft and laid them gently in the settle-bed. He lifted the older girls into the air so that they stood trembling on his shoulders like the Daffy-Duck Circus acrobats. They screamed till they wet their knickers. 'Can ye see the Big City?' he said. Time and again, with each of them, he repeated this performance. The Saintly Woman smiled and she laughed to herself over her long sock-darning needle as she listened to the wind whistling through the trees outside. It was good to see her husband home with the rage against the Malignities driven clean out of his body. Yes (she thought). I'll-Daze-Ye was just like a little child betimes, a balm to her mind.

The two older girls were soon asleep in the second four-poster bed in their mother and father's bedroom behind the hob. Their two brothers were asleep in the settle-bed on the floor of the Welcoming Room. In their beds in the loft the two little ones were already dreaming of the fairies in their storybooks. The pale moon shone down on them so that the mist and the dew on the bushes and the yard were covered in white gauze.

I'll-Daze-Ye entered the bedroom and stripped off his britches. He got in under the soft-wadded quilt and rested his head on the musty pillow. He crept close up beside the Saintly Woman in the four-poster bed that was placed next to the hen house wall where he could keep an alert ear out for the visiting weasel, the fox or the rat. He also kept a cute little ear alert for the two girls sleeping nearby in case they would wake and hear him breathing. Then when all was quiet and hushed he dangled his arms round his wife's neck and lifted her innocent chemise and placed his warm belly and thighs close to her own, enveloping her. He fell into the black caverns of a vast sleep with his wife's achingly-longing arms around his bruised and exhausted limbs. A few stars dimly appeared outside the window and one or two bats went off deftly hunting along the length of the river. It had been a giant-of-a-day - a diamond-of-a-day – a beautiful faction-fighting day to be forever remembered and cherished.

ELLIE-MAY

1

Tooraloo was the husband of Norry-What's-Your-Hurry, a woman who sometimes took half the day to stagger out of bed. They lived in Cuckoo Haven – halfway between Sack-and-Tack and the little village of Saddleback, a mile beyond Old Gentility's small farm. Tooraloo had the land and it was not in too bad a shape for a man from the hills. It was in a spot hidden in a huge shadow in a hollow out by the Eagles' Nest. Their lives were peaceful enough – sharing in the milking of their seven cows and going to the well each day for the four buckets of water. Norry was the sister of Hammer-the-Smith, who (apart from I'll-Daze-Ye) was the toughest man in our midst. He had arms and shoulders on him that our giant, Big Red, would have been proud to call his own.

Tooraloo was a useful pig-killer like Red Scissors. After wiping the blood of the pig on his trousers he was always sure to tell you that the dead pig never felt a *shnig* – meaning that he had given the poor creature the quickest and most sudden death possible with a belt of his sledgehammer straight into the forehead rather than the traditional slow death of the black-handled knife down the throat.

Norry-What's-Your-Hurry was his twin soul in that she made from the killed pig the finest sausages imaginable and also those other blood-puddings, both the white and the black. She also had the one and only butter-churn apart from the one on our own creamery road. Kind woman that she was, she was never slow to lend her churn to her neighbours. I tell you this – her butter was as good as any sold inside in the town. Of course, on those days when she was making her churn of butter she was in a good bit more of a hurry to get herself out of bed and for that day at any rate proved herself untrue to the name that one or two of her unkind neighbours had bestowed on her earlier in life.

They had only one child – Ellie-May. She was scarcely out of the schoolhouse of Dropsy and Hairy-Chin (that is, if she ever spent a day in their school) when she found herself carrying messages to the rebels on the run. It was the time of the Troubles when the light of Freedom was beckoning our men. She took them notes, hurriedly scribbled on bits of paper, all across the hills and out by the bog and on through Diddledy-goo and the foot of Chieftain Hill – notes telling the fighters the details of the enemy's whereabouts. From the constant running that she was doing she was beginning to build legs on her that would suit a racehorse and lungs on her that would suit a greyhound. When caught (good child that she was) she made sure she'd swallow the paper messages to avoid getting herself shot and thrown into the ditch. Her task of course wasn't always easy. One freezing January night she was forced at gunpoint to dig a trench a foot deep across a track where the Tans intended to spring an ambush on our men coming down from Sack-and-Tack with sackfuls of gelignite.

These wartime years greatly disturbed our households and were seldom (if ever) reported across the water in the Land of John Bull. The action of the Tans filled the hearts of our women with fear and an embedded hatred in the hearts of our men.

One thing was sure: our young boys were not the ones so much at risk as were the blossoming girls. And Ellie-May, though a mere child of 14, was a good-looking country girl. One afternoon she fell into the clutches of two merry Tan soldiers. That's when the sun went out of her life. For these brave boys did unmerciful things to her body. They must have given her an awful gruelling (said Father Sensibly) for they left her clothing floating on the waters of Growl River and *the river fairies* hung their heads in shame and could be heard crying in the woods for many days thereafter.

The rape of a child (she being so very young) was beyond all measure of understanding. The Devil was alive and unsmiling and doing very well for himself. There had to be an answer to this crime and Tooraloo and Hammer-the-Smith spat on the palms of each other's hands and swore an oath (*mighty* would be too gentle a word for it) that they'd go and seek revenge before the week was over. They were seen carrying two double-barrel guns and a pair of shovels out across the fields. They found the haunts of the two drunken soldiers and followed their tracks – in the very same way a weasel might track a single rabbit and avoid being misled by any other rabbit standing in its path. In short – they caught up with the Tans and shot them in the knees. Then they shot them in the genitals and their faces. Then with their two shovels they buried them in the soft earth of the bog – but not too deep down: 'Let the wild foxes and eagles come down (they said) and dig them up and feast on their entrails.' Just the briefest of Christian burial rites would do for the likes of them (they said) and they knelt down and said a hurried Act of Contrition for the young soldiers.

The first thing we noticed following this horrendous ordeal was how sad and silent Ellie-May had become, standing there at the half-door and vacantly staring out at the grey-blue glow of the dying day and the impending shadows on Chieftain Hill. No one could fathom out what sorrows lay in the recesses of her young mind. Some of the women huddled their heads together and they took a big bag of red apples up to her to chew on. Others went around scouring the ditches and made up a fine big nosegay of flowers for her bedroom altar. When they reached her place, they felt a bit sheepish and didn't know what to say to her. Nor did she know what to say back to them and they quickly came away – a few of them with flushed faces of anger and others weeping.

For the next few weeks she was seen to be acting more and more peculiar. The world seemed very small to her. She no longer ran with her messages to the rebels. She never came down past our doors to the shop for her mother's bag of messages.

And then a thunderstorm erupted inside in her chest. Like Slipperslapper in later years, we saw a new woman rising up out of the ashes of poor Ellie-May's soul as she cast the Tans' ransacking of her body to the back of her mind. Whereas women all over the world would have covered themselves in mourning-ashes after such wounds as hers and would have torn their garments into shreds, Ellie-May now replaced her agonies by dressing herself up in her grandmother's cast-off colourful clothes. She let her hair hang down loose like a horse's mane. She found half a dozen rags and tied them into her head like a rag-rope of ringlets. Then as soon as the first shimmering light of morning came on, she hopped out the doorway to greet the fairy-folk – full of exhilaration and wearing her father's big hobnail boots stuffed with brown paper – the ones with the shamrock studs in them. Her eyes sparkled like the shine in a sweet-gallon tin as she headed for the delicate field-flowers and went on towards the green pine woods. We couldn't help noticing that her legs had turned as red as ripe cherries from the way the Tans had belted her, making the poor girl look as if she had fallen into a heap of briars. Her cheeks were puffed out like the red radishes in Lord Elegance's garden and she was breathing hard, not knowing or caring where she was heading.

'The poor maddened creature,' sighed Dowager sadly when she saw the state of her. 'All she needs now, thanks to the way them bleddy Tans manhandled her,' said My-son-Jack, scratching his jaw, 'is a pair of honeysuckle trumpets hanging out of her ears.' And neither of them laughed.

Inside in the town Canon-next-to-God heard about the recent tragedy bestowed on her and reported it to Bishop High-Hat. Something had to be done to prevent this young girl from an incontrollable madness and ending the rest of her days in the House for Nervous Disorders. The holy man drove up the creamery road in his motorcar. Fingering his rosary beads, he entered the half-door and prayed to God that he would be able to soothe away Ellie-May's cares. 'God bless you, my child,' said he. 'For the good of your health,' he went on, 'and for the good of your Christian soul, it is time for you to go tend to your father's cows – time to forget the hatred that all wars bring to mankind.' And then he blessed her with a shower of holy water.

After that, he knelt down and said one or two decades of the rosary alongside herself and Tooraloo and Norry-What's-Your-Hurry. And though he had heard of the savage treatment meted out to the two Tan soldiers by the guns of Tooraloo and Hammer-the-Smith, he never said a word about their murderous killings. For priest though he was – and with the powers (some of the older folk still believed) to turn all of us into wild goats if he put his mind to it – the holy man knew that Tooraloo was as likely to put a bullet in his holy skull as quick as look at him.

2

Toorlaoo took himself off on a long journey to Monks Abbey and brought back with him the finest batty pony any of us had ever seen. It had an energetically high step and its speed could give any racehorse (including Jimbo's runaway ass at The Show Fair) a run for its money.

Once again Canon-next-to-God's motorcar came steaming its way up the slopes. Mindful of the fragile state of the violated young girl's disposition, he brought with him what looked like a gallon of holy water, intent on blessing the three of them – Tooraloo (the wicked Tan-slayer), Norry and Ellie-May. Most of all, he had come to bless the legs of the new pony. By this time Ellie-May had named her lovely creature *Beauty*. For beautiful indeed he was – himself and his foaming white mane.

Years later Norry was to remember this day as if it were yesterday. Unusual for her, the slowcoach couldn't fathom out why she had been in such a hurry to get out of bed so early in the morning – why nature was attracting her eye more than usual – as though the fairy spirits were calling her to come and join them. Maybe it was the guiding hands of her guardian angel for before the clock struck 8, she had said her morning prayers, had lit a good fire from the whitethorn twigs and thorny bushes and bounced out the door. The last thing she was expecting was the arrival of the good canon and his motorcar all over again.

At the same time Ellie-May was also awake – looking out over the half-door and dreamily admiring the silvery shine from the morning's first light lying on the pig house laurels, the ivy at the haggart-stick and the holly bushes at the hen house. She hadn't long crossed the yard to attend to Beauty's needs when her reveries were interrupted by the holy canon slamming the door of his motorcar. In a flash he saw that Ellie-May had fallen head over heels in love with her pet pony. She couldn't do enough for him. Fair play to you, Tooraloo, (thought the canon) when he realised what a sacrifice the man must have made out of his meagre savings and how far he must have travelled to bring back so fine a gift to his daughter.

Ellie-May bowed before the holy man. Then, as though he weren't in the yard at all, she began stroking the pony's hooves and forelocks. And though he was already as clean as a new pin she began to currycomb him so unsparingly with the wire brush that you could see your face glistening in his hide. Almost every day (said Tooraloo to the priest) his daughter was seen taking this blessed pony up to Hammer-the-Smith to get yet another pair of unnecessary shoes fitted onto him. The canon smiled.

A day or two later *Madam Misfortune* struck a severe blow when Ellie-May's beloved Beauty decided to take flight, leaving the poor girl profoundly heartbroken and the fat tears rolling down the side of her nose. Where had he gone? And more importantly – why had he gone? Had he headed back to where he came from – back to rub noses with some other pony – a pony (perhaps) that he simply couldn't live without? No – that was far from the mark.

It was springtime, the season of new love, and Beauty had been put out of his stride by a new arrival in the shape of a handsome chestnut mare belonging to Lord Elegance's niece (*Rowena*), a damsel fresh in from a finishing-school in the faraway spa-town of Bath. The graceful mare took one look at Ellie-May's fine young pony. The pony took one look at the charms of Rowena's mare. Ah (the smell and appearance of them) – was ever a love-match so instantly in bloom? In the blink of an eye Beauty forgot the previous day's grooming, forgot the currycombing, forgot the petting and pleasuring and the sugar-lumps he'd been getting from Ellie-May. As soon as the mare glided passed, he darted off after her to where his heart had flown – up into the hills.

Ellie-May sat alone and bereaved outside the half-door and began bawling like a banshee. Would she ever see her beloved Beauty again? Would she ever get him back? Nothing could console her.

And now *the kindly fates* kicked Madam Misfortune aside and their troop of *capricious fairies* started weaving their silk-threaded spells on their spiritual loom. For not too far away from the sad scenes in Tooraloo's yard lived a very shy fellow (*Neddy-the-Quiet-Man*). Up until now he had lived a life free from care or complication. If he were aware of the plans these mischief-making fairies had in store for him, who knows to what corner of the earth he'd have skedaddled to – or whether he'd have allowed himself ever to have been born? In his humble cabin beyond Slack-and-Tack he'd have continued to live his life of peace and quiet – that is if Beauty hadn't arrived unannounced at the turn of the road and begun grazing on the thistles outside his field-gate. As for Rowena's mare – she had vanished from sight and the pages of our history had to do without her.

Neddy had always been good with horses and took his reins and blinkers and headed towards Beauty. With whispering words of kindness, he managed to cajole and soothe him out of his lovelorn misery and coax him back as far as the haggart. He kept him there till the time was ripe for the amorous creature to grow calm enough to be mounted and ridden back to Ellie-May.

The second day after his escape Beauty and Neddy were seen arriving back into Tooraloo's yard, bringing light and cheerfulness with them. How quickly the sun leaves the clouds behind for suddenly a grateful Ellie-May had laughter-lines around the corner of her eyes again. It was like a Christmas day and she showered the quiet man with several cups of tea and filled his plate with ham and buttered soda-cake.

Tooraloo ran back from the hayshed. He opened the bottle of whiskey and warmed Neddy's gizzard with one or two glasses of its fine medicine. The quiet man was enthralled by all these acts of kindness. Nor did the exquisitely blue eyes of Ellie-May go amiss on him. In short – she was soon to become his newfound wealth.

This was not what Neddy's father had planned for his son since the day of his birth - the long step into Clare to seek out a goodly wife and a sealed dowry for himself. Now that Neddy had rescued and returned Ellie-May's lost pony, his world was about to be turned upside-down. In her eyes he'd become the saviour sent to her from heaven – the object of her genuine affection henceforth and before the month was finished the two of them had consummated their lot with the blessings of Canon-next-to-God and of Holy Mother Church. Their wedding-banns were proclaimed in Copperstone Hollow and the graces of the Marriage Sacrament now locked the two of them in merry harness – man and wife.

3

Sometimes there is a short hop from happiness to sadness. Within the year they were given the present of three babies, a thing unheard of and although the three unnamed-as-yet little ones (their very own *Faith, Hope and Charity*) had brought Neddy and Ellie-May's a happiness nothing short of delirium, life turned out to be far different at another cabin a few strides down the lane. Here lived Ellie-May's young cousin – the wayward *Test-Me*. They shared the same grandmother. Test-Me gave birth to a strapping baby boy almost at the same hour of day as Ellie-May. However, there were to be no shouts of joy from her and her sad-eyed parents (*Mary and Joseph*), no roaring bursts of celebration, no toasting with the whiskey-glass.

Test-Me was 17. She was like a delicate young dove, a simple doughy-skinned girl with girlishly long hair and knew nothing of life's mysteries until they came along and hit her flat in the face. Her baby boy arrived most unexpectedly – a wonder indeed. Was it a Virgin birth? No, it was the shame of the house and the talk of the countryside. The little infant was whipped away from under her legs before the screaming girl could even catch a glimpse of him or cradle him in her arms and before she could even give him an honest name he was whisked away to town to be fostered.

The old gossips did not have a field day of it this time round and were hushed away from the end of the lane. The moment was far too painful for the rest of us to dwell on – especially for Mary and Joseph, the misfortunate parents of Test-Me. All we could do was pray that the matter would be quickly put to one side and forgotten like last year's flood – that we could all get on with our lives as though nothing shameful had happened in our midst. The men of course shrugged their shoulders as only men do. They had seen it all before as soon as their young heifers came into heat. It was (said these soothsayers of ours) an unfortunate accident that could have happened to any young girl when she came into heat. 'It could have happened (they told the women) to any of yeer own daughters, ye high and mighty old hypocrites!'

But, damn the bit (said the women) – what on earth came into Test-Me's slobbery head to have rolled up her skirts yet again and get herself this second child? For she had already delivered her firstborn son only the year before when she was 16 and scarcely out of her own cradle – at a stage in life when every other sixteen-year-old was still walking barefooted round the fields and wearing their ankle socks – even when going for a frolic to the Platform Dances-in-the-Fields.

Canon-next-to-God was normally a mild and sympathetic man. But on this second occasion he turned himself into Pontius Pilate and was seen giving the poor girl no comfort whatsoever. Setting aside his other duties, he attended to this second tragedy with split-second haste. He purred his motorcar stealthily up the creamery road and in along the lane. The wheels of another motorcar followed silently behind him. We had never seen two motorcars together before this day – unless of course in a procession to a funeral. Was there a funeral somewhere today? Perhaps. My-son-Jack watched them passing by. 'Something is in the air, ma'am,' he said to Dowager.

On the flagstones stood Test-Me's father, waving down the cars. The following scene was like a Lenten tragedy as out from the second car hopped two young Guards, looking every bit like the reliable law-enforcers that they were.

It was a grey morning – the light falling sadly in between the dripping trees. 'Where are we off to?' said Test-Me. And seeing the official-looking eyes of The Guards and the solemn look of her priest she was filled with alarm. On a journey,' said her priest. 'And why are The Guards coming with us?' said she. 'They're driving ye to yeer grandfather's place in Galway where ye'll be safe from the evil old gossips,' said he. 'Ye wouldn't want those yokes constantly standing at the end of yeer lane or knocking at yeer door, would ye?'

The car plunged out of the yard and on over the hill. From time to time Test-Me looked back beneath the interlacing trees. Then in uncomfortable silence they drove the rest of the way out beyond Chieftain Hill and in less than an hour they were outside the gloomy walls of a convent. The place looked like a cemetery with the semi-circular sign in black letters over the gate.

It is said that the screams of this misfortunate girl could be heard ringing echoingly back across the Tipperary hills. Test-Me fought her captors as though she was a young tigress – knuckling the skulls of the stout-armed nuns who had come out the gate to drag her away from her weeping father and from the door of the motorcar. Oh, how they pulled at her! Oh, how they dragged at her hair, to try and cast her inside the walls of their sacred convent. Test-Me proved tougher than a barnacle on a Kerry boat and wouldn't let go of the car-door handle. It took half-a-dozen of the angry red-faced nuns and their unholy curses (their veils a-flying and their sleeves rolled up to their armpits) to get a proper run in at her. They hacked at her wrists and some of our more wily and unreliable gossips swore that Test-Me proceeded to take a good few mouthfuls of flesh from their arms with her bare teeth.

To behold her anger – to behold her tears and fear – it shook her weak-willed father to his boots. You should have seen the hatred in her eyes as she cursed him into hell. 'It's for the best, my poor daughter,' cried he. She was like the pig that refuses to leave the pig house door and parade to the place of slaughter and it took several more minutes to disengage her from the door handles. 'Can't ye pair of eejits do something rather than stand there like open-mouthed fools?' said the frustrated nuns to the hapless Guards. Whereupon one of the

Guards (the impudent pup) came up behind Test-Me and gave her a kick in the arse, which sent her floundering headlong into the arms of the holy nuns and the job was done.

Canon-next-to-God made the sign-of-the-cross on his chest. He blessed the heroic young Guards. He thanked the good God-in-heaven. He thanked the grieving father. He thanked the nuns. He almost thanked the motorcar – so nervous and ashamed of himself was our holy man. Like a second Judas he was now the unhappiest mortal in the whole of Tipperary and would stay that way for many a moon to come. For at heart he had been nothing but a good man all his life– himself and his gallons of holy-water.

Test-Me was gone forever. From that day forth her father would not be allowed to set eyes on her - as if her wasted beauty had been buried alive in a grave. The hapless girl had paid the price for her little bit of pleasure behind the ditch. For the next five-and-forty years she'd slave in the nuns' laundry-room as a knuckle-skinned skivvy – the price of redeeming her soul and getting herself a chance to reach heaven. It was the only way (we were told) of absolving the rest of us from the taint of her sinfulness. We had to grin and bear it. Poor Test-Me. Enough said.

4

Neddy-the-Quiet-Man settled down with his beloved Ellie-May at the end of the lane. Their marriage was proving to be a true-love match – with his heart inside in her heart and with her heart inside in his heart. No longer did she need to go on nursing her wounds and mourning her afflictions after the savagery of the Tans. Like any young mother she had enough work to do in caring for her three little ones and looking after her new man. When the day's work was done, she'd sit near the spinning-wheel at the fire. She'd sing her loving-songs (*coo-coo-coo! coo-coo-coo!*) into the ears of her delicate little threesome.

It was unfathomably strange for us to see how quickly Ellie-May had shed her grief. However, here among us a woman's happiness could never be left alone for too long and the ever-creative niggardly tongues soon got to work. *The jealous fairies* came hopping out over the ditch and wooed a number of our women into malicious bouts of gossip. How could one single woman have given birth (they whispered) to three separate babies – and all at one and the same time, I ask you? This had never happened before, had it? After all, Ellie-May wasn't a sow – or was she? This brought them more than a sniggering laugh and they began telling one another (at the well, at the shop door, at the church gates) that there was a simple reason why the holy canon had been sent for at the time of the babies' births – that he'd never have been summoned unless there was something very wrong indeed. It was clear (they said) that something abnormal had occurred in the life of Ellie-May. They couldn't get to the bottom of it – at least not yet.

Little by little an inkling of what might be the truth began to dribble its way into Neddy-the-Quiet-Man's ears. The fact that three babies had been born meant only one thing – there had to be three fathers as well as three babies. What sort of eejity talk was that? Neddy couldn't believe what he was hearing. In his sorrow the poor man was often found sobbing bitter tears abroad in the cowshed. It was rare for anyone to see a grown man crying – unless it was a man crying tears of joy when the mare had her beautiful foal. That was understandable. Once or twice they saw a man crying even more when the mare fell down dead in a drain abroad in the field. But Neddy seemed to be weeping for nothing that anyone could lay their hands on. This was a new one on them. You'd wonder (said the men) why on earth a quiet man like Neddy had never sought the advice of his priest, why he had never spoken to Doctor Glasses, why he had never shared a few drinks with Hammer-the-Smith (Ellie-May's uncle) and told him of his worries and the predicament he was in. More than anything else (quiet man though he was) why hadn't he the gumption to stand in front of Ellie-May herself and ask her to explain herself, ask her to admit to having strayed from the marriage-bed in the company of two other unnamed heathens?

All that Ellie-May could see were the dark clouds that had taken a hold of her husband's spirit. For the life of her she couldn't understand why he was looking so sad and miserable. Maybe it was in the breed of Neddy to turn a sort of sad and mournful as he grew older. It had happened before to a number of our men. But little did she know that her poor husband was going demented at the thought of two scoundrels having had their pleasure with his beloved Ellie-May. Soon his bouts of rage became the devil's-own curse and he swore that if he ever caught up with the two joy-boys that had bedded his wife he'd hang them from the crossbeams outside the town jail.

5

A week since the gossip of those cackling women had trickled its alarm into poor Neddy's ears another bit of stray news reached our ears – even before the creamery carts had started out with the milk: Shy-Dennis had left his outpost and departed for good during the stealth of the night. This was a very strange thing for any of our men to be doing. But then we gave ourselves a little thought: Shy-Dennis was an odd sort of creature, wasn't he? Everybody knew that. He was forever tramming his hay in the middle of the night, forever gazing up and counting the millions of stars like a blessed Magi searching for the right star to guide his hayfork, forever riding his aged mule round the fields before the cockerel had a chance to wipe the sleep from its eyes.

We heard that he and his mule had been spotted passing the Engine House at the railway yard in town. Tom Tatters, the town's hobgoblin, said Shy-Dennis was on his way to a convent in Kilkenny (like Soolah Patricia and Kate Solitary before him) and taking with him his whole fortune (a tidy sum of 500 pounds) stitched inside in his saddle-pack. The news came back that he'd reached the convent gates a week later, by which time he looked an unholy wreck. He told the startled nuns (whether it was true or not) that he had at last come home.

'Who on earth are you?' gasped the nuns. 'What is your business at this hour of the night?' they demanded, looking this strange character up and down and the long black coat he was wearing with the bit of string wrapped around its middle.

'I am Saint Joseph,' replied the poor confused fellow. 'and this is my ass.' Fair play to them, the nuns took him in and gave him a bowl of soup. They were just about to send him swiftly on his way when he produced his fortune from out of his saddle-pack. 'I have brought ye mee fortune'.

You can imagine how their worried faces suddenly changed colour and shone like the blessed sun. All talk of his leaving was thrown up in the air and was flung out the window. Shy-Dennis was as welcome as the flowers in May. The nuns must have danced the finest of jig-steps for the next week and a half.

For less than the price of a song and at the stroke of a solicitor's pen Neddy and Ellie-May (he hadn't yet told her of his misgivings about the rascals that had helped father their triplets) put their stamp on Shy-Dennis's tumbledown shack – what we scurrilously called *the mansion*.

Tooraloo and Norry-What's-Your-Hurry were more than a trifle sad to see the two of them leaving the old homestead and drive away in their ass-and-car. They waved the white handkerchief after them. You'd think that they were bound for the Land of the Silver Dollar even though they were merely travelling a hop and a jump away – to the other side of the creamery road.

Within a week the quiet man and his pick-axe and pitchfork had eased away a great deal of his anger and had laid out six excellent drills in his new haggart for his seed potatoes and cabbage shoots. Ellie-May washed the floor of the new Welcoming Room till it shone and glistened like a haystack in the snow and she brought back a big new table from town. When the fire was lit with the whitethorn logs, their new cabin was as good as a palace and soon Neddy began to forget his troubles. The two of them were like those cosy little lovebirds that you'd see in a cage at The Daffy-Duck Circus.

6

Their newfound joy (isn't it always the way?) was soon tempered with a cutting sorrow when Neddy's beloved father (*Rahilly*) came to his untimely end. Doctor Glasses had repeatedly warned him that eating out of the burner those big feeds of fat bacon after killing his three yearly pigs would bring him his final reward – that he'd cover his arteries in heaps of grease from the meat and that it'd be the end of him. With the first spasms of pain he knew that our good doctor was only too right and told Neddy that the sentence was on him – that he'd seen the blessed angels coming down to greet him and fetch him into the clouds.

He got out his best white shirt and his black suit and put them on. He took the rosary beads from off of the nail and went and lay down on top of the bed, the rosary bead neatly twisted in his fingers, looking a bit like the holy Saint Francis. The neighbours knew that something was amiss when there was no morning smoke rising up out of his chimney and they came in the door and found him dead on top of the bed – laid out neatly in his fine suit of clothes and ready for his coffin and his Maker.

Like the ending of a spell, Neddy blinked out the happy-death candles and, with just the silence in the room and allowing nobody else in the bedroom door, he said farewell to the ghost-of-his-father and spent the rest of the week grieving over him. Ellie-May held his tearful cheeks in her hands each evening and kept repeating: 'God is good! God is great!' But Neddy couldn't make head or tail of it all. His father's death had been so unexpected for he had been as healthy as a snipe throughout his life.

7

There now came a new and unhappy chapter. In less than a week the hopeful expectations of every man-jack-of-us were to be realised when it was found that Neddy (the fine decent man that he was) had a second string to his bow – apart from taming lovesick ponies in their tracks. For he inherited his father's whiskey-making still. Within a short while his ingenuity was seen to bear our men a most wonderful harvest with the smell and the smoke of his new medicines. If there were titles to be handed out, if there were diplomas or medals, rosettes or labels to be awarded for the making of fine potheen, Neddy was about to be crowned *the Absolute Master Brewer*. His potheen was second-to-none and he was seen as the expert in choosing the best spuds, the best barley, the best wheat and rye for the whiskey-droplets that trickled out from his copper wires and into his green bottles.

The first of the visitors ran their boots up the hill at breakneck speed. They sniffed and they sniffed and then they sniffed some more. They were as busy as wasps. Neddy waited in silent hope. Slowly they gurgled the first few drops. Once they had drained four or five thimblefuls, their taste-buds were beyond any repair that Doctor Glasses might achieve. They couldn't get enough of the blessed stuff and they ran back down the hill even quicker than they'd come up. They told us that the pour of it had rattled the few teeth left in their heads and that it had burnt its way down their throttle like a bird singing love-songs to them.

Before the month was out a dozen of our younger men had made imaginative excuses to skedaddle up the hill to Rahilly's former dwelling-place. By next morning when the sun had cleared the gauze away from Old Sam's orchard these same young buckos shambled home and completely forgot what day of the week it was and with mouths on them as dry as the parched road. Within the hour they were mountainously asleep and all that could be heard were thundering snores that could have awakened the dead in the graveyard. But they'd be alive and kicking in a week or so to buckle back into the work of the farm.

These early adventurers were followed by a lively trail of older men stepping out fairly lively to shake hands with Neddy and shove into the drink. Like the youngsters they drank so much of Neddy's whiskey that they were seen staggering round the creamery road like a bunch of sick rats and for once in their lives the old gossip's vocabulary wasn't nearly diverse enough to describe what they saw.

8

It was Saint Stephens's Night and the Wran-Byze Dance was taking on its usual celebratory course above at Din-Din-Dinny's long-house – a stone-throw from Rahilly's turf-shed and Neddy's new whiskey-still. With our love of the music and dancing all of us were having a whale of a time – a-flipping and a-tripping round the cement floor and out into the cobbled yard. There was no dance (not even the Evening Institute Dance or the Platform Dance-in-the-Fields), which could compare with this Dance-of-the-Wran-Byze. It was the time when men threw down the hayfork, the spade and the shovel (the plough too if they had to) so as to get their feet out onto the dance-floor. Old and young alike were soon destroying the floor with the cut of their hysterical hobnail boots – that is, in between wiping the sweat from their foreheads and bouncing their broad-shouldered damsels on their knees near the fire.

The dancing was good and the drinking was even better and the whole crowd of men and women were feeling mellow as could be. Then one of the men (we later thought it was *Sykie from Knockahopple*) happened to look out the window to see was there a frost coming on and if the stars were any good. Then he whispered to the man next to him. In the clear of the moonlight the two of them could see a few little lanterns listlessly zig-zagging up along the hillside. 'Tis The Guards - the feckin Guards!'

Damn it - we knew it! The little feckers were coming to arrest Neddy. He'd be seeing the inside of the jailhouse this very night and he'd be there at least a month or two. There were a half a dozen lamplights in all and a group of young law-enforcers in the shape of the town's constabulary. Their shadows swayed across the leafy stream and drifted up the hillside towards the turf-shed. They were bent on an intensive search for the whereabouts of Rahilly's still.

Being young, however, and with the inexperience of youth behind their ears, they felt a bit fragile as they took their tentative steps across the middle of the field. Their hearts soon began to pound uncertainly, not knowing if the coast was clear or whether in between the bouts of singing and dancing the revellers might get a chance to clear away their glasses of potheen or (more importantly still) whether Neddy might get a chance to hide away the still and all its implements.

And now the full light of the moon could be seen behind the high banks of raggy clouds as we watched the smoke coming up from the chimney of Rahilly's turf-shed where seemingly Neddy was hard at his work, producing the medicine that our throats craved. Frantically we watched The Guards heading nearer and nearer to the gate of his haggart. There was no time to raise the alarm or to warn our good friend. We hadn't so much as a ferret's jingly-bell between the lot of us.

The Guards leaped in over the ditch. What was in the back of their minds? Had they no heart for poor Neddy? Surely, they had mothers and fathers of their own? The women on the dance-floor stood back and the music stopped. The half-sets and the Clare-battering steps were now gone from us and a dozen of our men reached for their coats. They hurried out across the fields and hid themselves in the stealth of the darkness.

The Guards had beaten them to Rahilly's yard where they surrounded the turf-shed. From their hiding-place our men could see the lanterns clearly, could see the young townies sniffing and whiffing like a pack of hunting-dogs – looking for the smell of the whiskey.

They gave a few raps on the door of the shed. How the hell did they know the place to be looking for? What animal had been bad enough to have told them where to look? It was now the moment of truth and the anger was boiling inside us. We couldn't let a bunch of schoolboy Guards draw a curtain over the antics of Neddy without giving them a few belts on their sore heads, a few smacks in their gobs – to take back to town with them.

If only Neddy had been listening to the persistent barking of his two trusty sheepdogs, warning him of the approaching Guards. And then we had a little thought: if Saint Peter had once been man enough to raise his sword in an effort to protect Jesus, surely our men wouldn't be so meek and mild as not to take their own opportunity this very night?

Meanwhile – where the hell was Neddy? I'll tell you where he was: inside sitting by the fire, a drunken husk of himself – and so preoccupied with the last of his whiskey-glass as not to hear or take eed of such warnings as a dog's howls.

Then, as we looked out the window, we had another little thought to ourselves. Maybe the Guards were human after all. Maybe they'd be men enough to step out of line – just this once – and join the rest of us and take in a little of Neddy's pure medicine? Just a few little sips. After all, it was a cold and frosty night and what better way to ward off the ague in a man's limbs than a drop or two of Neddy's fine whiskey?

Maybe. Perhaps. But there was no use cajoling ourselves for we knew that these young upstarts were fashioned from different clay than ourselves - from a newer school. They had been given their Christian ethics – had drunk the contents that lay in the good books of Bede, Augustine and Aquinas and had poured it down their throats at an early age like we were now drinking the whiskey. We could never have the skills of the tongue to persuade these lads to stay a little while in our company and have a few sups of welcome with us. After all, we were only the poor scholars from the hills – few of us having had the fine chances of the townies to get ourselves into the realms of high-falutin' scholarship. So now – we were at a loss what to do. Why couldn't these Guards go about their real business elsewhere – the business of tracking down a stray horse-and-cart without its lamp or breaking up the odd bout of boxing between a few rival tinker-families?

Enough surmising: it was time for inspiration and action. The women quenched the lamps while the men threw the whiskey-cask out the back window. Then with a few strong ashplants our fellows leapt into Rahilly's haggart. In the darkness the silence was broken. There was a fight. It was a great bleddy fight. It was nobly done – a beautiful fight as long as it lasted. Our men gave the Guards a right good belting and damn near killed one or two of them as they looked at the blood trickling from their own knuckles. They left two more officers with injuries that would require the repair of a number of careful stitches and gave the rest of them a few broken ribs and cracked jaws to take back home with them. In desperation and when they realised that our men were not play-acting and that they were getting far too rough with them, the Guards cocked their pistols towards our men's heads and our men fled like gnats in all directions.

Stiff in their limbs, the Guards nevertheless searched the most remote parts of Rahilly's turf-shed and found some of the kettles. They found the still. They found the copper worm. They found the pick and the shovel, which had dug and hidden the entire project. All had been piled neatly in the middle of the dung heap that lay behind the cowshed.

There was an unbelievable sadness in what next happened. With their sledgehammers they smashed to smithereens whatever needed to be smashed. They had found everything except a good few of the jugs and the rest of the kettles – all still full to the gills with the whiskey. These treasures Neddy had buried in God-knows-where. He hadn't been such a dull-witted eejit as not to know that some sneaking little shitty-arse would one day be the cause of his ruination.

Well-satisfied with the results of their sledgehammering and the death of the whiskey-still, the Guards hauled themselves and their wounds back towards the town. Along with them they took Neddy. It was a truly terrible sight. How mournful the rest of us felt – to see him hauled along like a common criminal in a pair of handcuffs. From the window we saw the last of the poor devil being dragged down the stumbling hillside by the belt of his greatcoat. The young men were taking him into the jailhouse. It was enough to make a horse cry.

9

Poor Neddy was in jail for a month. The penalty for getting him out of jail was enormous – 75 pounds - a pure fortune in anyone's eyes. He'd have to stay in jail until it was paid – every blessed shilling of it. Not to be beaten, we all rallied round – even the women. None of us had ever dreamt that our good friend would have been treated so savagely. We ran raffles by the score. We entertained several card-playing competitions far and near for the traditional pound of tea and the plucked goose and turkey. The Yellowboy's father and his limping wellingtons was persuaded to run a short race (like Jimbo had done) against a captured three-legged hare on a specially constructed wired-in course. Instead of pennies, many pound notes changed hands to see the outcome of this extraordinary contest. Our renowned hero, Bazeen, was persuaded to bob up and down in his pig's barrel so that we could take money from the spectators to see if their wattles could break open his skull and kill him outright.

In due course we heaped all the money together and paid the fine down to the last shillings and pence.

We decided that we would plan another dance in honour of his imminent homecoming from the jailhouse, a dance which would be the greatest dance of all time, a dance that would beat into a cocked hat even our famed Wran-Byze Dance and send it back into the realms of forgotten memory. It might take us a month-and-a-half to plan it and to send out all the invitations. We remembered that even though the Guards had destroyed all our future whiskey-making, they hadn't found the remaining kettles (thanks be to our merciful God-in-heaven) or the jugs and the green bottles. When the time came for the dance we'd have oceans of the medicine to swig down our throats.

The House-Dance that followed above at Din-Din-Dinny's was sure to live up to its name –*the grandest dance there'd ever been*. It was more than beautiful. Men, women and children came out to scrub their faces in every yard-stream – for none of us wanted to look an obstacle. We dug deep around the corners of our Welcoming Rooms to find our most resplendent outfits. We spat on our boots till they were polished like glass. Then we hastened across the fields and arrived in a thundering great heap in Din-Din-Dinny's yard. And before the hour was out, even the women were seen whaling into the remains of the whiskey-kettles and the bottles, jugs and jam-jars and were soon running like headless chickens round the floor from it. What the silvery moon in the sky or the roosting crows in the rookery thought of all the merriment we shudder to think.

'Down the throttle with it!' was heard again and again. 'Mee belly's on fire!' So good a drink (said Neddy) it'd burn a hole in a sod-o-turf.' In a merry crowd we made several attacks with our rattling hobnails on the sparkling dance-floor till the soles of our feet were red-raw from the churning of the music.

We danced the evening away. We danced the night away. We danced half the next day away. We toasted Neddy - 'The sound man that ye are!' We toasted Ellie-May for forgiving her man for getting himself locked up in the jail. We toasted Peace itself - 'As long as we all shall live!'

Throughout the evening the mild-mannered Creamery Manager had been sitting next to Doctor Glasses in the corner next to the fire. They'd been watching the fine old times and the ringing of the fiddles and flutes and the gaiety of the dancers. They'd been passing the hours warming their shins with the blaze from the turf-sods and imbibing glass after glass of the rawgut whiskey. In the end Doctor Glasses had eyes on him that glittered like a pair of marbles and his flushed cheeks were the colour of red radishes.

We could see that our medical genius was as full as a tick (said some) and as drunk as an owl (said others). We had never seen the poor man like this before for we all knew that he'd never let a drop of strong liquor past his lips until this evening's celebration. He'd be in bed for the rest of the week, his dreams full of all the wild dancing. For once in his life he'd have a head on him as heavy as a sack of flour. And another thing – for the first time in his life he'd find himself placed at the very top of his own surgery's sick-list.

Both himself and the Creamery Manager and the whole pack of us wouldn't have missed this evening's entertainment – not for all the world. So merrily had Neddy's whiskey roared insides all of us that not only the next evening but the next night and indeed the rest of the week flitted clean away and disappeared before we heard tell of them or knew they'd arrived or could lift a muscle or an eyebrow. The dance at Din-Din-Dinny's (we all agreed) had been a night and a half – a dance we'd take to our grave, every man-jack-of-us. Indeed, it had! Enough said.

--E.F.H